PRETTY PINK
ribbons

BY K.L. GRAYSON

ISBN: 978-0-9907955-2-0

Cover Photo Photographer: Tomasz Zienkiewicz Photography
Author Bio Pic: Elizabeth Wiseman Photography
Editor: S.G. Thomas
Cover Designer: Perfect Pear Creative Covers
Formatting by Champagne Formats

Champagne
Formats

Dedication

To my sister Casey. Your strength, determination and perseverance are inspiring. You're my best friend—my hero. The battle you fought was long and hard, but you fought it with a quiet graceful beauty and you *survived*. Thank you for everything that you have done to help me tell Laney's story. I love you.

Prologue

"LEVI?" HER SOFT VOICE RINGS through the bar, effectively kicking my heart rate up a couple hundred notches, and I take a deep breath. This is what she does to me. When she's around, my entire universe shifts and I know—*I know*—that this woman is it for me.

"Coming." I rush to light the last of the candles, taking a quick inventory to make sure I didn't forget anything. I've known for several months that Laney is different . . . special. But the other night when her warm body was curled up in my arms, head tucked under my chin, I realized just how perfectly she fits. And not just with me, but into my life.

A loud thud followed by a faint "shit" catches my attention and I run across the patio, through the door, toward the dining room. "You okay in here?"

Laney is bent over, rubbing her knee. She lifts her head and her dark hair slides away from her face, putting her hazel eyes—the eyes that I love—on display. Her nose crinkles and she cocks her head. "Why is it so dark in here? You know I'm afraid of the dark." I laugh, bending down to inspect her knee. "Are you laughing at me, Mr. Beckford?" I glance up in time to see a sly grin split her face and I return it before focusing my attention back on the bruise that is now marring her flawless skin. Leaning forward, my lips graze her knee and she sighs, threading her delicate fingers through my hair. "When you act all sweet like this, it's hard to be mad at you for laughing at me."

I look up and she places a soft kiss against my lips. "I have a surprise for you," I whisper, pulling away, knowing good and well what her sweet, innocent kisses can turn into. Sliding a hand along her back, the other under her knees, I lift her off the ground and she squeals, wrapping her arms around my shoulders. Burying her face in my neck, she starts peppering kisses along my jaw.

"I love surprises." Her voice is low and sexy as shit, and if she says one more word, I'm certain we won't make it out to the patio. Soft lips encircle my earlobe and she nips it playfully then sucks the sensitive flesh into her mouth. I swat her ass and she moans, the vibrations sending a rush of blood straight to my dick. *Fuck* . . . the things this woman does to me.

Stopping in front of the patio doors, I lower her to her feet. "Close your eyes." Her gaze snaps to mine and her eyes widen with excitement before she slaps a hand over her eyes. Gripping her free hand in mine, I gently lead her across the threshold into the warm summer air.

I couldn't have asked for a better night to do this. My dad closed Flame for the weekend to celebrate my cousin's wedding so we have the entire restaurant to ourselves, and the weather is absolutely perfect. I blow out a slow breath, hoping that this perfect night gets a little bit more perfect when I tell Laney just how much she means to me. "Open your eyes."

She smiles wide, her sparkling white teeth lighting up her face. Her hand remains locked across her eyes and I can't help but laugh. "Laney." I tug at her arm, but she doesn't budge. "You can look now."

"Wait," she laughs, pushing me away with her free hand. "I'm prolonging the moment. I haven't had a surprise since I was seven years old and my mom bought me a Cabbage Patch doll for my birthday." Laney's smile falters and something inside of me clenches. Laney doesn't have a lot of memories of her mom, and she has even fewer good memories of her dad. "It wasn't even new." I stood there, my hands hovering at my sides, at a complete loss for words. "I think she got it from a garage sale, but I didn't care . . . I loved that doll."

Stepping toward her, I lace my fingers around the back of her neck, drawing her to me. "Laney, I didn't—"

"No." She buries her covered face in my chest and takes a deep breath. "It's okay. I'm sorry I got carried away. I'm just really excited for your surprise, even if it's nothing . . . I'm not saying it's nothing, but if it was, I'd still be just as excited." She pauses, pulling away from me. "Wait. That didn't come out right."

My hand glides down her back and I pull her to my chest. I want to spend the rest of my life making her happy. Logically, I know it's way too early to talk about marriage, what with the both of us still in college, but the thought lingers in the back of my head. "I know what you meant." She nods and I kiss the top of her head. "I'm going to give you lots of surprises, Laney." She nods again. "I'm going to spoil you rotten. I promise, one of these days you'll be sick of surprises."

She lifts her face as though she is looking for a kiss, but her hand is still covering her eyes and she isn't anywhere close to my mouth. I grin. She looks so damn cute with her pouty pink lips puckered and ready. "Where's your mouth?" she huffs, lifting up on her toes. "Levi?" Slipping my arm under her butt, I lift her up and she instinctively wraps her legs around my waist. Gripping the back of her head in my palm, I guide her smiling face toward mine and her lips part, granting me access. Our tongues collide, sliding and pushing against one another. Kissing Laney is like getting a taste of heaven. If she'd let me, I'd probably spend most of my days walking around with my lips connected to her in some way, shape, or form.

"Can I have my surprise now?" she mumbles against my mouth, biting at my bottom lip. I groan and she smiles against my mouth, knowing good and well what she's doing to me. "Did that turn you on?" She waggles her eyebrows above her hand, her knowing smile completely infectious. If her eyes were open, I'd adamantly deny any such thing. But they're closed so I smile back, loving this playful side of her.

"Nope."

"No?"

"Not even a little."

She tries to pull back, but my arms lock around her middle and she giggles. The most perfect sound in the entire world. "I don't believe you." She wiggles her free hand between us until she finds the swollen bulge busting at the zipper of my jeans, causing her to burst into full-on laughter. "I knew it. *I knew it.* Good God, you're easy." I have no comeback because she's right. This girl can fucking breathe on me and I'll get hard.

"What do you expect? You're fucking gorgeous." I run my nose up the side of her neck and back down. Her laughing morphs to giggling and she scrunches up her shoulders when I suck on the spot just below her ear. How easily she forgets that I know how to make her squirm too. "What's a man supposed to do? You've got these perfect tits rubbing all up on me." My hand roams up her side, my fingers grazing the outside of her breast. She's no longer laughing . . . or giggling. I inch my hand up a little bit higher, tangling my fingers in her hair. Wrapping her dark waves around my hand, I give a firm tug and her head tilts back, a small whimper falling from her lips. But I know my girl and that was not a whimper of pain. I just turned the fucking tables.

"Did you like that, Lane?"

"Mmm-hmm." My cock throbs at the sight of her, skirt bunched up around her hips and neck stretched, begging for my mouth.

"You look turned on, Lane. How turned on are you?" My nose slides down her neck until my lips hit the swell of her breast, and her breath hitches.

"A five. I'm a five," she says breathlessly. Bullshit, she's a five. Letting go of her hair, I slip my fingers in the top of her shirt, yanking it down. Laney's breast pops free, her nipple tightening when it meets the warm breeze. My mouth waters at the sight and I lean down to suck her sensitive bud into my mouth. My tongue swirls and my teeth nip, and within seconds she is writhing against me.

"A five, huh?" I blow on her wet nipple and she moans.

"I hate you," she pants. "A ten. I'm a ten." Her eyes flutter, but I'm not quite done with her yet.

"Did I tell you to open your eyes?" I swat her ass and she grinds into me, shaking her head furiously. "You haven't seen your surprise yet. Do you want your surprise?" She squeezes her eyes shut and nods.

"Is it you? Can I have you?" Her words slam into me and suddenly our little game is so much more. "I just want you." That last part sounded more like a plea and my throat constricts. I can't wait any longer. I need to tell her . . . she needs to know.

I push down on her hip, and she reluctantly untangles her legs and slides to the ground. I fix her shirt and attempt to adjust her bra. She laughs at my awkward movements and reaches up with her free hand to help. When her clothes are righted, I entwine our fingers, bringing her hand up to my mouth.

"You have me, Lane." I kiss her knuckles and she takes a step toward me. "I'm already yours."

"Levi? There's something—"

"Wait." I press a finger to the center of her mouth. "Open your eyes first, Lane." She obeys and I spin her around. Her mouth drops open on a gasp, her hand flying to her mouth.

"Oh my God." She turns to look at me, and then back to the patio, then back to me. "Levi," she sighs. "This is . . . it's . . . you did all of this?" Her golden eyes glitter under the pale moonlight.

"I wanted to do something special for you. It's not much, but—"

Laney turns, stepping into me. She grips the collar of my shirt with her manicured hands and pulls my face close to hers. "What do you mean *not much?*" She glances over her shoulder and my eyes follow, taking in what she's seeing.

Flame sits on the banks of the Mississippi River and the patio overlooks a wide expanse of rippling water, providing a magnificent view of the Arch riverfront. Lanterns are strung along the railing, emitting a soft, ethereal glow, and a round table is tucked in the corner adorned with her favorite flowers.

Laney's grip loosens on my shirt and she twists around, taking off toward the table. "You made me dinner?" She lifts the silver cover that's hiding one of the plates, then quickly replaces it. She turns to me with a brilliant smile. "My favorite." I nod, watching her reach toward the bouquet of Calla lilies. She pulls one from the bunch and raises it to her nose. Her eyes close and she sniffs, her chest rising and falling on a slow inhale. Her face is the perfect picture of serenity.

This is it . . .

"Laney?" I stand in front of her and she smiles, slowly peeling open her eyelids. My heart is pounding against my ribcage, and if my palms get any sweatier, I'll be embarrassed to touch her. *Come on, Levi, do it.* The words are stuck in my throat, threatening to choke the shit out of me if they don't come out. I rub my hands along my thighs and take a deep breath. "You like the lilies?"

What the hell was that? I was supposed to confess my love, not ask if she likes the damn flowers.

She stuffs the lily back in with the bunch and squeezes my hand. "I love them." Damn it. I was really hoping she was going to say '*I love you*' . . . then I wouldn't have to be the first. Ever so gradually, she lifts herself up and when our lips meet, something stirs inside me. I feel like I'm home. She is my home. She kisses me softly several times, never deepening it. "This is beautiful. It's wonderful."

Now would probably be a good time to spit it out . . . get it off my chest. If only I could concentrate—or breathe. I should probably breathe first; that would be good. My lungs fill and I blow out a big breath.

"Are you okay? Do you want to sit down?" Laney pulls me to a chair and shoves me in it.

"I have to tell you something," I blurt, catching her off guard. She clears her throat and pulls out the chair next to me.

"I have to tell you something too." She looks away and then down at her hands, which are fidgeting with the hem of her shirt. She's nervous. What the hell is she nervous about? I'm the one about to lay my heart out on the line. Alas, my dad always told me ladies first.

"You go first." I scoot my chair forward until our knees are touching and she glances up at me, blinking rapidly. She wrings her hands together, her eyes searching my face.

"No." She shakes her head adamantly. "You planned this amazing surprise. You go first."

"No, really—" She shakes her head jerkily, dismissing me, and we both sit there . . . staring at each other. Neither one of us says a word and the air grows thick with awkward tension.

Damn it.

This is not how I wanted this to go. I wanted to tell her I loved her, hear her say it back, eat dinner and then make love to her under the stars. But really, I just want to tell her I love her . . . and hear her say it back.

Both of us, obviously disturbed by our lack of communication, start talking at the same time.

"I love you."

"I got in!"

"What?" she gasps, her face beaming. She moves closer, which is funny because suddenly I'm wanting to move away.

"What did you say?" My stomach hardens as a wave of nausea rolls through me. My mind is working desperately to try and figure out what she's talking about, but I've got nothing. "You got in?" I ask, brows furrowed. "You got in where?"

Her eyes sparkle with excitement. I want to be excited with her, but the pain I have gnawing inside my gut is telling me that this is going to change everything. Her knees are bouncing at a fast clip and she bites back a smile. "Do you remember when I applied to the CIA?"

I nod once, vaguely remembering her talking about some scholarship for the Culinary Institute of America. She never said anything else about it, so I just assumed it was a passing thought. I was wrong, obviously.

Laney loves to cook. In fact, that's how we met. She started to waitress and hostess for my dad at Flame, and I bartend for him on the weekends and occasionally during the week. She told me once that she wanted to be a chef and working in a restaurant was her first step in that direction. I'm not going to lie, the girl can cook. There were a few times when my dad even pulled her back to the kitchen to help out if someone called out or left sick.

"I got accepted, Levi." She catapults forward, throwing herself into my arms, but I'm too shocked to move. What is this going to mean for us? Where is the school? I never once considered the fact that she may move. She can't move—I love her. "Levi? Did you hear me? I got accepted!" Her eyes are gleaming, but for the life of me I can't find the strength to smile back.

"So, what does that mean?" I manage to stutter out.

She sits up, her hands locking on mine. "It means I get to go to college. On a full scholarship. I don't have to pay for anything, Levi."

"But you're in college." I don't see what the big deal is. What can she do there that she can't do here? Her whole life is here. She can't possibly think it's a good idea to just pick up and leave. And what about Luke? She can't leave Luke . . . she can't leave *me*.

Her smile fades, the light in her eyes dulling a fraction, and she stares at me. "I'm going to a community college, Levi."

"There's nothing wrong with a community college," I insist.

She shakes her head. "No, there's not, but I'm not doing anything there. This isn't where I want to be." Her words are a punch to the fucking gut and I stand abruptly, sending my chair toppling backward. "Wait"—she reaches for me, but I pull away—"I didn't mean it like that." Slowly, she stands. "There is nothing for me here." Another fucking punch. "My life is going nowhere, Levi . . . you know this." Jesus Christ, screw the punch, she's using a jagged-edge knife. I rear back at her harsh words and she hangs her head, a tear slipping down her flushed cheek.

Laney's mother died of cancer when she was ten years old, and a few months after her passing, Laney's dad became a raging alcoholic. Laney spent her entire childhood raising her brother. The only good thing her poor excuse for a dad ever did right was give Laney access to any money he ever had. I'm not sure where he got his money, considering he could never keep a job for longer than a few months at a time, from what Laney told me. But he got it from somewhere, and it kept food in her and Luke's bellies and a roof over their heads.

"What about me, Laney?" I yell, jamming my finger into my chest. "What? I'm nothing to you? Your life with me won't ever go anywhere?" My arms are held out to the sides, but she doesn't answer. Her head snaps up and she moves forward.

"No." Her voice is high and frantic. She looks bewildered at why I would say that. "That's not it at all. You're everything. You mean everything. This doesn't mean we're over, it just means I'm going away to school for a while."

My eyes lock on a barge floating slowly down the river—what I wouldn't give to drift away right along with it. "Where is it? Where is the school?"

"St. Helena . . . California."

My eyes snap to hers. "California?" She nods and my stomach twists. "When would you leave?"

"The semester starts in six days. There was a last-minute cancellation . . . that's how I got in. That's why it's so sudden."

Tears are swimming in her eyes, but that does nothing to subdue the anger that is boiling up inside me. She bites down on her bottom lip, a small quiver taking root in her chin, and I grip my hair tightly, spinning away from her. "Christ, Laney," I growl, my voice echoing into the empty night.

As hurt as I am by what she's just told me, it's what she *didn't* say that's bothering me the most. Those three little words that I was dying to tell her were not reciprocated and that slices right through me. Did she even hear me say it?

"This doesn't have to change anything." I can feel her body behind me, the familiar scent of her perfume wafting through the air. I hang my head in defeat. What am I going to do if I can't see her every day? She has become my life. I go to bed thinking about her, I wake up thinking about her . . . hell, I probably even dream about her.

Not to mention, she's bound to get noticed. A girl like her catches the eye of every hot-blooded male within a five-mile radius. I'm going to go insane not being able to be there, and it very well might kill me not knowing who she is talking to or what she's doing at any given time. And when am I going to see her? It's not like either one of us can afford to travel back and forth.

"This changes everything." There has to be somewhere closer for her to go to culinary school. This can't be the only option. "I don't want you to go. I don't want to be away from you."

Her eyes soften, but something about that pisses me off. Reaching out, she grips my forearm and gives it a gentle squeeze. I don't pull away, mostly because something inside of me is screaming that this may be the last time we touch. "It's only for a couple of years. I *have* to do this, Levi."

"I can't do a couple of years." My words come out surprisingly calm considering I'm about two seconds away from punching the goddamn wall.

Her hand falls from my arm as she takes a step back. "What do you mean you can't do a couple of years?" Her words are slow and careful.

I need her to pick me. I need her to pick *us*. If she just gives us a chance—a real chance—one where she isn't thousands of miles away, we can make this work. I just need to finish school, then we can work at getting her into culinary school and I'll happily follow her wherever she wants to go. If she leaves now, we'll never make it. I won't survive it. Jesus, I probably sound like a fucking pussy, but I *need* her. When she's not around, I feel like I can't even breathe. Right now I need to know that she feels the same way about me. I close my eyes and take a deep breath.

When I look up, big doe eyes are watching me . . . waiting. As much as I want to pull her to me and tell her everything is going to be okay, I can't. My stomach clenches hard and tight as rejection and a ton of other emotions that I can't even name rip through my body. "If you leave"—I glance over her shoulder, unable to look her in the eye—"we're over."

"You don't mean that?" She lunges toward me, but I step back. Tears streak down her face and my hands itch to make this right, to somehow make it work.

"But I do."

She sobs, frantically wiping the tears from her face. "We can make this work. You're making this into so much more than it is. Please, Levi, you have to understand that this is my chance to get out of this town and start a new life."

"A life without me."

"No," she says, shaking her head vehemently.

"Really?" I yell, throwing my hands out to the side. "How do you suggest we make it work? You won't be able to afford to fly home, and I can't afford to fly to California." Her mouth snaps shut. She knows I'm right. "What are we going to do, talk on the phone every night? Sure, that might work in the beginning, but what happens when school starts to get busy and those calls start getting missed? What happens when I start wondering where you are and who you're spending time with? Or vice versa . . . what if you start wondering where I am or who I'm with?"

Laney crosses her arms over her chest. She's frustrated. Good, so am I. "You don't trust me?" she scoffs. "You think I'm going to go away to school and just forget about you . . . forget about us?"

"I don't know, Laney, you tell me!" Adrenaline is coursing

through my body. My lungs are heaving, my heart racing.

"I trust you, Levi."

"Well, maybe you shouldn't." I don't mean it. I don't. But I'm hurt, and this is what fucking happens when I'm hurt. I'm stubborn as hell and I feel the need to hurt back, which judging by the look on her face, I hit my mark.

Her eyes are like daggers shooting straight through me, but I don't budge. "So what's it going to be, Laney?"

"You want me to choose? You want me to give up my dreams . . . my one chance to get out from under my dad?"

It kills me that I'm doing this to her. Lord knows I don't want to give her an ultimatum, but I know me, and I know I can't do long distance. I know that if she just chooses me, I'll move heaven and earth to make every fucking dream of hers come true. "Yes. I'm asking you to choose."

Laney's hand covers her face. Her shoulders bob several times as soft cries float from her mouth. A few minutes pass and then she straightens her back, wipes the remaining tears from her face, and looks at me sadly. "I'm sorry." She hiccups on another sob and her shoulders hunch forward. "I'm so sorry, but I have to do this, Levi."

Her words slam into me like a freight train. My mind goes blank, everything around me dissipating into a mass of emptiness. Without thinking, I reach for the vase and hurl it across the patio. Hand-painted glass shatters against the wooden deck, sending two dozen Calla lilies into the air. A faint scream echoes through the breeze, but my mind blocks it out as I grab one plate and then the other, slamming them into the side of the restaurant. A loud roar rips from my lungs, echoing through the quiet summer night.

"Levi, please." A shaky hand touches my arm and I whip around, wrenching free from her grip. The sight of her tear-streaked face infiltrates my soul and rips open my heart, a place that I will never allow another woman to ever go again. I can feel large steel walls slam down around my heart, effectively closing it off.

My eyes fall on hers, which are full of fear and anxiety. I don't want to scare her. That wasn't my intention, but she hurt me. And I've already been hurt by another woman, one who walked away from me without a second glance. Chose a different life . . . one I didn't fit into. Unfortunately, I was only twelve and didn't know not to trust and love another woman again. Well, this time I'm older, wiser, and I'll learn from my mistakes.

Swallowing hard, I turn to look at the destruction my anger left behind. Closing my eyes, I grip my hands behind my neck, tilting my head up to the sky. "You need to leave." My voice is soft . . . resigned.

"Levi, plea—"

"GO," I snap, just wanting her gone. She doesn't say another word. I'm not sure how much longer she stands there, but I know the minute she walks away because she takes my heart with her.

Chapter 1

8 years later

Laney

"ARE YOU SURE THIS IS a good idea?"

My hands freeze on the box in front of me. How the heck am I supposed to answer that? Sitting back on my calves, I blow a chunk of hair out my eyes. Mia is watching me, her eyes flitting nervously to the box in front of her.

"No"—I hang my head—"I'm fairly certain that this is probably the worst idea ever." With shaky hands, I close the box and secure it with a piece of tape. I take a deep breath, holding the air in my lungs for a few seconds before blowing it out, thankful that I'm still here . . . still breathing. It's hard sometimes, to not let my mind wander in the direction that it typically likes to roam. But I have to try. If I don't, then the negative thoughts will consume me. And I can't let them consume me because I have one goal . . . well, two really.

First, I *need* to survive. I don't care what I have to do or how hard I have to fight, I have to survive. Because goal number two is the biggie.

I need *him.* I need him in my life, however I can have him. I need his forgiveness more than I need my next breath, but I have to keep breathing to earn it.

So, there it is. As much as this is probably a horrible move, there is no other option because without him, my life will not be complete.

I can practically hear Mia's eyes begging me to look up, so I do. Tears are pooled in her beautiful baby blues and when her chin quivers, something inside of me shatters. The façade that I've had firmly in place falls, leaving me naked and vulnerable—a place I'm all too familiar with these days. "I don't have a choice, Mia." My voice cracks, and in the blink of an eye she flies across the room. Her body collides with mine, our arms wrapping around each other as we hold on for dear life.

"I know," she cries. "I just hate this. It's not fair." Burying my face into her hair, I inhale the scent of the one person who has kept me sane over the past several months.

Mia has been a godsend, perfect in every way possible. She has gone above and beyond in her friendship duties and I'm certain I'll never be able to repay her, but I'll spend the rest of my life trying . . . however long that may be. "Life isn't fair. I've learned that the hard way." She nods, wiping away her tears. "This is the last leg of my journey and then I can live my life for me."

She squeezes me once and then pulls away, cupping my tear-streaked face in her hands. Her own tears are once again cascading down her flushed cheeks and she sniffs several times before speaking. "If there is anyone in this world—*anyone*"—she tugs me a little closer—"who deserves to be happy, it's you, Lane." Her voice is scratchy and raw, and I know that she means each and every word. "Okay." Straightening her back, she dries her face with the sleeve of her shirt then levels me with a wobbly smile. "Enough of the blubbering. Let's get you home."

And this is why I love her. Mia knows when I need to be held, and even better, she knows when to let go.

Twenty-two boxes, five hours and one sexy tatted moving guy later, we are on the road, leaving Napa Valley and its beautifulness behind us. All of my belongings have been stuffed and stacked into a big orange truck, and with any luck, everything will arrive in one piece. As for Mia and me, that's questionable. Two thousand miles is a long journey, and I hope and pray that this heap of shit I call a car will make it without breaking down. The last thing we need is to get stranded, or worse yet have to spend money to fix up this hunk of junk—money that I most certainly do not have.

Lucky for me, Mia has the kind of job that allows her to make her own schedule, and by that I mean she works for her dad and pretty much told him when she was leaving and when she would be back. Mia is a trust-fund baby through and through, and although her parents can be rude and stuffy, Mia is the exact opposite. You'd never know that she is the daughter of one of the most influential men in the music industry.

Mia's dad offered for us to use his private jet, but it wasn't out of the goodness of his heart. I attribute it to Ivy, my bitch of a car. I get that he wants his daughter to arrive safely and in style, and he's concerned that my fifteen-year-old Chevy won't make it. But there was no way I was leaving her behind. As much as Ivy has a mind of her own, she's still mine, and she's the most valuable possession I have left to sell, should I need the money.

So here we are, making the one-and-a-half day trip back to St. Louis, where Mia has vowed to help me find a place to stay and get settled in before flying back home. I probably should have told her that I've already found a house, but at this point, the less she knows, the better.

Mia turns the radio down and I flash her a small smile before turning my eyes back to the road. She shifts, and when I glance back to her she's turned toward me, head leaning against the seat. I can tell by the look in her eyes that she is worrying again. It doesn't matter how many times I tell her that I'm fine and that I will be fine, she still worries. "What is it, Mia? I know that look." With my eyes trained on the road, I hear her huff out a short breath.

"How much do you have?" *Great.* This is exactly the sort of thing I don't want to talk about right now.

"It's none of your business." Mia punches me lightly in the arm and I laugh, grateful that I'm at least able to keep the conversation somewhat lighthearted. My eyes flit from her to the road several times. I know Mia, and there is no way she'll let me leave this car without getting what she wants so I finally give in. "Fifty grand."

"What?" she gasps. I use driving as my reason to not look her in the eye, because I know exactly what I'll see. It's not enough. It isn't enough to pay what I owe, to start over, or to get what I need. "Pull the fuck over." My stomach rolls with a wave of nausea, emotion slowly creeps its way up my throat and tears begin to build behind my eyes. I've been fooling myself to think that this will ever work long-term. I mean, seriously . . . who am I kidding? There is no way I'm going to make it. Tears start dripping down my face and neither one of us says a word. Signaling right, I slowly pull off to the shoulder of the interstate and an 18-wheeler whizzes by, violently rocking Ivy.

"How in the hell did you get fifty grand?"

"It's not enough," I mumble.

"That's not what has me concerned," she scoffs.

I should be slightly relieved that Mia isn't insinuating I haven't saved enough, but now I'm worried about her reaction to how I've been able to save that much in the first place. Finally building up the nerve, I look over at her. Her wide eyes are looking straight at me and I can practically see the wheels spinning in her head. Mia knows how much I made, and I know her well enough to know that she's working furiously to try and calculate how I was able to live and still save fifty grand.

Turning in my seat, I tuck a leg under my butt. "I've worked hard, Mia." Her eyes soften. "You know how much overtime I had been working prior to my surgery, and you know I don't spend any money unless I have to."

She laughs humorlessly. "Oh trust me, I know," she says, sarcasm dripping from her voice. "I know you've saved and I know you've skimped on things, but knowing you were able to save *that much* makes me feel like I've been naïve about just *how much* you've been skimping." California is damn expensive, and when Mia and I first met, yes, I was skimping on everything from water to food to electricity, just to make ends meet. But when I got sick, I promised her that I would start taking better care of myself.

"Can we please not have this convers—?"

"No!" she interrupts, slapping a hand on her leg. "We're going to have this conversation. Damn it, Laney!" Her jaw clenches tight and she looks away, running her fingers through her long blond hair before burying her face in her hands. I watch in shock as her tiny shoulders start bobbing up and down. It's sort of ironic that I'm the one that needs to comfort her. I gently rub a hand down her back and she jerks away, a light sob falling from her mouth.

"Mia?"

"Don't you get it?" she snaps, looking up at me. Mascara is smeared down her face and her eyes are pinning me in my seat, pleading with me to understand what she's saying. "I need you, Laney." She pounds her fist over her heart. "So you can't cut corners. This is your life!" My heart clenches at her words and I wish that I could give her some sort of reassurance that I'm not going anywhere—ever. But I can't. And she and I both know it.

Her brows dip low and her lips thin into a tight line. "Have you been lying to me?" I'm not really sure if she's asking, since the look on her face tells me that she already knows the answer.

"I haven't lied . . . exactly."

"What the fuck is that supposed to mean?" I absolutely hate that we are having this conversation, mostly because I know she's right. I haven't been living in poverty, but it's been pretty darn close. I needed to save up enough to pay the ungodly amount of money that I'm about to spend when I get to St. Louis, and that's not taking into consideration the heap of bills I owe that stupid-ass hospital in California.

It wasn't by choice, but I needed the extra money and every penny counts. Who cares if I've substituted fresh fruits and vegetables for canned soup and ramen noodles? Who cares that I haven't taken a single pain pill in order to save a couple hundred bucks? So yes, I've cut corners to save money, but look at me. I'm healthy—*well, sort of*—clothed and I've had a roof over my head. "Laney Renee, please tell me that you've been eating and taking care of yourself, because I'm not sure I can handle it if you haven't."

"You're overreacting."

"I'm not."

"You are. I promise you that it's not as bad you're probably thinking." She rolls her eyes. "Would you just trust me? I'm fine, I promise." *I'm going straight to hell for that lie.* "And look, cutting corners is going to help out in the long run. I'll be able to pay off some bills and I can start my treatments as soon as I get to town."

A slender hand slides down the front of her face at the same time she releases a long, slow breath. "Sure, it'll help out in the long run, but now I feel guilty wondering what in the hell you've been doing to be able to put away that much money." She looks down. I wouldn't dare tell her about all of the other things I've done to save a couple of pennies—that might throw her into a complete tailspin. Mia doesn't need to know that milk, juice and meat were not staples on my grocery list, or that I cancelled my cable and internet several months ago. It's not surprising that she didn't know since most of our time together was spent at her posh

K.L. GRAYSON

condo, especially during my recovery. The few times that she did come over to my place, she always brought a movie so it was never questioned.

Although I was able to hide a lot from her, she still knew that I had a pile of medical bills that were eating away at me. Mia has offered to pay off my hospital bill several times, but I can't take her money, mostly because I know that I'll never be able to pay her back. Sure, I have COBRA health insurance that I'm paying out the wazoo for, but it's shitty at best. I'm not naïve; this debt will most likely stay with me until the day I die.

Resting my hand on her leg, I squeeze it lightly and her sad eyes find mine. "I'm going to fight, Mia. I'm going to put up the biggest fight of my life, and I promise you that I'll try my hardest to beat this." She nods once, grabs me around the shoulders and tugs me toward her. I'm not sure how long we sit there on the side of the interstate, but it doesn't really matter because if there is one thing that I've learned over the past several months, it's that moments like this need to be treasured.

Chapter 2

Laney

"THAT'S IT?" DISAPPOINTMENT SEEPS THROUGH Mia's voice as she twists her head, stretching her neck to try and get a full view out the window.

"That's it."

From the corner of my eye, I see her slump back in her seat. "I'm not impressed. It's just a big metal—"

"—arch." There's no need for me to look; I have the damn thing and everything surrounding it memorized. It may just be an arch, but it symbolizes a time in my life when things were different . . . easier. The first boy to steal my heart—the man who still owns it—kissed me for the first time under the Gateway Arch, and many times after that as well. Our evenings were often spent walking around the grounds beneath the monument, sitting on the banks and watching the barges drift carelessly down the Mississippi River. We spent those nights making out under the stars, dreaming and talking about the future . . . a future that *I* robbed us of.

"Yes, an arch. But why an arch? Why not a triangle or a circle?" I blink, smiling softly, thankful that Mia pulled me from my thoughts before my memories took me down a path I wasn't ready to travel. Don't get me wrong, I'm totally going down that road, just not right now. Not today.

"Google it." I shrug, rolling the window down so I can stick out my arm and feel the warm air whip it around. I twirl my hand, letting it float through the air like I did when I was a kid. *"You're gonna get that arm ripped off,"* my mom would scold from the front seat. But of course, I didn't care then and I don't care now. I rest my head back on the seat, my arm dangling from the window as I weave Ivy in and out of traffic. The people of St. Louis think their traffic is bad, but this is nothing compared to some of the jams I ended up in while living in California.

"Is that your answer to everything, *Google it?*" I glance at Mia, laughing when I see her pull out her phone.

"You're googling it, aren't you?"

"Absolutely not."

I cock an eyebrow. "Okay," I reply in mock agreement, throwing my head back in laughter seconds later when she starts rattling off facts about the St. Louis Arch.

"It was a competition. People were competing to design a monument . . . obviously, the Arch won," she says dryly, pausing to read more. I shake my head in amusement at how engrossed she is in this. "It's six hundred and thirty feet tall and . . . OH MY GOD—" She slaps me on the arm and I glance between her and the road several times because there is no way in hell I want to miss my exit . . . and because I should probably drive with my eyes on the road. "We can go up *in* the Arch!"

"Um, no."

She scoffs. "Why not?" I will not look at her. I won't do it. She has these big huge puppy dog eyes and they get me every damn time. "Fine. Then we should at least put it on our bucket lists." I barely have time to register what she says before whipping my head in her direction. Her eyes are wide with regret, hand covering her mouth. She slowly shakes her head. "I'm so sorry. I didn't mean that. Please, don't listen to me. I'm a total bitch and I suck as a friend and I'm so sorry. Please forgive me." Words keep falling from her lips, and only when my tires hit the rumble strips on the side of the interstate do I look up in time to slam on the brakes, mere seconds before barreling into the back of another car. My fingers are clenched around the steering wheel, my heart beating wildly in my chest as my breathing comes out in labored pants. It could be because of the fifty-car pileup I nearly caused, but more likely because Mia is right.

I haven't lived my life. I take that back, I've lived it—safely— but have I really enjoyed it? I'm not so sure. I've always been a careful person, never one to step out of the box or take chances. I didn't drink before my twenty-first birthday, didn't cliff dive into the quarry on graduation day, and skinny dipping in the river with my friends was a big fat no-no. My fear of getting caught, getting in trouble, or worse yet, getting arrested, kept me from doing a lot of things. And looking back, I wish I had those memories. Memories of fun times, being a foolish teenager and breaking rules. Memories that I could call on when the reality of my life gets to be too much and I need an escape.

Tomorrow is not promised—to anyone—and I think it's time I start living what life I have left to its fullest potential. At the end of the day, when everything is said and done, I don't want to look back on my life with regrets. I want to be happy knowing that I took chances, went on adventures and tried new things. Moving back home doesn't have to just be about making amends with *him,* it can be a fresh start . . . a chance for me to start living. I can do things that I never would have dreamt of doing. My heart rate kicks up a few notches, a burst of warmth slowly spreading through my body at the thought of doing something wild and crazy, and I can feel my lips start to lift.

My mind starts racing with ideas. Things I can do . . . things that—surprisingly—I *want* to do. Skydiving. Bungee jumping. Skinny dipping. Cliff diving. Get a tattoo. Seriously, what's the worst that could happen? My life is already hanging in the balance, and who knows, maybe this will be good for me. Spice things up a little bit—have some fun. Go out with a bang, so to speak. My fingers itch to pull the car over and start making a list, but instead I reach across the console and squeeze Mia's leg.

"You're right," I whisper, my eyes trained on the car in front of me. "Let's make a list."

"Laney?"

"It's fine. Really." And I am fine, because I need this. I need to know that I'm still alive, and what better way than giving myself one hell of an adrenaline rush? She grips my hand in hers, but I refuse to take my eyes off the road because I know that if I look at her, I'll lose it. I'll start bawling like a damn baby, and right now I don't want to cry. I want to be excited about this new adventure that I'm going to take myself on.

"I'm so sorry," she says.

"I know. It's okay, really. I promise I'm not mad." I glance in her direction, and I can tell by her guilt-ridden eyes that she doesn't believe me. "Mia, this will be good for me. I think making a bucket list is a great idea." A couple of tears drip past her lashes and trickle down her face but I blink hard, focusing my attention back on the road. There is no sense in getting upset. This is my reality. Mia squeezes my hand a little tighter before I pull it from her grasp.

Thankfully, traffic has started moving and when I see the sign for my exit, I signal right and follow the ramp. Weaving through the city, I listen contentedly as Mia points out different shops and restaurants as we pass them, and each time she names something familiar it makes me realize how homesick I've really been.

I turn left down a one-way street, hoping that Mia doesn't catch on to the change in scenery. "Um . . . Lane?" Dang it. I knew she'd notice. I had no doubt she would've said something as soon as we pulled up in front of the line of houses, but I was hoping to put this argument off for a few more minutes.

"Yeah?" I ask absently, pretending that I'm concentrating on where I'm going.

"Where the fuck are you going?"

"Language," I scold.

Mia clutches her purse to her body. Out of the corner of my eye, I see her chewing on the inside of her mouth and I feel sort of bad for not being completely truthful with her about my living arrangements. "Seriously, Lane, turn around. This place doesn't seem very safe."

Mia was raised in a gated community with a silver spoon in her mouth, so the sight of run-down buildings and not-so-clean people walking the streets is freaking her the hell out. I'm not going to lie, I'm a little freaked out myself, but this doesn't affect me quite as much as her because I was raised in a similar neighborhood. After my mom passed away, my dad ended up in foreclosure on my childhood home. Money was tight and we ended up in the 'bad' part of town, where drug dealers were arrested on a daily basis and the sound of gunshots would often wake me up at night. I have absolutely no idea how Luke and I made it out alive, but we did. You learn quickly how to survive. You keep your head down, don't talk to anyone unless you have to, and when it's absolutely necessary, you suck up . . . to the right people.

My 'suck up' was in the form of food for protection. There was a young man, Benny, who lived in the apartment next to ours. His mom was a junkie and oftentimes he would go days without eating. Benny was an attractive boy of Latino descent. He was tall and strong with a hard face that most people found intimidating, despite his young age.

Once, Luke and I were being pushed around by some older kids at the bus stop and Benny stepped in to save us. That night I sat outside of my apartment with a container of ramen noodles and waited for him to come out of his home. Two hours later he finally came out, and it was there, on a shredded welcome mat between two apartment doors, that I first offered Benny food in exchange for protection.

"Don't worry, Mia. I've got it covered." I pull over in front of a small brick shotgun house and double-check the number on the mailbox with the number I have written down. "This is it."

Stuffing my phone in my pocket, I reach in the center console and grab my can of Mace, shaking it several times to make sure it's still full.

"What the hell is that?"

Turning in my seat, I look at a pale-faced Mia. I can't help but giggle at the look of horror in her eyes. "It's Mace." I wiggle the can in front of her face and a hysterical burst of laughter rips from her lips as she runs a shaky hand through her hair.

"Well, no shit, Sherlock. What concerns me is that we need it . . . why the hell do we need it, Lane? Let's just go." Her frantic eyes are pleading with me to start the car and drive away, but I can't. What Mia doesn't know is that I don't need her to help me find a place to live—thanks to Benny, I've already found one. I'm not a complete bitch so I do feel bad that I led her to believe we would be doing some house-hunting. But my idea of house-hunting and Mia's idea of house-hunting are *way* different. Although she has been my best friend for the past several years, there are still quite a few things Mia doesn't know about me—about my life. For instance, she doesn't know that the man peering in through her window is not a thug, but my new neighbor and a huge teddy bear.

The gentle giant taps twice on the window and I watch in slow motion as Mia turns around in her seat, taking in the man standing outside of the car.

"Ohmigod," she squeals, whipping back around, pinning me with terrified eyes. "Ohmigod, ohmigod, ohmigod. Please. Please move. Go, Lane. *Please.*" I wish I had the strength to compose myself, but I don't. I can't help the giggle that bubbles up from my throat, or the way I push her hand away when she tries to start my car. I'm a horrible friend—well, not really, but I'm sure she thinks so right about now. Pushing open my door, I slide from the car. I effectively mute her pleading screams as I close the door and then run at full force into a set of strong, waiting arms. Arms that I'd grown to love over the years. Arms that I trust and miss.

Chapter 3

Laney

"BENNY!" MY BODY SLAMS INTO his hard chest and he doesn't waste any time gathering me to him. Benny has never been an affectionate person—he's more a fighter than a lover—but I learned early on that it's only because he was never really loved. No one took the time to show him affection. I inhale deeply, reveling in my first taste of home. "I missed you," I mumble, my face smashed in the crook of his neck.

"Christ, Laney, it's so good to see you." His rough voice is thick with emotion and I squeeze him a little bit tighter, thankful that we've kept in touch over the years.

"Me?" I pull back to look at his face, but he doesn't put me down. "It's good to see *you.* Look at you, Benny." His grip loosens and I drop to the sidewalk, my eyes roaming his body, taking him in. "You're such a handsome devil"—he flushes and I nudge his arm—"but that's nothing new." He glances down, rubbing a hand on the back of his neck. *I embarrassed him.* His eyes shift to my car and he jerks his thumb.

Mia is watching us, but I can tell her eyes aren't on me. Her bottom lip is tucked between her teeth, her telltale sign that she's found something she likes. She's sizing Benny up, probably trying to decide if she should jump him or run away. Mia has always been able to get whatever man she wants. With her golden blond hair, ice blue eyes and killer curves, she's never had to ask and she sure as hell has never had to beg.

I shift my gaze and find Benny staring back at her with a look of confusion, most likely because seconds ago Mia was ready to bolt just at the sight of him. Not that I can blame her . . . Benny is nothing less than intimidating. He also happens to be incredibly good-looking. Every inch of his six-foot-three frame is a chiseled mass of muscle, and a majority of those muscles are decorated in every tattoo imaginable. But if you can look past the bright colors and bulging biceps, Benny is nothing more than a beautiful soul who was dealt a shitty hand.

His head is cocked to the side, brows furrowed, as Mia's wandering gaze roams up his body and back down before she catches my eye. Her eyes widen in embarrassment, no doubt because I caught her ogling, and I can practically hear her huff before she crosses her arms over her chest and turns in her seat. I slap Benny's arm and he shakes his head as though I just pulled him from a trance. I have no idea what in the hell is going on here, but if I get a vote, I think she should jump him. Benny might be a little rough around the edges, but he had a difficult childhood and an even harder start to adulthood. The guy could use a good woman to ruffle his feathers a little bit.

He looks at me for a beat and then shifts his attention back to the car. "I should probably go apologize to Cinderella." I snicker, knowing that not only does that nickname fit Mia to a T but also how much she would utterly despise it. Waving my hand in the direction of my car and the seething woman inside it, I give him my permission to go right ahead. He saunters across the sidewalk and I turn to look at my new home.

Home.

Eagerly, I make my way up the sidewalk. Black faded shutters frame the windows, paint is chipping from the front door, and when I reach for the knob, it wiggles loosely in my hand. But all of that is superficial. Unlike me, all of that can be fixed. Pushing open the heavy door, I walk in and smile at the sight that greets me. Dark hardwood floors as far as I can see are scuffed and worn, but I smile because it's a testament to how much this house has truly been 'lived' in. Someone, most likely Luke or Benny, has polished the tattered wood to near perfection and a soft blue rug sits in the middle of the living room.

"I've got new furniture coming, but it isn't here yet." I freeze, excitement bubbling up inside of me at the sound of his voice. Spinning around, I find Luke leaning casually against the door-frame leading into the kitchen. His hands are tucked deep in his pockets and his knowing eyes are watching me. I haven't seen my brother in two years and he's definitely changed in that time. His eyes are hardened and his hair is longer, now sweeping across his forehead.

When I first moved to California, Luke and I went three years without seeing each other. We were both in college and neither one of us could afford a plane ticket. But nothing—and I mean nothing—was going to keep me from my brother. He was all I had left. We talked on the phone almost every day and decided that once we were able to save up enough money, we were going to meet and go on vacation together somewhere since we never took vacations as children. Our first trip was on my third summer away, and we met in Chicago for five days of much needed re-connection. Since then, we've been to Florida and Colorado, and thanks to my little friend that has decided to take up residence in my body, our next destination has yet to be determined.

"You didn't have to get me new furniture. I've got a couch and chair coming here from . . . home." It's weird referring to California as my 'home,' even though it has been for the past eight years. St. Louis has been and always will be my *home*. It holds all of my memories, both good and bad, and it's the one place that I will always come back to, no matter where I am in life.

Pushing away from the wall, Luke takes three long strides,

putting himself directly in front of me. To an outsider, we probably look like complete idiots. Here we are, brother and sister, and we haven't yet made one move to hug. But to us, it's normal—it's what we do. We size each other up, reminding ourselves that the other one is, in fact, real . . . and here. Which is what I'm certain Luke is doing now, considering he hasn't seen me since my diagnosis. "I know I didn't have to get you furniture, but I wanted to. Both the couch and chair were old when Dad had them. Plus, I figured a new set of furniture for your new home . . . it was the least I could do for the girl who practically raised me." And this is exactly why I have the best brother in the entire world.

Luke reaches for me at the same time I reach for him. We cling to each other for several minutes, neither of us saying a word or making a move to pull away. Sometimes you just need this. You just need to know that there is someone in your life that will love you, no matter what—someone that you never have to worry about leaving. Because that's what most people do, don't they? That's what I did anyway. "I love you, Luke." I fight back the tears, determined not to let my emotions taint what should be a happy reunion.

"I love you too, Laneybug." I hear the front door open and then shut, but I refuse to move. I have two years' worth of hugs to make up for and there is no way I'm ready to let go.

"She sure does have a thing for hugging hot men today, doesn't she?" Leave it to Mia to find my brother attractive. I smile into Luke's chest at the same time he lifts his head to see who the sassy mouth belongs to.

"You think I'm hot?" Benny's voice sounds smug and I can just picture him staring at her with his typical 'bad boy charmer' look.

"No. Not at all—"

"But you just said—"

"I'm sleep deprived," Mia quips, "leave it alone." Luke laughs a deep throaty laugh and I pull away from his embrace in time to find Mia sizing him up—only this time she's met her match.

Luke takes a step toward her and offers her his hand.

"You must be Mia." Her eyes flash with joy and she slips a perfectly manicured hand into Luke's. He lifts her hand to his mouth, never breaking eye contact, and places a single kiss to her knuckles. My brother, forever the charmer.

"And you must be the man I'm going home with tonight." Luke barks out a laugh and Benny rolls his eyes, pushing past us. I watch his retreating form walk into the kitchen before turning my gaze back to Mia.

"Mia, stop hitting on my brother." Her eyes flit between me and Luke, a seductive smile curling her lips.

"Laney, there is no way that this is Luke. The Luke that you've shown me pictures of is nothing but a boy. This guy here"—with one hand still clutched in his, she lifts the other to his chest—"is all man."

Luke's head twists in my direction, a shit-eating grin plastered across his face. No. There is no way that this is going to happen. "Down girl. He's my brother, for Christ's sake."

"Chill, Mama Bear," Luke says, letting go of Mia's hand. "I still remember the rule."

"Rule? What rule?" Luke and I laugh. Mia stares at us, waiting for an explanation.

"Luke here isn't allowed to touch any of my friends," I answer, giving her a cheeky smile.

Mia's eyes roll in disbelief, but I don't expect anything less from the girl who has never had to follow a rule a day in her life. "Well, that's no fun."

"Well, that's Laney, forever the fun sucker." I slap Luke in the chest and he laughs, bending down to kiss my cheek. "Just kidding. You know I love you." I grunt in response. "Okay, I've got to run," he says, digging his keys out of his pocket. "I have a meeting in twenty minutes, but Benny has everything else taken care of. If you need me, call me. Got it?"

"Got it," I nod.

Luke turns to Mia just as Benny walks back into the room.

"Mia, it was a pleasure meeting you." Her answering smile drips with sweetness. Luke turns back to me. "I'll see you tomorrow, and please don't forget to tell me when you schedule your first appointment. I want to be there with you." I know he means it; I can tell by the pleading look in his eyes. Plus, I know how much it killed him when he couldn't be with me during my surgery. As much as I would prefer to do this by myself, I know Luke wants to support me however he can. It's hard because he wants so badly to wave a hand and make all of this go away, but the truth of the matter is that he can't.

No one can.

"I'm calling first thing in the morning. I'll let you know as soon as I have an appointment."

"Perfect." With one last peck on the cheek for me and a quick wave 'goodbye' at Benny, Luke is out the door. Spinning around, I find Mia lounged on the blue rug, messing with her phone. Benny is poised on a step stool screwing a new light bulb into my ceiling fan, and I take a moment to look around. I'm not sure how I got here, figuratively speaking, but now that I'm here I have no intention of leaving. The thought of endless possibilities puts an enormous smile on my face.

"What are you grinning at?" Benny's warm smile flashes at me from up above.

"I'm happy." I move across the room to unpack one of my bags that mysteriously made its way into the house. "I can't wait to decorate my new home, and I'm excited that I can see you and Luke whenever I want." I shrug, loving that I have Benny next door and Luke just a few miles away. Ideally, I'd love to buy a house, but for now I'll have to settle for renting. "I'm just happy to be home." And it really is as simple as that. No matter what life throws at me, no matter where it takes me, right here and right now I am happy, and that's really all I can ask for.

Chapter 4

Laney

"MIA?" I NUDGE HER SHOULDER lightly, not wanting to startle her. "Mia?" She squirms in her seat before lazily blinking her eyes.

"Hmmm?" Sitting up, she stretches her arms and yawns. Her once silky hair is matted and plastered against the side of her head. She rubs a hand along the back of her neck. The past two days have really taken a toll on her. The same night we arrived in St. Louis, the moving van showed up, and the next morning my new furniture arrived. Needless to say, we've spent nearly every waking moment since then hauling boxes into the house, unpacking them, and putting all my stuff away. I fussed and argued with Benny and Mia, telling them that the boxes could wait, but Mia insisted that the house be in perfect living order before she leaves to go back home. I wish I could say that I'm as exhausted as Mia, but they wouldn't let me lift a finger even after my reassurance that I'm no longer bound by post-surgery heavy lifting restrictions.

So here I am, bright-eyed and bushy-tailed, itching to do something, and Mia is so spent that she can barely keep her eyes open. "Mia, go to bed. You're exhausted and you need some extra sleep." She moans, lifting her hand as though it takes every ounce of strength she has.

She looks at her watch. "But it's only seven."

"Who cares what time it is? Go to bed and get some rest. I'll wake you up in the morning and we'll go out for biscuits and gravy." I'm certain the promise of biscuits and gravy for breakfast will do it. Mia is a biscuit and gravy addict, and how in the hell she is able to eat as much of it as she does and still keep her movie star figure is beyond me.

"Deal." She pushes up from the couch and stumbles down the hall to my room. That's the only downfall to these shotgun houses . . . they're small. Mia offered to sleep on the couch while she's here, but I was having none of it. I offered to share my bed and we've spent the past few nights cuddled up next to each other.

Sliding from the couch, I walk out the front door and take a seat on the porch. My eyes drift to the blanket of stars in the sky and I stare at them in wonder. My mom used to tell me that I could wish on any star any time I wanted, but if I ever saw a shooting star I could make two wishes. I couldn't begin to tell you how many wishes I've made on these stars over the years. Some of them have come true, others not so much. But it's still fun to believe.

I search for the North Star, and out of nowhere a shooting star darts across the sky. I squeeze my eyes shut. I don't even have to think about what my two wishes will be. There are only two things I want in life, and as fun as it is to close my eyes and hope, I know that it will take more than a little bit of effort on my part to help make these wishes come true.

Standing up, I dust off my butt. I hustle inside and leave a quick note for Mia that I'll be right back. Grabbing my keys and purse, I head back out, double-checking that the door is locked. "I was wondering how long it would take you." Benny's deep voice startles me and I spin around, my purse clutched tight against my chest.

"You scared the heck out of me." He chuckles, stepping down

from his porch, hands buried in his pockets.

"I saw you out here a minute ago. You always did like looking at the stars." It shouldn't surprise me that he remembers. "How many wishes did you make?"

I look down, embarrassed. "Two," I whisper. The grass crunches under the weight of Benny's shoes, and I watch as his black boots stop in front of me. His warm hand cups my chin and he lifts my face.

"We all make wishes, Laney. We all hope and dream and pray, so don't be ashamed." I nod. Benny has been through so much in his life, much more than I've been through, and I can't even imagine how many times he's probably wished and dreamt and prayed. "The key is to wish for things that aren't unattainable." My eyes burn and I swallow hard. "I don't know what you wished for, Laney, but I hope they come true." He steps back and turns toward my house. "Go. You've waited two days, and frankly I'm surprised you were able to wait that long." I smile. He knows me well, and therefore he knows exactly where I'm going. "I'll be here in case Rapunzel wakes up."

"Rapunzel?" I ask, confused.

Benny laughs. "What can I say? It's fun to piss her off." He shrugs his shoulder and I shake my head in mock admonishment. Then he walks me to my car, opens my door and I slide into the seat. "Just be careful, okay?"

"Careful is my middle name." I flash him my brightest smile. He shuts my door and taps the hood of my car twice before he disappears into the night.

It's not a far drive, maybe two or three miles, but the closer I get to Flame, the harder my heart slams inside my chest. My palms are sweaty and butterflies have taken flight in my stomach, and I'm grateful that I forgot to eat supper. The parking lot is crowded, so I pull along the side of the restaurant, knowing from my time working here that there's a small alleyway leading to the back where no one ever parks. It's mostly a place where the bartenders would come to smoke.

I exit the car and slowly wander around the front of the building. My hand glides along the warm brick. This place was like a second home to me, and not just because of the boy who worked here. It was an escape, a sanctuary of sorts. I looked forward to working because if I was here, then it meant I wasn't at home. Plus, when I was here, I was eating real food, not just soup or whatever else I was able to scrounge from our bare fridge.

I stumble but quickly recover before what would have been a nasty face plant into the ground. I look down at the offending culprit and notice for the first time a walkway where there never used to be a walkway. My eyes follow the path until it ends at a beautiful building that is now attached to Flame. In large blue script, the word 'Blue' is written above the front entrance.

Following the path, I walk toward Blue, my eyes taking in everything I see. The front of the building is made entirely of glass. Of course, I can't see in because the windows are heavily tinted, but the architecture is absolutely breathtaking. Dan Beckford, Levi's father, owns Flame, and I can't help but wonder when he built Blue. Of all the times we've spoken over the years, he's never mentioned it. Honestly, I can't say I'm surprised because there is something else—or I guess I should say *someone* else—that he never mentions. Don't get me wrong, I've tried . . . several times, in fact. But the old man just won't budge. Then again, why would he? His son gave me an ultimatum, and I didn't choose him.

A loud thud catches my attention and I whip around, wishing I had carried my Mace with me. Not that this is a bad neighborhood—because it isn't. Faint shouting is coming from around the building and I jog across the lot, back toward my car. The closer I get, the louder the shouts become.

"You're a prick!" I round the corner, and in the blink of an eye I'm being plowed over by an angry woman. I feel something sharp stab into the palm of my hand as my body slams backward on the concrete. I wince, but somehow manage to keep my eyes locked on the beautiful woman as she trips over me. She's able to catch her balance before mumbling a clipped "sorry." Her heels click loudly against the asphalt and I stare at her in awe, wishing for nothing more than to be able to walk that steady in a pair of heels that tall. "Tell Dan to call me when he grows a brain and fires your sorry ass," she throws over her shoulder.

My gaze snaps to the unfortunate soul who is on the receiving end of her heated words. When my eyes land on Levi, my mouth falls open. I knew there was a tiny chance I might see him tonight, though nothing could have prepared me for it. Levi was always a good-looking young man, but I don't need more than the light of the moon to see just how generous time has been to him.

His thick frame walks right on past me without a second glance and I welcome the moment of reprieve. Because this is it. This is the moment that I've thought about over and over and over again for the past eight years. And as I watch him stop, hands poised against his hips as he goes head-to-head with an irate woman, every speech I had ever concocted falls to the wayside.

Levi is dressed to the nines in a dark purple button-up shirt that is tucked neatly into a pair of black fitted slacks. His sleeves are bunched up around his elbows, and when his hands flex on his hips, I get the most magnificent view of his chiseled forearms. The yelling continues, but honestly, I couldn't tell you a darn word that is being said because I can't seem to tear my eyes off this stunning man. His feet are spread slightly, planted firmly on the ground, and the material of his pants stretches tight against his butt and thighs. Sweet baby Jesus, what I wouldn't give to be wrapped around him like that.

You could be, but you blew it.

I close my eyes, remembering what it felt like to be surrounded by Levi. It was nothing short of perfect. His touch alone had the ability to calm me in ways that nothing, or no one else, ever could. When I was with him, I felt safe and loved, and at that time in my life those were two things I didn't feel very often. I didn't need him to say the words, because every time he looked at me, I could see it in his eyes. I could feel it in his touch. He loved me.

I know he did.

Walking away from Levi isn't my biggest regret . . . although it's a close second. God knows I would give up just about anything to be able to turn back time and make that decision all over again. My biggest regret is that I walked away without telling him how *I* felt—without telling him how much he meant to me.

A thick lump forms in my throat as my mind replays that night. *I love you.* I can still hear the excitement in his voice as he professed his love for me for the first—and only—time. If I could turn the clock back, I'd throw myself at him, tell him he's the most important person in my life and I'd never let him go. But I can't. Because while he was confessing his love, I was ripping his heart out . . . and that's something I'll never be able to forgive myself for.

Somewhere in the back of mind, I register the silence that has enveloped me. I listen for the angry voices but come up empty. I peel my eyes open to find a scowling Levi staring down at me. His hands are hanging loosely at his sides and his dark blue eyes are swirling with a thousand different emotions as they search my face.

"Laney." My name is but a whisper, but the sound of it on his lips sends shivers up my spine.

"Hi, Levi."

Chapter 5

Levi

SOMEONE SPIKED MY DRINK. THERE'S no other explanation for why I'm seeing Laney Jacobs sprawled out on the ground, staring up at me with those fucking doe eyes that have haunted my dreams for the past eight years. Except it really is her because she just said my name in that unmistakably sexy voice I couldn't forget if I tried.

My mind is stuck. Completely frozen. And despite any attempt otherwise, I'm unable to keep my eyes from roaming every inch of her. She must be just as shocked as I am because she too is staring at me like she just saw a ghost, and I can only imagine what we would look like to someone that happened to walk by.

She opens her mouth several times but nothing comes out. *Yeah, I know the feeling.* I honestly never thought that this moment would come, and now that it's here, the only thing running on repeat in my head is—

"What the hell are you doing here?" Her eyes widen a fraction and she purses her lips. Seriously? What the hell did she expect me to say? *"Welcome home. How've you been? Let's have dinner."* Fuck no. I've got to give her credit, though. Even with my harsh words, she still keeps hers eyes locked on mine. And holy shit . . . those eyes. I used to find them hypnotizing. Sage and emerald green with swirls of soft caramel. I could get lost in them for days on end with no sense of time. It's a damn good thing they have absolutely no effect on me at all anymore.

None.

Zilch.

Nada.

She's splayed out on the parking lot, leaning back casually on her palms as though she just sat down to relax. Her short little legs look a mile long in her cutoff jean shorts. She's wearing a loose-fitting t-shirt that does nothing for the sexy little body that I know she's got hiding underneath. And what I wouldn't give to have it wrapped around me again for just one more night.

She clears her throat and my gaze snaps to hers. Warmth slides up my neck, seeping into my cheeks. I clench my jaw. Hard. *Fucking embarrassing.* I don't mind getting caught ogling a beautiful woman, but I sure as hell don't want to get caught ogling *this* woman. Surprisingly, she doesn't look smug. No, she looks . . . hopeful, which does nothing to help me sort the through the jumbled mess of emotions I've got floating around. Sitting up, Laney brushes her hands together, knocking off the dirt.

"This is my home," she whispers, peeking up at me under a thick set of bangs that weren't there the last time I saw her. I shouldn't be surprised. Deep down I knew she wouldn't stay the same, but I can't help but wonder what else about her has changed. Are Calla lilies still her favorite flower? Does she still eat triple fudge ice cream and French fries when she's sad? Where has she been? Where does she work? Does she still love fried pickles and deep-dish pizza? *Does she ever think about me?*

Laney was my world, and as I stare at her for the first time in eight years, the pull to be near her and touch her is stronger than I ever remember it. But it doesn't seem to matter what I'm feeling, because the memory of her walking away from me—from us—is still very vivid in my mind.

"No." I shake my head, brow furrowed. "Your home is in California. If this was your home, it wouldn't have taken you eight years to come back." She flinches. Her eyes dart frantically around the parking lot before she squares her shoulders and holds up her hand.

"Could you help me up?"

"No," I answer quickly, astonished that she would even ask. There's no way I can touch her. I've worked too damn hard to purge her from my system, and I'm terrified that one touch of her silky skin is all it would take to erase the past eight years. My gaze drifts to her hand. If I close my eyes, I'm certain I could still feel the way the pads of her fingers used to roam across my chest, trail down my abs, grab onto my c—

Fuck no. I push away the memory before I actually let it in and look at her with a cool indifference.

She watches me carefully for several seconds before slowly lowering her hand back to her lap. "I should've never left," she whispers. And there it is. The icing on the fucking cake. Her words slam into me at full force and I run my hand through my hair, gripping it tight.

"But you did," I growl, hating that Laney's been back in my life for all of two minutes and she's already got me worked up like this. She bites her lip, her eyes shimmering.

"Worst mistake I ever made," she says with conviction. Fucking hell, I don't want to hear this shit now. This woman walked away without a second fucking glance, and then a couple of weeks after that, she ripped my heart out again. As if the first time wasn't enough. So yeah, eight years ago I would have welcomed those words . . . but not now.

"Fuck!" My hands fist at my side. "What the hell do I say to that, Laney?" The look of regret and guilt written across her face is almost my undoing. "You walked away from me, remember?" My voice, along with my blood pressure, is rising with each word as I stab a finger into my chest. "You're the one who left me."

Her eyes stay locked on mine. I have absolutely no idea what's going through that pretty little head of hers and it's driving me insane.

"You gave me an ultimatum, Levi. I realize that I made more than my fair share of mistakes and I'm adult enough to admit that, but it wasn't just me who was wrong. You forced my hand. You forced me to choose between you and my future—"

"Don't you get it?" I yell. "I *was* your future, Laney. Me!" My chest is heaving and my hands are shaking. Adrenaline is running rampant through my veins and suddenly I feel exhausted. I don't want to do this. This isn't me. I haven't lost my temper since that night eight years ago. Only Laney seems to bring this out in me. Well, not tonight.

"Listen"—I take a deep breath and lace my fingers above my head—"I wasn't prepared to see you tonight and I'm not ready to hash things out with you." Laney bites on the inside of her mouth, and just when I think she might very well burst into tears, a look of understanding slides across her face. She pushes up from the ground and it takes every last ounce of strength I have to keep from reaching out to help her up. She rubs her palms along the sides of her shorts and a bright red streak appears on the faded material.

"You're bleeding," I breathe, moving toward her. She lifts her hand, absently examining it.

"Huh. I guess I am." She shrugs her shoulders as if it's no big deal.

"Come on." I tug on her elbow then release her almost instantly when I realize my hand is touching her skin. She doesn't say anything, just looks down with a saddened gaze. "I have a first-aid kit in my office. Let's clean that up." Surprisingly, she doesn't fight me, instead choosing to follow behind quietly as I push the door open and weave my way through the back of the restaurant toward my office. I lead her into the adjoining bathroom where she props her hip against the sink while I make quick work of finding the peroxide, antibiotic cream, and Band-Aids. I concentrate on my breathing—in and out—and my rage from a few moments ago gradually fades.

"Where's Dan?" Her words roll casually off of her tongue—

too casually. Something doesn't sit right with me. *Has she talked to my father?*

"He's finally stepping back. He's getting too old to do this anyway." She nods. I lay everything out on the sink and keep talking. Why, I have no idea. "Mason was supposed to take over Flame since I'm running Blue, but with all of the changes we've had going on, we've both been stretched a bit thin."

"Blue is yours?"

"It is," I confirm, turning the faucet on to let the water warm up. I don't want to talk to her about Blue. Frankly, I don't want to talk to her at all. I need to get her the hell out of here. I'm so damn confused. One part of me wants to push her away, while the other part is struggling to pull her close and all these damn feelings are fucking with my head.

"It's beautiful," she says, her warm breath fanning the side of my face. I take a deep breath and look up. It blows me away that she's here, in my office, talking to me about Blue. I can see every emotion running across her face—I always could read her like a book—but hope and fear seem to be battling for control. Her bright eyes are begging me to see her, her hands are itching to touch me, and I can tell by the way she keeps biting her lower lip that she is feeling the exact thing I'm trying *not* to feel. Our connection.

"Here." I shove the wet cloth at her, mad at myself for even entertaining the fact that we still have a connection. Because we don't. Nope, she broke that bond. Sure, it took me awhile to get over her, but I did.

"Oh. Okay." She grabs the cloth and dabs at the cut on the palm of her hand. I watch her as she scrubs gently at the dried blood and dirt.

"Does it need stitches?"

"No," she shakes her head and laughs. "It's just a little cut. But I'll let you kiss it and make it all better if you want."

"Don't," I command, pushing past her, aggravated that she would even think it's okay to go there. I can hear her feet pad be-

43

hind me on the wooden floor, but I don't stop until I'm shielded by my big mahogany desk. "You need to go." I slam my hands against the smooth wood and lift my head. "I can't do this with you. You need to leave."

She furrows her brow. "What exactly is it that you can't do?"

"Why the fuck are you here?" I demand, throwing my hands up. "Christ, Laney. I don't even know what to say to you. I haven't seen you for eight years—eight years, Laney! And now you're back and telling me it was all a mistake and that you regret it, and now you want me to just forget—" I trail off, not wanting to finish, because she doesn't deserve it. She doesn't deserve my time. She doesn't deserve me.

"I'm not going anywhere, Levi." I watch her carefully. Laney always was an incredibly strong woman, never hesitating to ask for what she wanted or to speak her mind. I can see that hasn't changed.

"Why did you move home?" I curse myself as soon as the question leaves my mouth, because I'm not sure I want to know. If she tells me she moved home to start a family with her new husband, I may very well punch a hole in the wall.

She swallows hard. "I've got my reasons for moving home, but you're not ready to hear them."

"What the hell does that mean?" I roar.

She walks up to me, on the opposite side of the desk, and leans forward. "It means that you are part of the reason I moved home." I don't miss the fact that she said *part*. "But I can see that you're still very angry, and rightfully so. You should hate me, because I hate myself. So until we work through those feelings, you're not ready to know why I'm home."

"Maybe I don't want to know." Because I don't.

"Oh, trust me," she says, averting her eyes with a grim look on her face, "you'll want to know." She takes a deep breath and looks back at me. "Who was the girl?" Her question catches me off guard, so it takes me a moment to process what she just said.

"Jenny?" And then it hits me. I've been so wrapped up in

seeing Laney again that I totally forgot my best chef just fucking walked out on me. I sigh, falling back into my seat. This night can't possibly get any worse. "She's my head chef."

Laney's shoulders relax. Who did she think she was? "Not any more, by the looks of it."

"You're right." I flick my computer on, waking it up. Time to look for a new chef. "Listen, I've got a ton of stuff to do. Why don't you go in the bathroom and bandage your hand up and then head on out. Good luck with everything. It was nice to see you." I lie. It isn't nice to see her. It fucking hurts like hell and I want her to go back to California . . . or stay . . . hell, I don't know what I want.

My eyes flit across the screen as I browse through my dad's files. I know he has a folder with possible applicants in here somewhere. I see Laney fidget with her shirt from the corner of my eye, but I don't spare her another glance. I've had enough for tonight, and the quicker she is out of here, the quicker I can forget about her again.

"I'll do it," she says, garnering my attention. She takes a hesitant step forward. "Let me fill in for you"—I give her a hard look and she takes a step back—"at least until you find someone else." It's tempting. But I can't. There is no way I can work with her day in and day out. It's impossible. "Please," she pleads, sitting in the chair in front of my desk, her hands folding neatly in her lap. "Please let me help you. I don't have a job yet so my schedule is completely open. Well, except for an appointment I have on Thursday that I can't miss, but we can work around that."

Laney is more than capable of filling in. I'm ashamed to admit that I've kept tabs on her over the years, but because I did, I know she accomplished what she set out to do . . . and then some. After a heated argument with Luke a couple of years ago, he finally caved and told me that not only did Laney graduate with her bachelor's degree in Culinary Arts, she also received a bachelor's in Baking and Pastry Arts Management. Plus, I'd be lying if I said that I've never googled her name just to see what popped up. Suffice it to say that despite my resentment toward her, I am very proud of her accomplishments.

"I can't pay you what you made in California." I don't even want to know what she was raking in there, but no doubt it was well above anything she will make around here.

She shakes her head and scoots forward in her seat. "It doesn't matter what I made in California." Her teeth bite down on her lower lip and her eyes flit around the room as though she's contemplating what to say next. Then her gaze lands on mine. "I don't care what you pay me, I'd just be happy to help you."

I'm at a loss for words, desperate to come out of this situation unscathed. But I'm not sure that's even possible at this point. The sincerity in her voice, and the vulnerability and remorse in her eyes make it hard to tell her no. I should tell her no. But I can't. Partly because I'm in desperate need of a new chef, but mostly because something deep inside of me is screaming at me to tell her yes.

Laney is staring at me, patiently waiting for an answer, but I'm not really sure how to proceed. I have a gut feeling that my answer to her question could dramatically change my life. And I'm not sure I want anything *to* change. I'm happy. Content.

I run a hand down my face, aggravated for even thinking that I would actually let Laney back into my life. I've made my decision and I'm sticking to it, and there isn't anything she can do or say to change that. But as much as it pains me to see her and for old wounds to reopen, I want this closure. "Fine. Be here tomorrow at three." Her eyes widen with excitement and suddenly I feel the need to set her straight. "But this doesn't change anything. This doesn't make us friends and it certainly doesn't mean we're ever going to be more than that again. Got it?"

She grins and pushes up from her chair. "You won't regret this, Levi." Grabbing a piece of paper and a pen from my desk, she scribbles her number down. "In case you need to get ahold of me." She slides the paper and pen across the desk before turning around. My eyes drift down her back and land on her tight little ass. She stops dead in her tracks and twists around. My eyes snap to hers. She has a mischievous grin on her face and I berate myself for getting caught . . . again. "Levi?"

"Yeah?" What else could she fucking want?

"You look fantastic. It was really great seeing you." I nod, unable to form words because, well, I don't really know what to say. "I'm not with anyone. Not married. No kids. Just thought I'd make that clear up front . . . you know, in case you were wondering."

"I wasn't." *I so was.*

"Are you . . . married?" I can see it on her face. My answer matters. As much as I want to lie and say yes, I can't.

I shake my head slowly. She smiles, seemingly pleased with my response, then walks out the door, shutting it quietly behind her. I bury my face in my hands.

What the fuck did I just do?

Chapter 6

Laney

"CRAP. THIS IS GOING TO hurt." I cringe when the buzzing noise starts up, even though it's not even directed toward me.

"Like a bitch. It's going to hurt like a bitch." I glare at Mia but she just laughs. "I can't believe we're doing this!" she squeals. "Well, I can believe I'm doing this, but not you." She was so excited when I told her I made plans to cross off my first bucket list item. Mia already has a few tattoos, but I don't have any and that's about to change. Soon, I will be inked.

"Why not me?" I scoff.

"Seriously? Do you have to ask?"

"No," I concede, hating that I'm so damn predictable. I don't want to be predictable. "Mike?" I whisper, not wanting Mia to hear me.

"Yup?"

"I don't want a pink ribbon." Ohmigod. I can't believe I'm doing this.

"Sweetheart, I'll do whatever you want, but you need to decide now." And I do . . . I make a split-second decision.

"Can I have a piece of paper?" He hands me a notepad and pen. I quickly write down what I want it to say and hand it back.

Mike looks at it for several seconds, grabs the pen and starts drawing on the paper. He flips it around and I smile. "It's perfect." I look up at him and nod. "Let's do that."

"Are you sure?" he confirms. "It's permanent. Once it's there . . . it's there."

"I've only got one life, Mike." My voice is laced with conviction. His warm brown eyes smile down at me and he nods.

"Give me a few minutes to get this ready." He walks away and I'm left staring at Mia. She's lying on her stomach, her eyes closed. Her shorts are pushed low on her hip, and I watch in awe as the needle penetrates her skin several times before the blood is wiped away.

"Does it hurt?" Mia opens her eyes and surprisingly, she looks sleepy.

She shrugs. "Nothing compared to what you've been through." Her eyes flick over to the empty seat next to my table and then back at me. "What's going on?"

I smile, content with my decision. "I changed my mind."

Her eyes widen. "No pink ribbon or no tattoo?" she asks.

"No pink ribbon."

"What are you getting?" She won't judge me, but for some reason I'm not ready to tell her. Right now, I'm content just knowing that I'm stepping out of my box—in a big way.

"You'll have to wait and see," I tease, knowing it'll tick her off.

"Bitch," she huffs, eliciting a laugh from the tatted-up man at her side.

"Okay, Laney. Are you ready?" Mike slides his chair next to my reclined seat and sits down. I watch as he opens a couple of sealed packages.

"As I'll ever be."

Crap. What did I do? I can't believe I got a freaking tattoo. And holy *hell,* did it hurt.

Standing in front of my mirror, I strip out of my shirt, lift my right arm and slowly peel back the thick white bandage along the side of my torso. My tattoo sits off to the side of where my breast should be and is easily covered up when my arm hangs down at my side. Mike told me to leave it covered for four to six hours and it's been five, so I think I'm good. With the aftercare instructions in front of me, I methodically perform each step, since the last thing I need right now is an infection of some sort.

I slip on a clean shirt and walk back to my bedroom. Mia is sitting on my bed, looking through one of my old photo albums. "Are you going to show me?" she asks, not bothering to look up.

I had every intention of showing her. I should show her, but for some reason I don't want to. I can't explain it, but it's like I have this secret that nobody else knows about. It's my little secret. My little slice of heaven in a word, and I don't think I'm ready to share it with anyone yet.

"Will you be mad if I don't?" I ask, walking over to my closet and pulling a pair of black pants off the hanger. I slip my jeans off, shimmy into the slacks and sit down on the bed next to her. Only when the bed dips under my weight does she shut the album and look at me.

"Do you regret it?"

"The tattoo?"

"No. The piercing." She rolls her eyes and shoves me playfully.

"No," I reply, surprised at how easily I answered. Because I don't regret it. This tattoo is special to me in a way that no one else could possibly understand.

"Then, no. If you don't regret it, I won't be mad." She shrugs her shoulder and smiles. "I'm just really proud of you." And I know she is, I can see it in her eyes.

"Thank you." I take a deep breath. "I'm really proud of me too." She nods and we both fall into a comfortable silence. I'm not sure what Mia's thinking about, but I'm thinking about to-morrow because the closer I get to tomorrow, the more nervous I become. I shouldn't be. I've been preparing myself for weeks now, and I should want to get started so I can get it over with. Unfortunately, it's not that easy, because as much as it is a means to an end, there is no guarantee it will work.

If I'm being honest, I'm scared . . . and if I'm *truly* being honest with myself, scared probably isn't even the right word. *I'm terrified.* I've spent way too much time on Google, and as much good information as it's given me, there's been just as much bad—and the bad scares the crap out of me.

I close my eyes and count to ten . . . slowly. It's been my thing ever since surgery. Right before I went under, the anesthesiologist told me to count to ten, and somewhere around four I drifted into a peaceful sleep. So now when I find myself getting worked up and anxious, I stop and count to ten. Usually by the time I get to one, I've been able to calm myself down.

"Are you scared?" Mia asks. I look at her, but she's looking down at her hands. I guess we were thinking about the same thing. I throw myself back on the bed and stare up at the ceiling. The fan is on low and my eyes lock on a single blade, following as it goes around and around. Once again, I find myself counting.

I've tried really hard to put up a good front with Mia. I don't need to drown her in all of my worries. What I do need is for her to stay positive, and if she's going to stay positive, then she has to think I'm staying positive. But it doesn't matter how good my façade is, sometimes the truth seeps through.

"Yes. But it's a different sort of scared. It's not the-boogie-man-is-gonna-get-me sort of scared or a crap-there's-a-spider sort of scared." Mia lies back on the bed and I feel her soft hand grip mine. I squeeze it, allowing her to anchor me to the here and now. "It's hard to explain, but it's a panicky type of fear. When I start thinking about it, my heart starts racing, my mind goes a mile a minute and I can literally feel adrenaline pumping through my body. But the adrenaline makes me shaky and nervous, and it doesn't matter how many deep breaths I take or how many times I count to ten, it's still there nagging at me. Because when push comes to shove, it's still my reality. A reality I have to face, and sometimes that alone is terrifying." I can feel Mia watching me so I turn my head. Her eyes aren't filled with pity, thank God, because that's the last thing I want. But they are shining with sorrow.

"I wish it was someone else," she croaks, swallowing hard. "There are thousands of bad people in the world, but it happened to you." I watch her eyes fill with tears and then I look away. It's pathetic of me really; that I'm unable to look my best friend in the face when it's obvious that she is struggling with this almost as much as I am. But I've cried my fair share of tears and although I'm certain my tear ducts have yet to dry up, I don't want to cry tonight. Somehow I know that if I watch Mia break, then I'll shatter right along with her.

"I'm glad it's me." She gasps, startled by my words, and I rush to try and explain. "If it wasn't me, it would be someone else, and I would never wish this upon someone else. You know that saying that God will only give you what you can handle?"

She nods.

"Sometimes I tell myself that he just thinks I'm really strong and I can handle it, whereas someone else couldn't."

"Does that help?" she asks. "Does that make you feel better about it?"

"No, but it eases my mind. Sometimes when I'm having a good day, it brings me peace, however temporary it may be. But no, it doesn't make me feel better."

"Peace," she whispers, seemingly trying the word on for size. "I want you to have peace."

"Are you going with me tomorrow?" I ask, needing to step away from the heavy talk, even though tomorrow will bring more of the same.

"I think I'm going to let you and Luke go. I was there for you through your surgery, and I think that Luke wants to be the one there for you through this." I understand where she's coming from, and a part of me wants Luke to be the only one to go. But as much as Luke is my brother, Mia is my sister.

"There's plenty of me to go around," I joke. "And I'm sure Luke won't mind sharing."

Mia smiles and shakes her head. "Not this time. I think he needs this more than you know."

I sigh, bringing my arm up to rest it over my head. "Yeah. You're probably right."

"Of course I'm right." She slaps my legs and sits up, effectively shutting down the conversation. "I'm always right. Now let's find you a hot little shirt that will drive Levi crazy tonight."

"I don't need a hot little shirt; I wear a jacket when I cook."

"You do?" she asks, furrowing her brow. "I thought maybe that was just on TV."

"Nope," I laugh. "I wear one every time I'm in the kitchen, and since I'll have the coat on, there will be no need for a 'hot little shirt.' Plus, I think Levi is avoiding me."

"What? Why?"

"Because I haven't seen him at all since I started. On Monday, Mason was there waiting for me and he did all of my intro stuff, and then on Tuesday I jumped right in with the rest of the crew. I haven't seen him once." I hate that I haven't seen him. I want to see him.

"But didn't you say that he told you Mason was supposed to be running Flame and he runs Blue?"

"Well . . . yeah." I kind of forgot about that. I just assumed that since Levi was the one to 'hire' me, he would be there when I started my shift. But he wasn't . . . it was Mason. Don't get me wrong, it was really great seeing Mason. I always did have a sweet spot for that kid. But he isn't really a kid anymore and his rugged good looks mimic his older brother's in just about every way, making it a little hard to be around him.

Mia pushes up from the bed and saunters to the closet. She thumbs through the hangers quickly before stopping at a red blouse. "What time do you get off tonight?"

"Tonight, I get off at nine. Why?" I'm not sure what she's cooking up, but it can't be good. She tugs the blouse from the hanger and grabs a skirt next to it.

"Where are your black heels?"

"I'm not wearing heels to work. They'll kill my feet."

"No, silly. I mean for after work." Bending down, she starts rummaging through my shoes, standing up quickly with an excited grin when she finds what she's looking for.

"Found 'em!"

"Tell me again why I need an outfit with heels?"

"Because we're going to have a few drinks after you get off." No. No, that isn't going to work.

"I can't, Mia. I have to be at the doctor's office at nine o'clock in the morning and I need to have a completely clear mind."

"And you will have a clear mind. We're only going for one drink . . . okay, maybe two. But it'll help you relax and maybe you'll sleep better."

I roll my eyes and push up from the bed. "I'll sleep just fine without the alcohol."

"No, you won't. You'll toss and turn and worry about it all night, and then you'll be exhausted in the morning and you won't hear a damn word the doctor has to say. This way, you'll have a few glasses of wine—just enough to make you sleepy—you'll go home and crash, get a good night's sleep and you'll wake up refreshed and alert. And somewhere along the way, you might catch a glimpse of Levi."

Mia doesn't know about the ultimatum Levi gave me eight years ago. All she knows is that I left him. She thinks I chose school over him and walked away . . . which is what I did. But it's not the whole story. I don't want her to know the whole story because I don't want her to think poorly of Levi.

Yes, he gave the ultimatum, but I pulled the trigger. I made the choice, and if she is going to think poorly of anyone, I want it to be me. However, this is Mia and she'll never think poorly of me.

She just tells me I was young and stupid, and if I really want him back in my life, I need to do a little groveling. Which I'm prepared to do . . . if he ever shows his face and gives me the chance.

"Fine," I concede, knowing it's much easier to comply with her. "What are you going to do until I get off?" She tosses my shoes on the bed with the rest of my outfit and starts digging through her suitcase.

"I'm probably going to hang with Benny." Her head pops up over the edge of my bed. "Maybe I can get him to come out with us." She looks hopeful so I really don't want to burst her bubble, but Benny doesn't go out. If he does, he sure as hell wouldn't go to Blue. Benny isn't a 'club' kind of guy.

"Good luck with that," I mumble, slipping on my shoes. "I'll text you when I get off."

"Sounds good," she says, her head once again buried in her suitcase. Shirts are flying left and right, and I duck when a sandal flies at my head.

"And you'll bring my outfit so I can change when you get there?" I ask.

"Yup." I duck again but not soon enough, and I take a red lace bra to the face.

"Mia, how many clothes did you bring?" I toss the bra on the floor at the same time she pops back up with a black scrap of material clutched in her hand.

"Got it!" She wiggles her hips in excitement and waves the silky shirt in front of her. "Benny is going to shit when he sees me in this."

Well, that catches my attention. A cat-ate-the-canary grin slips into place at the thought of my two friends hooking up. "You have a thing for Benny," I taunt, resulting in a stink eye from Mia.

"Do not," she huffs. "I just think it's fun to mess with him"— she shrugs—"and he's sort of hot so . . ." She trails off and I shake my head.

"Please don't play games with him. He's been through a lot,"

I say, no longer joking. She looks up at me and I half expect her to ask me what all he has been through, but she doesn't. I'm glad because it's not my story to tell.

"I won't play games with him, Lane," she says, her face sober. "I really like Ben. He's a great guy." *Ben?* Since when does she call him Ben?

"So he's Ben, huh?" I tease . . . sort of. I really want to know what that's about.

"I don't know." She sits on the bed again and fiddles with the hem of her shirt. "We've been hanging out the past couple of days that you've been at work and we've had a lot of fun together. I enjoy spending time with him."

Mia hasn't always had the best luck with men and most of the guys that she associates with aren't so 'great,' so I'm sure she appreciates being around someone as kind and attentive as Benny. Even if he calls her every princess name known to mankind.

I pat her leg and she looks at me. I'm not sure what I see floating around in her eyes, but it almost looks like she wants my approval.

"Have fun tonight," I say with a wink, reaching for my purse. She follows me through the house, and I stop to grab my recipe book then shove it in my purse. Just as I reach for the door, it opens and Benny walks in. I give him a knowing smile and push past him. "Don't do anything I wouldn't do," I throw over my shoulder as I walk to my car. I swear I hear Benny say, *"Well shit, that doesn't leave us with many options."*

The drive to Flame is short and it's still fairly early, so the parking lot is empty when I arrive. I gather my things and head into the restaurant. The hostess—I think her name is Jamie—is setting up the tables and I wave at her. A soft melody floats through the air and I smile. Everything about this place is familiar and it makes me happy. It makes me feel safe.

Mason pushes his way through the heavy door that leads to the kitchen and stops right before plowing into me. "Hey, Laney," he says with a smile, but I keep going in the direction he just came from. As much as I love Mason, he's not Levi, and I'd be lying if I said I wasn't disappointed to walk in here—yet again—to no Levi. It probably sounds stupid of me, but I really thought I'd gotten somewhere with him the other night. I know he was shocked to see me, but there were points during our conversation that he looked genuinely happy. So the fact that he has gone MIA when he knew I would be here working rubs me the wrong way.

"Hey, Mason." I know he follows me because I can hear him behind me. I set my purse down on the counter and reach for my white jacket that's hanging on the back of the door. This I can handle. Put me in a kitchen, let me cook, and I'm good to go.

"You okay?" he asks. Pulling my recipe book from my purse, I turn to find Mason watching me, his hip propped against one of the sinks.

"Fine, you?" I can tell by the look on his face that he knows I'm lying. He smiles and points toward my book.

"What's that?"

I smile, giddy about what I have planned, hoping that he doesn't mind. "This," I say dramatically, picking up the spiral-bound book, "is my recipe book. I was hoping we could try a few new dessert items out."

"That's a great idea—"

"No," Levi interrupts, barreling through the door. "We aren't changing the menu." His words are clipped and final, his eyes hard—and oh so sexy.

"I'm not trying to change the menu. I'm just trying to spice it up. You have the exact same dessert options that you had eight years ago," I defend, hoping I'll get him to cave. Mason looks at me apologetically but doesn't step in . . . and I don't blame him. His big brother is a force to be reckoned with, and you have to be prepared to go up against him. Lucky for me, I'm prepared. "How many desserts do you sell a night?"

Levi looks to Mason, who shrugs. "I don't know . . . maybe ten to twenty, roughly."

"That's it?" Levi barks.

"It's because your dessert options are boring, Levi," I tell him. "People don't want to buy a dessert from you that they can just as easily make at home. They want something new and exciting, something fresh. They want to pay for something warm and delicious here so they don't have to go home and spend hours prepping and baking."

"I think it's a great idea," Mason says, grabbing my recipe book and flipping through it. "Plus, Flame is mine so it's my decision."

"Wrong," Levi snaps, pulling the book from Mason. "Flame is ours. It doesn't matter if you're running it, we both make the decisions." Levi stops and I watch as his eyes roam over one of the pages. He looks up at me and then back down at the recipe. "Can I borrow this?"

I hesitate, biting on the inside of my lip. That recipe book is like a Bible to me. When I'm feeling any sort of emotion, I bake, and even though I know all of those recipes by heart, I don't want anything to happen to it. Levi must notice my hesitation because he adds, "Just for tonight. I'll look through it, pick out a few and you can make them for Mason and me, then we'll go from there. That okay?"

I nod, happy that he's at least considering it. Levi walks out without a second glance and Mason smirks.

"What? What are you smiling at?" I ask him.

"You've got his undies so twisted up he can't fucking see straight." How the hell he got that out of the little conversation we just had, I have no idea.

"Really? Have you noticed that he's been conveniently missing since the moment I started here?" Seriously, how am I supposed to weasel my way back into his life if he won't even come near me?

Mason shakes his head. "He hasn't been missing." Now this piques my interest. "He's been watching from afar. I'm telling you . . . you coming back home has got him all sorts of discombobulated." I was hoping my return would affect him, but I'm not sure I like hearing it put quite like that.

"Why do you say that?"

Mason runs a hand along his neck and looks down before he meets my curious gaze. "Fuck. I shouldn't say anything because it's none of my business." I watch him, eyebrows raised, urging him to continue. "Fine," he moans, shoving his hands in his pockets. "You being here has messed with his head, Lane. Don't take that the wrong way, because I think he's genuinely glad to see you. But he wasn't expecting it, and now he doesn't know what to do or how to act. I think he's been hiding out because he's afraid to be around you."

I can't say I'm surprised. I think if my situation were any different than what it is, I'd be confused and nervous too. But it's not, and I don't necessarily have time on my side to mess with those types of feelings. "I'm not sure what to do with that, Mase."

"I'm not sure there is anything you can do," he replies, his eyes apologetic. "I think it's just something that will take time. He needs to get used to you being here, but I think seeing you every day will help with that. Personally, I'm thrilled you're back."

Mason and I always did have fun working together, but it was more of a brother-sister type of friendship. When Levi gave me the ultimatum, Mason sided with me, which did not sit well with Big Brother . . . at all. "He'll come around, Lane, just give him time."

There's that word again. *Time.* If only I knew how much *time* I have left.

I give him a tight smile and walk toward the door. "Where are you going?" I hear from behind me.

"To talk to Levi." I push the door open and pause to look back at Mason, who has a huge grin on his face. "Aren't you going to try and stop me?"

He shakes he head. "Hell no." And that's all I need. The door swings shut behind me, muting Mason's laughter. I have absolutely no idea what I'm going to say to Levi, but I feel like I have to say something. I don't want him to be uncomfortable, and if my being here is making it that hard on him, then I'll leave. I stop in front of Levi's office door and take a deep breath, running a shaky hand over my ponytail.

Knocking twice, I push open the door, and the scene in front me stops me cold. My breath hitches and my heart stops. Levi is standing in the middle of his office, his arms wrapped tightly around a woman whose face I cannot see. His gaze meets mine and he stills, his beautiful blue eyes as wide as they can be.

I look around the room, my eyes landing on anything they can possibly find except for the painful sight in front of me. I swallow hard, pushing back the thickness building in my throat. "I—I'm sorry. I should have . . . I shouldn't have just . . ." My words come out broken and when I look at them, Levi drops his arms from the woman he was holding.

She turns around and watches me carefully for a few seconds before speaking. "Hi," she says, lifting her hand in a tiny wave and then looking at Levi, whose eyes are locked on mine. I can't tell what he's thinking, but he looks shocked and maybe a little apologetic. My eyes drift to the beautiful woman at his side. Her hair is long with thick waves. She has stunning green eyes and a dimple that probably gets her whatever she wants. And based on what I saw when I walked in here, what she wants is Levi.

"I'm sorry," I mumble. Embarrassed, I turn around and all but sprint back toward the kitchen, ignoring Levi as he yells my name. I walk faster, hoping he'll leave me alone, but he doesn't. He yells my name a second time, only this time I can also hear his feet hitting the floor behind me.

A large hand locks on my elbow, and he spins me around to face him. His brows are dipped low and his chest is heaving. I peek over his shoulder to find that the woman from his office is leaning casually against the wall. *Great. A freaking audience.* She must sense my apprehension because she pushes away from the wall and walks up to us.

"I'm going to head out." She places a kiss on Levi's cheek

and he nods, not taking his eyes off of me. "It was a pleasure meeting you." Her voice is laced with kindness and there isn't a touch of sarcasm. She smiles softly before walking away.

Levi lets go of my arm. He's looking at me like he can't figure out what to do with me, and oddly enough, I feel the same way. I don't know what to do with me either. I've never been good about thinking before I speak, so it's no surprise when words start falling from my mouth. "You said you weren't with anyone."

His mouth ticks up in a smirk. "No. I said I wasn't married. I never said I didn't have a girlfriend."

Tears burn at the back of my eyes and I blink several times, willing them to stay away. "Fuck," he growls, running a hand down his face. He looks up at the ceiling for a few seconds and then his eyes find mine again. "But I don't have a girlfriend."

Air rushes from my lungs and my shoulders instantly relax. I can't even explain how relieved I am to hear that. "I shouldn't have made you think that we are together. Her name is Harley and we're close friends." He looks down for several beats and mumbles, "She's engaged."

"It's okay, I shouldn't have barged in on you like that. It wasn't fair of me." Levi nods, his eyes still trained on the ground. For the first time, I notice how exhausted he looks. His shirt is untucked and a little wrinkly, which isn't at all the way I remember him from the old days. "Are you sure you're okay with me working here?" I blurt.

His head snaps up. "Why would you ask that?"

"I don't know." I shrug my shoulders. "You've avoided me the past couple of days and Mason—"

"Mason needs to mind his own damn business," he snaps. "And I haven't been avoiding you. I've been . . . I've been busy." I purse my lips and cock a brow. Mmm-hmm, and I'm the freaking queen of England.

Levi steps toward me and every hair on my body stands at attention at his close proximity. "I'm glad you're here, Laney."

A smile tugs at the corner of my mouth and when he returns it, I know he's being sincere. "One day at a time, okay?"

I nod, repeating his words, "One day at a time."

One day at a time.
It keeps playing over and over in my head as I spend the next several hours cooking. How many days is it going to take? Will I ever get the chance to make it right? It's a darn good thing that I'm at work tonight, because as long as I'm cooking, I'm able to keep my mind from wandering too far down that beaten path.

With a gentle touch that I've mastered over the last several years, I place the veal in the center of the plate, top it with a sweet marsala wine sauce and hand the plate to one of the other chefs, who adds the baked potato and mixed vegetables.

"That's it for you, Laney." Mark flashes me a sweet smile. "You're good to go."

"I can stay if you need me."

"Nope," he replies. "You've worked your tail off this week. Enjoy your day off tomorrow."

Enjoy my day off . . . that's not gonna happen.

My phone vibrates in my pocket and I dig it out to find a text from Mia. *I'll be waiting in the bathroom.* I rush in that direction, suddenly excited to get all dolled up and go check out Blue. And not just because a certain someone might be there . . . okay, that's probably the biggest reason. But I really am looking forward to a glass of wine and some girl time with Mia.

I walk in the bathroom and as soon as I see Mia, I let out a low whistle. "Look at you, hot mama!"

Mia starts laughing and twirls in a circle. "Thank you. Thank you." She gives a little bow. "I couldn't get Ben to join us, but I did get a scorching hot look from him when I walked out of the bedroom."

"You probably gave the poor guy a heart attack. That shirt doesn't even have a back."

Mia cranes her neck to look at herself in the mirror. "Is it too much? I thought you said the place was fancy?"

"I've never been inside of Blue, but it looks fancy."

Mia shrugs her shoulders. "Oh well. Now"—she claps her hands, turning toward the sink—"let's get you dressed." Flicking the lock on the door, I start stripping out of my clothes. I shimmy into the skirt and blouse, slip on the heels and pull my hair band out. I finger comb my hair and Mia hands me my makeup bag.

"Thank God you remembered that." I don't usually wear makeup to work; there's just no point when you work over a hot stove all day. I spend a few minutes applying my makeup as Mia fusses over herself in the mirror.

"Done," I announce, tossing my makeup bag in the backpack Mia brought, along with my work clothes. "How do I look?"

She turns to me and grins. "Fantastic. But you always look great. I wish you would dress like this more often." She reaches in her purse and pulls out a small bottle of perfume. She sprays me twice and when I give her a questioning look, she shrugs. "What? You don't want to go in there looking like *this* and smelling like *that*."

"Smelling like what?" Mia picks up our bag and we make our way out to my car. I sniff my hair . . . food. Who cares? We're going out for one drink, and I'm certainly not going out to pick up any guy—except maybe Levi. *Hmm . . ."* I think I need more perfume." Mia snorts with laughter and when I unlock the car door, she tosses the bag in. "Wait." I pin her with a questioning gaze. "How did you get here?"

"Benny." Her eyes take on a dreamy look and she gets a goofy grin on her face. When the fog clears and she finally sees me, she sobers up. "What? What are you smiling at?"

"You," I laugh, pushing her toward Blue. "You are smitten over Benny."

"Am not."

"Are too," I sing as she pushes through the front door of the bar. A beautiful young woman is seated behind a large wooden podium.

"Good evening, ladies," she says, walking toward us. She's wearing a pencil skirt, white tuxedo shirt, and red tie. To top it all off, she's wearing the most gorgeous pair of red peep-toe stilettos that I've ever seen. And then it hits me. Levi works side by side next to her every day, and if I had to guess, I'd say there are probably several more where she came from. "Are you ladies here with a party tonight or would you like a table?"

"We'll just sit at the bar, if that's okay?" Mia looks to me for confirmation and I nod.

"Absolutely," she says and points us in the direction of the bar. "Tatum and Riley are the bartenders tonight and they'll be more than happy to serve you." Mia and I smile and as we make our way to the bar. Meanwhile, my eyes roam across the room. The ceiling is open with exposed wooden beams. The tables and booths are all sleek lines and warm colors. This place screams sophistication but not in a stuffy sort of way. I'd call it *inviting*.

Mia and I each pull out a stool and scoot up next to the bar. "Hi. My name is Tatum. What can I get you ladies tonight?" Yup, I was right. Another beautiful woman. I take a deep breath and roll my eyes, more at myself than anything. I'm not a jealous person, but the thought of Levi working with these perfect women all night long puts a little damper on my self-confidence. Although I've been told I'm pretty, these girls are stunning. Mia nudges my arm and I look up.

"What? Sorry, I missed the question."

"What would you like to drink?" Tatum's voice is low and husky, but her smile is incredibly bright.

Mia hands me the drink menu. "What are you getting?" I ask her.

"Pinot Noir."

My eyes skim the page and when they land on the prices per glass, I set the menu down. "Can I just get a water, please?"

"What?" Mia scoffs. "No. I'm buying tonight."

"Shut your mouth. You are not buying tonight. I just changed my mind." There is no way she is going to believe that, but I don't have any other option. I can't pay that much for a glass of wine, especially when I don't have any money actually coming in at the moment. A warm hand lands on my back and I twirl around.

"Hi." Levi looks at me for a brief second before shifting his attention to Mia. "Good evening," he says, offering Mia his hand and a warm smile. A huge grin splits Mia's face. She's seen pictures of Levi, albeit a much younger version of him, but he hasn't changed that much—if you don't count the broadened shoulders, thick biceps, and thighs that look like cannons. Mia knows exactly who she's talking to as she slips her hand in his.

"You must be Levi." Her voice is silky smooth. Levi cocks his head in confusion, and if it's at all possible, her smile gets a little bit bigger. Crap. I know that look. She glances at me, and she must register the look of dismay on my face because she shoots me a quick wink before refocusing her attention on the larger-than-life hunk of a man standing next to us. "Laney's told me all about you. All good things, of course."

A smug little grin floats across Levi's face and he looks at me. "All good things, huh?"

"There only are good things. There's nothing bad to tell." The words are easy for me to say, but I can tell they aren't so easy for Levi to hear. His smile falters. Clearing his throat, he turns away from me and watches Tatum as she places Mia's glass of wine in front of her before handing me my water.

"Why are you drinking water?" he asks. I open my mouth to respond, but Mouthy Mia beats me to the punch.

"I told her I'd pay for her drink, but she's being stubborn." She peers around Levi to look at me. "You're stubborn." I stick my tongue out at her. Real mature, I know. "They aren't that expensive," she mumbles, taking a sip of her wine.

I blanch. There's no way Levi missed what she said and the

curious look in his eyes confirms that. I turn to the bar, determined not to discuss my financial situation. Levi bends down so we're cheek to cheek.

"What are you drinking?"

"Water," I answer sarcastically, lifting up my glass.

"Still a smartass, I see," he says with a hint of humor. "Let me rephrase. What would you like to drink?"

"She loves Moscato." I pin Mia with a glare. *What?* she mouths. I shake my head. Levi leans across the bar and flags down Tatum.

"What's up, Levi?" she says, planting her hands on top of the bar. Her eyes drift over to me and she smiles. There is a gleam in her eye, but I can't quite pinpoint what exactly I'm seeing.

"Could you get Laney a glass of Moscato?"

"Sure thing, boss." She turns to walk away and I don't miss the little wink she gives me.

"She likes you," Levi whispers. His warm breath fans the side of my face and I feel my bones melt into a big pile of goo. He smells *so* good.

"She seems nice," I whisper back. Levi smiles, and I have to hold on to the bar to keep myself from toppling out of my chair. I've seen this smile before, but it's been a really long time and oh boy, have I missed it. I can't believe he's being this nice to me. His behavior has been so hot and cold the past few days, but I'll take it regardless.

"You don't get it, do you?"

"Get what?" I ask as Tatum walks up and hands me a glass of Moscato. She leans her elbows on the bar and looks at Levi and then back at me.

"I take it you're already spoken for?" My eyes widen as what she's asking sinks in. Mia throws her head back and laughs right along with Levi.

"Um. Actually, no, I'm not," I reply, slightly dumbfounded that she is hitting on me. I don't think I've had anyone hit on me or even flirt with me in at least three years. And it feels good.

"But you're not gay." She isn't asking . . . she knows. I smile at Tatum. She's a beautiful girl and I'm sure she could have her pick of any woman she wants—just not this woman. Because this woman's heart already belongs to someone else.

"I'm not, but you can bet that cute little tushy of yours that if I was gay, I'd be on you like white on rice." Tatum's face lights up and she points a finger at a stunned Levi.

"She's a keeper." She turns toward me. "You're a keeper. I like you, Laney."

"Back at ya, Tatum." I reach for my glass with a smug grin and take a sip. I may have always played things safe, but I've never once been called shy.

Levi hasn't moved an inch and I can feel his body behind me. He has one foot propped on the bottom of my chair and if I shift to the left, I'm certain that I would be cradled between his legs. We fall into a comfortable silence, all of us sipping our drinks as we take in the crowd around us. A small band has taken the stage and is playing a sweet jazzy tune that I find myself swaying to.

"So, Levi, what are those?" Mia asks, pointing up to the ceiling.

Levi's eyes follow hers and he clears his throat. "Those are cages."

Mia rolls her eyes. "Well, no shit. What are they for? Do people have sex in there?"

"Mia, this isn't a sex club." He chuckles. "No, no sex in the cages. But girls do like to dance in them."

"Like the girls that work for you? Or any girls?"

"Some of my workers do and sometimes the patrons do. It's purely for entertainment, and the girls are not allowed to strip. Dance only."

"Laney," Mia says. "We are *so* going to dance in one of those."

"There is no way you'll ever get Laney up in one of those," Levi interjects before I can respond.

Mia stares at him with a cocky little grin. "I got her to get a tattoo. I'm sure I could get her in one of those. She just needs to

.L. GRAYSON

be nice and sauced up first."

Levi spins toward me, the shock evident on his face. "You got a tattoo?" he asks incredulously, his eyebrows pushing into his hairline.

I smile around the rim of my glass. See? People would never expect that from me, which makes me incredibly happy. *This* is how I want to live my life.

"I did," I answer, matter of fact. "It was on my bucket list and I checked it off."

"And," Mia adds, "she didn't even cry."

"Nope. Not a tear."

"I don't believe you," Levi says skeptically. "It's not one of those fake tattoos, is it?"

"No," I laugh. "It's real. Want to see it?"

"Actually, yes, I do."

"Okay, well—" I reach for the hem of my shirt and raise it slightly, pretending that I'm going to lift it over my head. Of course I'm not going to, but he doesn't know that.

"Hell no!" Mia snaps. "I didn't get to see the tattoo, but you're going to show him?"

"Whoa . . ." Levi reaches for my hands and tugs them away from my shirt, all the while looking around to make sure no one else saw. "What are you doing?"

"I was going to show you my tattoo."

"Not cool," Mia mumbles under her breath. "Sisters before misters."

"And you have to take your shirt off to do it?" Levi asks, completely ignoring Mia.

"Yup. Probably my bra too." Levi's eyes blaze hot with lust and I can't help but smile. He's always been a boob man, and that's probably what he's picturing right now. "Another time?" I ask sweetly, resting my hand on his arm. Something in him relaxes, I can almost see it. It's like he has this wall up and I just knocked a few bricks off the top. His eyes dance with a playful familiarity as he watches me.

"Another time," he says, his voice low and rough. He reaches for his beer that Tatum had placed on the bar earlier. "You ladies enjoy your evening. I'm going to go talk to some friends. Mia, it was a pleasure meeting you." Levi flashes both of us one last smile and Mia looks at me with a twinkle in her eye.

"He's fantastic. And I'm guessing by that goofy-ass grin on your face that whatever just happened here made your entire night."

"It made my entire week," I answer, thankful that Mia convinced me to come out tonight.

Chapter 7

Laney

*B*AKING POWDER . . . BAKING POWDER . . . *you've got to be around here somewhere. Aha! There you are.* Pulling the box from the shelf, I measure out two teaspoons and pour the essential ingredient into the bowl along with the flour, shortening and salt. I stir in warm water and mix the dough until it's nice and smooth, then cover the bowl and let it sit. But there's no time for me to sit, because if I sit then I think. I've done a lot of thinking already and frankly, my brain hurts. There is only so much information one brain can or should process in one day and I've hit my limit . . . and then some.

Quickly, I move through the kitchen, pulling out more ingredients. The dough has to sit for twenty minutes, which is more than enough time to start making something else. I set the timer and get to work.

This is how I deal with things. I cook, or bake, it doesn't really matter which as long as it involves me in a kitchen. And after the day I've had, I needed a big kitchen in a big way and mine at home wasn't going to cut it. I spent nearly the entire afternoon at the treatment center with my doctor and a few dozen nurses, who instructed, poked, prodded and hauled me from room to room until they were certain I had every piece of knowledge I needed to proceed with my treatments. Dr. Hopkins was nice but overly cheery, and there were several times that I wanted to slap the smile right off of her face. Didn't she know what I was going through? Didn't she understand the storm that was raging inside of me while she spoke of labs, scans, tests, appointments, side effects and every other medical thing she could throw in there? Shouldn't she have known that while she was talking about tissue, staging, blood cells, and hair loss, I was thinking about one thing and one thing only?

Surviving.

"Laney, I've spoken to your oncologist and your surgeon from California. I know that they've both talked with you in great detail about your diagnosis and the treatment plan that would ensue after your mastectomy, but I just want to start by recapping so that you and I are both on the same page."

Dr. Hopkins is sitting in front of me with a file, which I assume is mine. It's thick, and when she flips it open I see the words written in bold lettering at the top of the page.

Name: Laney Jacobs
Diagnosis: Stage III Invasive Ductal Carcinoma

My eyes linger on the page, but I'm not reading anything. There isn't anything in that file that I haven't already been told, and it all really boils down to one thing.

I have breast cancer.

There was—or is, who the hell knows—a disease growing inside of me . . . killing me.

"Laney?" A gentle hand touches my knee and I look up to find Dr. Hopkins watching me. "Are you okay?"

That's a stupid question. *No, I'm not okay. I had my breast removed, for crying out loud, and now I'm about to have some extremely toxic chemicals pumped through my body for the next several months in case there are any 'bad cells' left floating around. So no, I'm not okay.* "Yes, doctor. Sorry, please keep going." Luke wraps his hand around mine and squeezes it gently. I squeeze back, thankful that I'm not doing this alone.

She nods with a knowing smile. We spend the next hour reviewing my diagnosis, surgery, and upcoming treatment plans. "So if it's okay with you, Laney, I would really like to get started as soon as possible. You're six weeks post-op, and the sooner we can start your chemotherapy, the better."

I look at Luke, though I'm not sure why exactly—it's not like he really has a say in this. But his soft smile is all the reassurance I need. "I'm ready to get this started," I answer with false bravado.

"When can she start?" Luke asks. He scoots forward in his chair—as if it will help him hear her better—but his hand stays locked in mine.

"Well," she says, looking at me with a hopeful smile. "We're going to draw your blood here today, so as long as all of your blood levels look good, we can start tomorrow."

"Tomorrow?" I pull my arm away, my fingers sliding from Luke's tight grip, and I run a shaky hand across my head. "I . . . I wasn't expecting it so soon." I'd thought maybe she'd say next week, or the week after that, to give me time to adjust and process everything. But isn't that exactly what I've been doing the past several weeks?

Dr. Hopkins must notice my hesitation because she scoots her stool closer to me. I hold up my hand, signaling her to give me a minute. Her eyes are soft and understanding. "I know this is hard, Laney, but it's necessary." I nod. "If you need the weekend to prepare yourself, we can start on Monday. It's your call."

She's right. I need to get this over with. I need to make sure this horrible disease is gone for good so I can get back to my life.

"Tomorrow is perfect." My voice hitches, and I try for a smile but fail miserably. Luke wraps his arm around my shoulder and whispers in my ear.

"I'm here with you every step. Got it? Every. Single. Step." I nod again, because apparently that's all someone can do in this *situation, and then wipe away a tear that slips from my eye.*

"Great." Dr. Hopkins stands up, shaking first my hand and then Luke's. "Sit tight for a minute. One of the nurses is going to come in and give you information about the treatments and talk to you about side effects and what to expect."

A loud beep pulls me from a fog and I look down to see that my whisk is sitting in a chocolaty batter. Honestly, I have no idea how I even got to this point. It's sort of like arriving at a destination and then realizing that you don't remember actually driving there.

Another timer goes off and I walk to the stove, slip on an oven mitt and pull out the pan, loving the way the sweet cinnamon smell fills the kitchen. Closing my eyes, I inhale deeply, allowing my body to savor the familiar scent—a scent that may very well become foreign to me in the near future.

"You must be Laney." A short, plump woman pushes her way into the room and extends her hand. Yes, another formality that I'm just not in the mood for. I shake her hand nonetheless, and she sits on a rolling stool and opens up a folder. "My name is Tara and I'm one of the nurses in the oncology unit so you'll probably be seeing a lot of me." She flashes me a quick smile, but her attempt at making me smile falls flat. "Okay, this folder is for you. You get to take it home and you'll want to comb through it and read everything thoroughly, but right now I'm going to hit on some of the important stuff." She hands me the first paper. My eyes slide across the page and my heart stops momentarily before slamming violently into my rib cage.

SIDE EFFECTS OF CHEMOTHERAPY

I suck in a deep breath as my eyes travel over the words, one by one, each word crashing into me like a freight train, each one affecting me a little bit differently.

Nausea . . . vomiting . . . diarrhea . . . constipation . . . bruising . . . bleeding . . . fatigue . . . loss of appetite . . . loss of smell or taste . . . loss of hair.

Each word is a knife to the gut, but the last three feel like someone takes that knife, jabs it in as far as it could possibly go and then twists it until every last bit of my insides are shredded into tiny little pieces.

I am a woman, and there are two things that help distinguish me as such—my hair and my breasts. A giant lump forms in my throat and my bottom lip starts to tremble. My hand slides across my lap and into Luke's, whose tight grip is probably the only thing holding me together right now. It's bad enough I've already lost one breast and that in the place of my once perky, plump tissue I have a jagged scar over sunken flesh. But now, on top of that, I'm going to lose my hair. I don't want to lose my hair, I don't want to wear a wig, and I certainly don't want the looks of pity that a bald head will undoubtedly draw.

Luke nudges my arm and I look up as I struggle to keep my emotions in check. He nods to Tara and I shift my attention, but the fear of everything that is about to happen to me has my blood pumping so hard through my body that it's now pounding behind my ears. The only thing I seem to hear is the beat of my own heart, and I suppose I should at least be thankful I can hear that . . . it means I'm still alive. I watch Tara absently, and I'm able to decipher a few things she says.

"Your treatments will be every other Friday for six months . . . Treatments will take approximately four to five hours . . . You'll get your blood drawn before each round of chemo . . . We'll give you medicine in case the nausea and vomiting get to be too much . . . Make sure you're eating healthy . . . Be sure and drink lots of water . . . Feel free to bring someone with you during your treatments . . . Don't hesitate to ask any questions." My eyes clog with tears and I look down, rubbing my temples, willing myself to calm down.

"Laney? Laney . . . are you okay?"

A large hand settles on my shoulder and I whip around to find myself face to face with Levi. He steps back, his hands up in the air. "Sorry. I didn't mean to startle you." I look at the knife in my hand and then back up at him. "Are you okay?" he questions.

I lower the knife and mumble an apology before turning back toward the counter. What was I doing? Oh yes, the dough. I finish cutting the rolled-out dough into three-inch chunks, and then I check the oil to make sure it's warmed up to the right temperature before I drop the chunks into the sizzling pot. I turn back toward Levi and find him standing in the exact same spot as before.

"I'm fine," I shrug. "Why would you think I wouldn't be okay?" I ask as nonchalantly as I possibly can. He eyes me curiously for several seconds.

"Well, for starters, you're crying." I rub my arm across my face and sure enough . . . tears. The strange thing is that I don't even remember crying. Levi chuckles, but I'm not really sure what he's finding funny about the situation.

"What? What are you laughing at?"

He shakes his head and steps toward me. I watch as he slowly lifts his hand and wipes it gently across my cheek. "You just smeared flour all over your face." His hand leaves a trail of heat against my skin and when he pulls back, a part of me wants to grab his arm and insist that he keep touching me. But that might be a little much.

"Thanks," I mumble, still breathless from his touch. "I've just had a really bad day." His blue eyes are staring tenderly into mine, and I want nothing more than for him to tuck me against his big warm chest and hold me and promise that everything is going to be okay. "Like really, really bad."

A part of me wants so badly for him to ask me what's wrong. And not just so I have someone to talk to about it, but so that I have *him* to talk to about it. Logically, I know he isn't there yet. He isn't quite ready to make amends, and until he's ready to make amends, he isn't ready to learn about my diagnosis.

"Is that why my kitchen looks like a tornado went through it?" he asks, looking around the room. I nod coyly and he smiles in return. "Glad to know that hasn't changed."

Cocking my head, I ask, "What do you mean?"

"You," he says, waving his hand in my direction. "Anytime

75

you were upset—about anything—you wanted to be in the kitchen. It didn't matter what it was, and it didn't matter what you were making, you had to be in here."

I slide my hands down the front of my apron. "Well, you're right. That hasn't changed." We stand there staring at each other, and I can't help but wonder what all hasn't changed with him. In the past, when Levi was upset, he liked to be with me, and it didn't matter what we did as long as we were together. I wonder what he does now when he's upset.

"What are you making?" He halts our trip down memory lane and strides over to the pot that's sizzling and popping on the stove.

I follow him, noticing that he doesn't look quite as rumpled today as he did the other day. "You look better today," I say, the words just falling from my mouth.

"Did I look bad the other day?" he asks, a hint of amusement in his voice.

"No, you just looked stressed."

"Mason and I have had some things going on with the business," he says with a shrug, as if it's not a big deal.

"Careful. It'll spit at you," I warn when he gets too close to the bubbling pot.

"What is it?" he asks, peering over the edge from a safe distance. They've been in long enough, so I pull the fried dough from the oil, one by one, and place them on a cooling rack. Picking one up, I bounce it from hand to hand, blowing on it to cool it down so it won't burn his mouth.

"Here." I hold the tiny chunk of heaven in my hand and Levi takes it. "Take a bite." I grin, excited for him to try what I've made. He doesn't hesitate and I watch as he bites into the crunchy layer, his eyes instantly rolling back into his head.

"Oh my God," he moans around the food in his mouth. "This is amazing." I pop a bite into my mouth and smile as he asks, "Can I have another one?"

I cover my mouth so he doesn't see my half-eaten food when

I answer him. "Please. Eat as much as you want. It's your kitchen, so it's really your food anyway." He puts another bite in his mouth and it hits me. I shouldn't have come here. Sure, maybe at one time I would have been welcome to come here at—I look at my watch—midnight, but I'm not sure I still have those privileges. Even though Blue is open, Flame is closed, and I had to use the key Mason gave me to get in. I really should have called first.

"I'm sorry," I furrow my brow, hoping that he isn't pissed. "I shouldn't have just come in here like this." I shake my head at my lack of consideration. "I wasn't thinking. I needed to clear my head and this seemed like the perfect place." Levi swallows his food and watches me intently as I keep talking. I can tell that he wants to ask me what I'm talking about, but he doesn't. "I couldn't be alone at home because Mia and Benny were there. So I came here . . . out of habit, I think, but I still shouldn't have come. Or at the very least I should have called you first. I'm really—"

"It's okay," he interrupts softly. "You were going to make me samples of some desserts anyway"—he peeks in the oven—"and by the looks of it, that's exactly what you did." When his eyes meet mine again, he looks happy, not unlike the way he looked last night at Blue but far different from how he looked the night he hired me.

"That's it? You're not mad?"

"No," he laughs. "I'm not mad. Now show me what else you've got." He's really thrown me for a loop. It's not that I expected him to be furious, but with our history and the less than warm welcome I initially received, I anticipated a little bit more of an argument. But don't get me wrong, I'll take this. Plus, I get the impression he's trying to take my mind off what's bothering me . . . and it's working, so I'm going to go with it.

"Okay." I walk across to the counter where my creations are and hand Levi a fork. I slide the first dessert in front of him. "This is tiramisu." He dives right in and I giggle at his eagerness. Levi always did have a sweet tooth. "It's a classic dessert that's easy to make and I think your patrons would love it."

"It's so good," he says, sliding the fork into his mouth again. My eyes stray to his lips and I watch as they lock around the utensil, sliding it out ever so slowly, ensuring that he doesn't miss one morsel of his bite. I blink, my lips parted, as his tongue slides over his bottom lip and—

"What are these?"

"What's what?"

"These," he says, lifting up the container and waving it in front of my face.

"Oh, those. Yes." I clear my throat, slightly embarrassed that I just lost my train of thought watching a man eat—then again, it's not just *any* man. I'm hoping that Levi didn't notice, or maybe he's just gentlemanly enough to not mention it. "These little darlings are Espresso Cream Pies. Here, try one." I lift the container and he pulls one out, his eyes dancing like he's in heaven.

"This," he says with conviction, pointing to the tiny pie. "This is fabulous. I want these on the menu." A small bubble of hope forms inside of me, and for the first time in I don't know how long, I find myself getting excited about something.

"Wait!" I run over to the oven and pull open the door, first checking to see if it's done. This is the one that's important and I need it to be perfect. Pulling the pan out, I set it on the stove. Levi walks over and stands next to me. His eyes lock on the pie in front of us and he stares at it blankly for several seconds before looking at me.

"Is that . . . ?"

"Butterscotch Cream Pie," I answer excitedly. "Yes, it is."

A small smile tugs at the corner of his mouth and that little bubble of hope I felt blossoms into something much more. "My grandma used to make that," he whispers.

"I know." His eyes widen in disbelief and he seems to be at a complete loss for words. That's okay, I can talk enough for the both of us. "I don't have her recipe, but I've been working to perfect that pie for the past eight years and this is as close as I can get to your grandmother's." Something in Levi's expression shifts, though I can't quite pinpoint what it is. An appreciation of sorts . . . maybe? "I hope you like it."

Chapter 8

Levi

I CAN'T BELIEVE SHE MADE ME Butterscotch Cream Pie. And on top of that, Laney said she's been perfecting the recipe for eight years. Eight freaking years.

I'm fully aware that I'm staring at her like a fucking idiot, but I really don't know what to say. *She made my Grammy's pie.* I can't remember her ever eating my Grammy's pie. How the hell did she even remember my Grammy used to make it?

I've been working really hard at keeping my distance and not allowing myself to get too close, but *fuck me,* she's making it hard. If I don't get a grip on what I'm feeling now, I'll most likely get in way over my head. But I can't just ignore this . . . this is so much more than just a pie. I'm just not sure I'm ready to explore exactly what *it* is.

"Well?" she asks hopefully, shoving a fork in my direction. "Are you going to try it?" She looks so damn cute in her pink apron, hair piled messily on top of her head and flour smeared across her face, and the sight of her tugs at something deep inside of me—something I haven't felt in a very long time. Something I'm not sure I ever want to feel again. Unfortunately for me, Laney is my weakness . . . my kryptonite. One look from her makes me want to forget that the past eight years ever happened and beg her to start right back where we left off. I can't let that happen.

"This doesn't change anything," I blurt, needing to remind her—and me—that what we had is in the past. Laney's smile slowly falls, along with the fork that she is holding up, and I resist the urge to reach out to her.

I know I'm partly to blame here. I bought her a drink last night, mostly because it killed me that she thought she couldn't afford it, and I stupidly let my guard down, even if it was only for a couple of minutes. It's no secret that she hurt me, but after seeing her again and being around her again, I'm reminded why I loved her so much. She's spunky, tenacious, caring, and her smile could light up the darkest night. And although I know I can't let myself love her again, I would still very much like to be friends with her.

"But it can, if you let it," she says, stepping toward me. And this is where the challenge lies. Laney has a determination like no one I've ever met, and if I have any hope at all of walking away from this intact, I need to tread lightly. "We need to talk about what happened that night, Levi."

"We did talk about it."

"No," she shakes her head vehemently. "I tried to talk about it and *you* blew me off."

"Fine. Talk," I concede, leaning against the counter, knowing that this isn't going to go well. She blows out a slow breath and looks up at the ceiling as though she's praying for the strength to get through this. "Well . . ." I urge, wanting her to get on with it. If she insists on reopening these old wounds, the faster the better so I can close them back up . . . for good this time.

"I made a mistake, a terrible one, and I want to make it right." She takes another step toward me and I take one back. She sighs. "I should have never left. I should've stayed here, with you." *You're damn right you should have.* I bite down on my lower lip, trying desperately to keep my thoughts to myself. "I'm more than willing to take the fall, but let's face it, you weren't innocent in all of this either."

And that's all it takes to set me off. Blood slowly rises, seeping into my cheeks, and I fist my hands at my side. "You left *me*," I spit, pounding a fist into my chest as I step toward her. "*You* didn't choose us. *You* chose to leave."

"But the ultimatum should've never been given," she argues. "I wanted to be with you. I wanted to make it work, and yes, I know it was going to probably be the hardest thing we've ever done, but I was willing to try. I had faith in us."

She's right. I know she's right. I shouldn't have given the ultimatum, but selfishly, I wanted her here with me, not thousands of miles away. And also, I just wanted her to pick me.

"My mom left us," I growl, looking away because it's easier than looking her in the eyes. I hear her sharp intake of breath. I never told her this. She'd asked, but I never told her the truth because it hurt too much. The one woman who should have loved me unconditionally walked away.

"You told me your mom died in a car accident," she whispers. I look over and her eyes are glistening under the bright fluorescent lights. Telling her my mom died was the easy way out. Mason and I told all of our friends our mom had died, because to us, she did die. She cut us out of her life, so we cut her out of ours.

"Yeah, well, I lied." I shrug. "She left us. I was only twelve, and Mason was ten. Don't"—I shake my head—"don't look at me like that."

"Like what?"

"Like you pity me," I snap, running a hand through my hair and down the back of my neck. "Don't pity me. We're better off without her, and—I'm getting off subject. I'm telling you this because I trusted her. She was my mother. She should have loved me and cared for me, no matter what. But she didn't. She was selfish. She saw a better life for herself and she took it without batting an eyelash."

I can see the instant Laney registers what I'm saying to her because her hand flies to her mouth and she slowly starts to shake her head. "So you see," I nod, not giving her the chance to talk. "You left, just like she did. You saw an opportunity to better your life and you took it. And you know what, I'm not even mad about it anymore because now I get it. I get why you did what you did, but it doesn't mean I agree with it. And it certainly doesn't mean that we can go back to what we were because I can't put myself out there like that again. You broke my fucking heart, Laney. You shredded it in two and it took me eight years—*eight* goddamn years—to get over it. And you know what? Now that you're home, I'm still not sure I'm over it." I can see a flash of hope behind her wet eyes and I continue quickly. "I gave you the ultimatum because I wanted you to choose me. I was in love with you and I needed to know that, when push came to shove, I was your first choice."

"You were my first choice," she sobs, running an arm across her tear-soaked face. "I didn't want to choose. I wanted both, but you insisted so I made a rash decision, one that I've regretted every single day since the day I left."

"I don't believe you," I argue, remembering our conversation shortly after she left.

Please pick up. Please pick up. "Hello?" her voice is soft, timid, and nothing like my Laney.

"Laney, baby, thank God you answered. I've been trying to call you for days." This is the third time I've called her today, and probably the hundredth time this week.

"I know," she says softly. I can tell by her thick voice that she's been crying. I hate when she cries.

"Please don't cry, Laney. I'm sorry. I'm so fucking sorry." I take a deep breath, trying to remember what I've been rehearsing in my head for the past couple of days. When words fail me, I say 'fuck it' and go for broke. "I didn't mean it, Laney. I didn't mean to make you choose. I was just scared and afraid that I was going to lose you, which I did, and now I'm miserable. I need you, Laney. I miss you. You're all I think about, baby, and I want you back."

"Levi—"

"Just hear me out," I interrupt, feeling like if I don't get to say what I need to say, I'll lose my chance. *"We can make this work, but I can't be away from you. Laney, I've done nothing but think about you. When I close my eyes, it's your face that I see. I can smell your shampoo on my pillow when I lie down at night and I miss you, baby. Please let me make this right,"* I beg, not caring one bit that I'm waxing poetic.

"How are you going to make it right, Levi? You said yourself that we will never make it being this far apart, and I can't move home. I need to do this, Levi. I have *to do this."*

"I know," I plead, dropping my head into my trembling hand. *"I know you have to do this, and I want to do this with you."*

"You . . . you what?" Is she really that surprised? Does she not know that I wouldn't drop absolutely everything to be with her? Of course she doesn't. I'm the one that told her it could never work out if she left.

"Don't sound so surprised, Laney. I love you. I want to do this with you." I stand up and pace the length of my room in a desperate attempt to calm my nerves.

"But what about your classes? What about your degree? You're so close to graduating, Levi. You can't stop now," she says incredulously.

"Sure I can. I can get a job out there with you and we can work on getting you through school, and then when we come home, I can finish up my degree." It really is that simple. Although when I mentioned it to my dad, I thought he was going to maim me.

"Levi—"

"It's not a big deal, Lane," I insist, wanting—needing—her to let me do this. *"I work for my dad. I'm getting my degree so I can do a better job of running the businesses that are already going to be mine. My education can wait."*

"Levi—" Resignation rings loudly through her quiet voice and dread settles low in my stomach. I push forward.

"Let me do this, Lane. I need to be with you. God, I wish I

would have never given you that ultimatum. That was so wrong of me and I'm so sorry for the way I acted. I need to see you and I need to make it right." I'm putting my heart on the line, desperately hoping and praying that the woman who owns it still wants it. I can hear Laney breathing through the phone, but she's quiet. Too quiet.

"Laney? Do you forgive me? Please, *can we please make this work?"*

"I forgive you, Levi. Of course I forgive you," she breathes. A rush of air leaves my lungs. I didn't realize just how badly I needed to hear that until she actually said it. "But we can't make this work. I'm sorry." My entire world stops spinning as her words plow into me. What does she mean we can't make this work? *I'm giving up everything to make this work.*

"We can. I'm going to move out—"

"I don't love you," she whispers. Her voice breaks on the last word and a deep sob sounds through the phone. My hands to start to shake, my heart is beating wildly in my chest and I'm about two seconds away from completely losing it. She just confirmed my worst fear.

"Laney. Please don't do this," I beg, hoping that maybe she's just still upset from the ultimatum I gave her. I'll never forgive myself for being so thoughtless. "I promise that I can make it up to you and I will make you happy."

"Levi . . ." Her watery voice is soft and it breaks my heart that I'm not with her right now, that we're doing this on the phone. I want to hold her and comfort her, and if she really doesn't love me, I want to look into her eyes when she tells me. "I don't want to be with you. I'm sorry, Levi. This is the hardest thing I've ever had to do, but what we had . . . it was young love, it was fun, but I'm ready to move on and I need to do it here, without you."

A stabbing pain shoots through the left side of my chest and I rub at it, trying to get the pain to stop. Emotion clogs my throat and I swallow hard, determined not to cry. I can't believe this is happening. I know she never said the words, but never in a mil-

lion years would I have believed that Laney doesn't love me, and the fact that she's reducing what we have to nothing but 'young love' tears me to fucking pieces.

Laney is crying, begging me to forgive her, pleading with me to stay friends, but I can't do that. I can't just be her friend. Something deep inside of me—my heart maybe—is telling me that she's full of shit, that she doesn't mean it, and to push her on it, but my brain knows better. My brain remembers what it's like to be tossed aside and it instantly kicks into survival mode.

"Don't you get it, Laney? I wasn't your first choice, because you didn't even love me."

"Don't *you* get it, Levi?" she sobs, throwing my words back at me. "I lied. I lied because I loved you so damn much and there was no way I was going to let you put your life and your dreams on hold for *me*. I couldn't do it." She wipes angrily at the tears running down her face and my breath hitches in my throat, my heart skidding to an abrupt stop.

"No." I shake my head, refusing to believe her. "No. You didn't love me. You said so yourself. We were nothing but young love—"

"I had to make you believe me." She steps toward me, her hands fisted together above her chest. "I knew what you were going to do, and I couldn't let you throw everything you'd worked for away just for me and my dreams. I would have never forgiven myself for that, Levi . . . *never.*" She looks around and waves her hand in the direction of the restaurant. "And look at you now." She smiles, blinking past the tears. "I don't regret it, because *look at you now.* You're successful and so very talented, and I'm amazed by what you've done."

I'm speechless. I have no idea what to say. In the past eight years, aside from that one fleeting moment when she'd first said those devastating words, I never let myself believe she was lying—that she was doing it to protect me and *my* future. And in all honesty, she's probably right. I would've thrown away my dreams, and sure, I might still run Flame, but would Blue even be here? Would Mason and I be working toward opening up restaurants in other cities? Probably not, because I most likely would have never gone back to school.

Spinning around, I blow out a slow breath. Does this change anything? Does the reasoning behind her decisions make this better? I'm not sure, but I can't help but feel better about it somehow. Regardless, I'm still pissed as hell because that's eight long years that we could've been together. I run a hand down the front of my face and close my eyes, absorbing everything that Laney just told me.

"That night here at Flame," I say, twisting toward her. "I told you I loved you, and you never said it back." That's probably what bothers me the most. She tells me that she loved me, she tells me that she said those things to protect me, but the night I first said those three little words, she never said them back.

She shakes her head, the movement so slight that I almost don't catch it. She takes two small steps forward, positioning herself directly in front of me. I swallow hard at the determined look in her eyes. I hope that I'm making the right decision—that I'm not somehow making yet another huge mistake. Because if she keeps pushing, I'm going to let her back into my life. Her eyes soften and she gives me a hesitant smile. Ever so slowly, she lifts her left hand. Her eyes drop to my chest and then snap back to my face, but I can't take my eyes off of her . . . the girl that I gave my heart to all those years ago. I can hardly believe she's standing in front of me, telling me that what we had was, in fact, love. She places her tiny hand over my heart and I suck in a breath, overwhelmed by what her touch still does to me.

"Levi, I love you. I loved you then, I've loved you every single second of every single day for the past eight years and I'm going to love you until the day I die." She rests her other hand on my cheek and I fight the urge to close my eyes. It hurts to look at her right now, but I can't look away. "I will say it over and over again, every single day, until you believe me. You're it for me, Levi. I can't imagine spending whatever time I have left on this beautiful earth with anyone else but you. And I won't spend it with anyone else except you."

"You don't even know me anymore." Except she does. I haven't changed much and I bet she still knows all the important things.

"I don't see it that way." She shakes her head, smiling wistfully. "Sure, there are things about the two of us that have changed, but the one thing that has stayed constant and true are my feelings for you. They haven't wavered—not once."

Both tenderness and doubt fill me, and I hang my head. "I don't know what to say, Laney," I reply gently. "This is a lot to take in." I look up and Laney nods, then nudges me backward until my butt hits the counter. I go willingly . . . of course I do.

"Do you believe me?" she asks, hope in her eyes. "Do you believe that I lied to protect you? Even if you don't agree with it, do you believe it?"

"I want to believe it." She nods, accepting my answer. And it's true, I do want to believe her . . . and I think I do. It's just a lot to take in, and even if I do believe her, does that change anything? Can we ever be more than friends again?

Laney's other hand trails up my neck, sending a shiver straight down my spine. Christ, her touch is amazing. I've been touched by a lot of women over the years—more than I'd like to count—but none of them compare to Laney.

"Will you close your eyes for a second?" she asks, her eyes trained on my mouth. *Oh no. No, no, no.* I'm not sure I can handle this. Laney was always my addiction—my drug of choice, so to speak—and if she does what I think she's going to do, I'll never make it. I might as well throw in the towel now and hand her my balls on a silver fucking platter.

"Why?" I whisper, hating that my body is already betraying me. Before she even answers, my eyelids drift shut and I feel her push up on her tippy-toes, the front of her body brushing lightly against mine. All of my concerns and fears quickly dissipate as if they were never even there, and instead I'm consumed with the feel of her fingers pushing into my hair and the steady beat of her heart against my chest. It feels good . . . too good. I tell myself to ignore the attraction, but it's virtually impossible with her body squished up against me and the growing bulge between my legs.

"I don't want you to see the girl who made a terrible mistake when she walked away. I want you to *feel* the woman who came back, the woman who loves you so fiercely she can feel it in her bones." The front of her body molds against mine and a low groan rumbles from my chest. I smell the sweet scent of her breath just before her soft lips touch mine. Heaven, help me—her lips are amazing.

Aw, hell.

Her mouth is warm, supple and so much more perfect than I remember. I pull back just a fraction. My hands move to her neck, my thumbs framing her jaw, and I angle my mouth over hers. When my tongue pushes between her lips, she lets out the sexiest little moan. Then she weaves her free hand into my hair and squeezes.

There is nothing sexier than Laney when she's on a mission, and right now that mission is me. I would've expected her movements to be hurried and frantic, what with everything we've talked about tonight, but they're not. Her mouth is moving lazily against mine, and if my eyes were open, I'm certain they'd roll straight back into my head. She pulls back all too soon, pupils dilated. "Better than I remember," she whispers, running her fingers over her swollen lips. I smile, loving that I made an impression and not at all because I'm a cocky little shit.

She pushes away from the counter with a satisfied grin and turns away from me. My hand snaps out, catching her wrist before she gets too far. She stops, looking at me over her shoulder.

"Where do you think you're going?" I ask.

Her satisfied grin turns into a mischievous smirk. She pulls loose from my grip and saunters back toward me, not stopping until she's invaded every bit of my personal space. Which, of course, I don't mind at all. If there is anyone I'd want in my personal space, it's this girl.

She rests her hands on my chest and tilts her face to mine. "I've got to clean this kitchen up," she says with a smirk. I look around and see that she's right. This place is a disaster. The sink is full of dirty dishes and she's managed to sprinkle flour on almost every surface of the kitchen, in addition to the chunks of dough scattered around the floor.

"I'll help you clean," I offer, not quite ready to say goodnight. She shakes her head and grips my shirt in her hands. "What do you mean *no?*"

"We've had a long night," she says. I nod. She's got that right. "We've successfully hashed out—"

I shush her with a finger to her lips and her eyes widen in amusement. "I don't want to talk about that anymore. It's over. I'm ready to move past it." She grins behind my fingers and it's infectious. Christ, how I've missed her.

"So where does this leave us?" she asks when I drop my hand. *Isn't that the million dollar question?* Unfortunately, I've never been good at any sort of game show, and I have absolutely no idea what the answer is.

I shrug. "I'm not sure. I know I want us to be friends." And maybe more than that . . . someday.

"Then that's where we'll start, as friends." A tiny part of me had been hoping she would keep pushing me for more because I know that, despite my loud bark, I never would've bit. I'd have given in to her in a heartbeat. But this is good too. I like this. I'm glad I found her here tonight, and I'm really glad we got to talk and hash things out. I already feel lighter, like a weight has been lifted from my shoulders—a weight that I've been hauling around with me for the past eight years. It's an amazing feeling.

Bending forward, I kiss her cheek then trail my lips to her ear. "Friends," I whisper, noticing the goose bumps that pop up on her neck just before I walk past her toward the door.

"Hey, boss?" I turn around and look at her. Her bangs fall into her eyes and she pushes them away from her face.

"Yeah?"

"I'm going to need off every other Friday starting tomorrow." She's no longer smiling; in fact, she looks a little nervous. I want to ask her why she needs off, but something inside of me says to let it go. Judging by the strained look on her face, I'm going to go with my gut and trust that if it's something important or serious, she'll tell me when she's ready. Plus, I don't want to push it. We've already come so far tonight and I want to end it on a good note.

"That's not a problem." She nods jerkily and I ignore the sinking feeling that is taking place in the pit of my stomach. "So I'll see you Monday?"

"See you Monday."

Chapter 9

Levi

"YOU LOOK LIKE HELL, BRO." Mason slaps my back, pushing past me to grab a chip from the bowl on the table. My best friend, Harley, decided to have an impromptu barbeque and so here I sit at her kitchen table on a Sunday afternoon with her adorable son, Max. "And you just got pummeled in Connect Four by a five-year-old."

"Five and a half!" Max yells, slapping Mason's hand away when he tries to ruffle his hair.

"Get up, Levi, let me have a shot at this." Mason pushes me from my seat and makes a show of stretching his neck and cracking his knuckles. Max laughs and begins to copy his movements. Mason is so good with Max—well, actually he's great with every kid. I'd never tell him that because his head would swell to epic proportions and Mason's head is big enough the way it is.

"Kick his butt, Max." I hold my fist out. Max bumps it and then scowls at Mason. I walk outside and step up to the grill next to Tyson, Harley's fiancé. "I am so glad that it's you doing the cooking and not me." Tyson slides me a glance and smiles. The stupid man hasn't stopped smiling since he proposed to Harley, and I can't blame him—she's one hell of a woman.

Before Tyson was in the picture, Harley and I spent a lot of time together. There was even a brief period when I actually thought we might end up together. I didn't love her, not like that, but I love her as a friend and Max means the world to me. I was determined to make sure they both had a great life, but Tyson has that honor now, and I was more than happy to pass the torch.

"Levi," Harley says tenderly, walking toward Ty and me. She stands up on her tiptoes, kissing me on the cheek, and Tyson growls. Harley and I just laugh. It's hilarious watching him get all territorial when she's around me. The guy seriously has nothing to worry about. He put a huge-ass rock on her finger and she's head over heels in love with him. "Walk with me," she says, tugging on my arm. "I haven't talked to you in a while."

Wrapping my arm around her shoulder, I pull her into my side and we stroll over to the picnic table and sit down. "That's not true. You came to Flame the other day and saw me, remember?"

"Ah, yes," she says as she straddles the bench to face me. I can tell by the look on her face that I'm about to get pelted with a million and one questions, and I'm sure it has everything to do with Laney. "You're referring to the day I brought you donuts for breakfast." I nod, waiting for it. "The day that a cute little brunette came barreling into your office and then freaked out and ran when she saw us hugging." *I knew it.*

"So how's Max?"

"Nice try," she deadpans. "Spill it. I want details. Who is she, why did she look like her heart was breaking and why don't I know who she is?"

"Christ, you're nosy." I narrow my eyes at Harley, trying to figure out how much I want to share with her, mainly because I really don't know what's going on between the two of us myself.

The thing is, I haven't been able to stop thinking about Laney since I walked out of the kitchen three nights ago. She's consumed my mind. I've thought about her voice and the way her eyes lit up when she showed me the pie she made. I've thought about her fingers tugging on my hair and the way her body molded to mine. I've thought about how perfect she felt and how much

I've missed her over the years.

Unfortunately, I also can't stop thinking about that sickening feeling I got when I walked away. I spent the better part of the weekend staring at my cell phone, convincing myself that I didn't need to call and check on her. But I wanted to. I wanted to hear her voice again and see her beautiful face, which sort of pissed me off and ultimately led me to shoving my phone in the top drawer of my desk and locking it. How on earth did she manage to weasel her way back into my head in one night?

I've convinced myself that it's just me being nostalgic. She's a shiny new toy all over again and that's all it is. It'll wear off. The more I see her, the more I'll realize that what we had really is in the past and we are better off friends. Yup, I'm going to go with that.

"You can sit here and stare at me all day. Hell, you can even give me the silent treatment, but you are not moving from that spot until you spill the beans." Harley's relentless, and I know she's not kidding. She will hound me until I tell her who Laney is.

"Laney was the first girl I ever loved," I answer, rubbing my hand down the front of my face. "I'm going to need a beer for this." Harley shoots up and darts across the yard, grabs a beer from the cooler and runs back. She pops off the top and hands it to me with a cheeky smile.

"Keep going."

"Okay. Long story short, we were young and in love and it was incredibly intense. She got accepted into culinary school across the country. I yelled. She cried. She left. She's back. There, that about sums it up."

"Wait a minute," Harley interjects. "Back up. Why did you yell?"

"Because I didn't want her to go. But that's a moot point now anyway because we've talked through all of that."

"Okay, but what exactly did you guys talk through? What happened?" I groan, taking a long pull from my beer. I'm not comfortable giving Harley all the details of my past with Laney. I don't mind her knowing about Laney, that's not the problem. It's just that Laney was the love of my life and what happened between us is personal. Plus, Harley is extremely overprotective of me, and I don't want her to think badly of Laney for not choosing me.

"Harley, I'm not going to give you the details. It's not just my story to tell."

"Oh my gosh!" Harley gasps, her eyes wide as though she discovered the meaning of life. "You love her. It's okay, I understand. You don't have to give me details."

"No," I shake my head frantically. "No, I don't love her. I *did* love her—*did* being the operative word here." The whole time I'm talking, Harley is shaking her head and it's starting to tick me off.

"I'm sorry, I don't believe you." I open my mouth but Harley holds her hand up, so I take another drink of my beer instead. "Levi, you used to tell me everything . . . sometimes too much. But you told me stuff about the girls you were with because you didn't care. You didn't care about them and you certainly didn't care about their feelings." I cringe at what she's saying and she pats my leg. "You're not telling me about Laney because she means something to you. Her feelings mean something to you."

I blink. Damn. I sometimes forget how perceptive Harley is.

"So can you tell me what's happening now?" she asks with a smirk, eyebrows raised. "Because I know something is happening. When she walked into your office, she looked like someone kicked her puppy." I can't help but laugh because that is sort of what she looked like, and it was adorable. I'm not going to lie, when Laney walked in and I saw her face, I was actually quite amused. I know it's an asshole thing to think, but I like that she was jealous. I just hadn't been prepared for her to run off before I could introduce Harley and set things straight.

"Eight years ago we went our separate ways, and now she's back and wants to make amends." That's the easiest way to put it.

I'm itching to tell her about our kiss, but that make me feels like a fucking pussy so I take another chug of my beer. I don't want to make it seem like more than what it was. Because it wasn't much, I don't think. Yes, it rocked my world and brought back a flood of emotions, but I'm trying to forget that part. Which is proving to be difficult considering that every time I think about her, I get hard.

"Wow," she whispers. "Sounds a lot like Ty and me." Tyson and Harley had been best friends since childhood, and Tyson, being the idiot that he was, left for medical school and never looked back. Okay, that's not true. He looked back about five years later, realized he'd made a huge fucking mistake and came crawling back on his hands and knees. And now here they are, the perfect couple, happily in love and planning a wedding.

I run a hand down the front of my face and nod my head, because it does sound a lot like Ty and Harley. I sigh, deciding that maybe it would be okay to talk to Harley about some of what happened.

"She made it very clear that she still has feelings for me, which is why she had the 'kicked puppy' look. Previously, she'd asked if I was married and I told her no, so when she walked in and saw you, I think she thought I lied to her."

Harley frowns. "I'm sorry that she thought that. I can talk to her if you want."

"No," I wave her off. "I talked to her and told her we were just friends. Anyway, we spent the majority of that evening hashing stuff out and I think it really helped. There were things that both of us needed to get off of our chests. I just wish we could've said them eight years ago."

Harley nods in understanding. "So where does that leave you now?"

"It leaves me with a friend and a constant hard-on. *Ow!*" I laugh when Harley slaps the side of my head.

"Promise me something?" My eyes roll back into my head and I groan. I hate it when she starts off with that. Harley is glaring at me with her lips pursed and brows furrowed. I wave my hand, urging her to get on with it. "You always told me that you're never going to settle down. You said you'll never open your heart back up to the possibility of love." I nod. She's right, but the vow I made myself eight years ago doesn't seem as strong today as it did at the time. Not that I'm going to tell her that. "You're an incredible man, Levi. You've got this big huge heart that's made of solid gold, and I really don't want to see it go to waste. So promise me you'll keep an open mind. Don't close yourself off to the possibility of love. If you have feelings, then you need to act on them, and if you don't, then you need to be upfront with her so you don't lead her on."

"Thank you, Hallmark," I answer sarcastically, turning to look at Tyson when he busts out laughing. Harley shoots him a stern glare and he just shrugs his shoulders.

"Leave the man alone, babe!" Ty hollers, making his way toward us.

"Do you promise?" she asks, completely ignoring her fiancé.

"I promise." That's not a complete lie. I do plan on keeping an open mind when it comes to Laney, but I'm still not so sure about the whole love-and-forever thing. That part may take a while.

"Levi!" Max yells, plowing out the back door and into the yard. "Wanna play soccer?"

"Absolutely." If her loud huff is any indication, I'm certain Harley wasn't done—but I sure as hell am. This little boy is growing up way too fast, and if he wants to play soccer, then soccer we will play.

Chapter 10

Laney

I WILL NOT CRY.

I will not cry.

Dang it.

Tears burn hot behind my eyes and despite my silent pleas to keep them away, I just can't. The water from the shower is pouring off my body and I just stand and let it all out. I can't fight my emotions anymore. I can't hold everything in. I've been on the verge of tears all weekend and it's been pissing me off.

I should be happy and optimistic. My first treatment went off without a hitch and I feel pretty good, if you don't count the extreme fatigue that is plaguing me despite having slept for ten hours last night. I have no nausea, no vomiting, and yet I feel like I'm dying on the inside. Oh wait . . . that's because I am.

The thought of dying is what does it—it's what finally pushes those tears past the confines of my lashes. And this time, I let it. I let it consume me. I let it own me in hopes that purging it from my system now will give me a renewed strength to fight it later. Wrapping my arms around my stomach, I fold my body in two. Tears race down my face, emotion crawls up my throat and a loud sob rips from my lungs.

I can't believe this is happening.

I don't want to die.

I'm not ready to die.

I have way too many things that I still want to do in life, like get married, and have babies, and grandbabies, and travel to Italy . . . or better yet, Paris. I want to kiss my husband atop the Eiffel tower under a blanket of stars. I want to go whale-watching off the coast of Alaska, ride in a hot-air balloon over a reserve in Africa, and make love on the beaches of Bora Bora.

For the first time, it hits me that I may not *ever* get the chance to do those things. I've thought about dying, but only in the abstract. I've never actually thought about all of the things that I could potentially miss out on.

My trembling hands ball into fists and I pray for the strength to make it through this. *If I can just make it through this.*

Stay positive.

Think good thoughts.

That's what the nurse told me.

"Good morning, Laney." Her smile is way too bright for an oncology unit, if you ask me, but I suppose there's a reason for that. "My name is Heather, and I'm going to get you started." I follow behind her, but I don't talk. She leads me into a small private room that has a hospital bed, one of those really uncomfortable hospital recliner chairs and a TV. An IV pole sits in the corner and I look away, trying to ignore the bags of clear fluid that are already hanging from the metal hooks. "First treatments can be emotional, so everyone gets the option of having theirs in private. You're more than welcome to receive your treatment out on the floor with the rest of the patients, if you'd like. It's completely up to you."

"This is fine," I mumble. Heather smiles and pats my arm.

"I can't imagine how scary this must be for you, but we're going to make it as painless as possible. Feel free to take your shoes off and relax, make yourself comfortable. Most patients prefer to sit up in the chair, but you're going to be here for several hours so if you'd prefer to, you can lie in the bed."

I kick my shoes off and sit in the chair, the tight plastic squeaking when I work to make myself comfortable . . . as if somehow sitting a certain way could manage to accomplish that. "Is there someone here with you today?" I nod my head. Luke, Mia and Benny are all sitting not-so-patiently in the waiting room. They're like a bunch of mother hens that wouldn't take no for an answer, but it warms my heart to know that they all cared enough to want to be here with me. My mind drifts to Levi. I wonder if he would've wanted to be here with me . . . had he known. "Once we get you hooked up and started, I'll be sure and get them for you."

"There's three of them." I laugh, and Heather looks at me and smiles. "I tried to convince them that I'd be fine, but they insisted on coming. I don't know why," I say with a shrug. "I have no idea what they're going to do for the next five hours."

"Support you."

"Huh?"

"That's what they're going to do for the next five hours. They're going to support you. Believe it or not, this is usually just as hard on the loved ones as it is on the patients themselves. They need to know they can help out, even if it's just in the form of support." I look away, tears pricking the back of my eyes. She's right. I never really thought about what this is doing to them. I shouldn't be so hard on them for hovering. "Let them, okay?" I look back at the petite nurse, who seems to be imploring me to do as she says with her eyes more so than her words. "I see a lot of patients come and go, and some of them do this completely by themselves. No loved ones to sit by them or encourage them or hold their hand when they're scared or sick, and I can't imagine how that would feel. So let them. Let them worry about you. Let them sit here for five hours and watch this drip into your arm." She points to the IV bag. I'm thankful Heather told me that. I needed to hear it. "They're doing it because they love you and they're scared." I give her a tremulous smile and she nods. "Okay then. What do you say we get this started? Are you ready to get your first treatment out of the way?"

100

"Let's do it."

And I did.

With three nervous Nellies hovering around me and asking a ton of questions, I did it. It wasn't at all what I expected either. It didn't hurt. I had a small wave of nausea hit shortly after it started, but they gave me some 'extra stuff' in my IV that stopped that.

Benny and Mia handled things pretty well—under the circumstances, anyway—but Luke's reaction just about broke me. The look on his face told me everything I needed to know about what this was doing to my baby brother. Eyes wide and glossy, he shoved the emesis basin at me right before he stood up and walked out the door. I wanted to go after him and assure him I was fine, but I couldn't. Not only was I unable to get out of the chair but also because I wasn't fine.

Luke came back after a couple of minutes and didn't say a word. He simply pushed his chair as close to mine as he could get it, wrapped my hand in his and didn't move until my treatment was over. He never said anything about it, but I can't help but wonder if he's worried about losing me the way we lost our mom.

I know I need to stay strong for them, the people who love me endlessly, but I also need to stay strong for myself. I can't let myself get wrapped up in the *what ifs*. Because when I allow them in, even just a little bit, they take over and my mind shoots off into a thousand different directions. I have to stay strong. I *can* do this. Pushing the fear away, I regain control of my emotions.

I will be fine.

I will survive this.

Squeezing my facial cleanser into my hands, I rub them together and lather up my face, washing away my tears and insecurities. With precise, habitual movements, I wash my hair, shave my legs and then step out of the shower before wrapping myself in a towel. Pulling open the bottom drawer of my vanity, I reach for my blow dryer and then stop, my hand hovering in the air. My hair is a pain in the butt to blow dry; it's long and it takes forever.

Maybe I should get it cut, something cute and spunky. It's going to fall out anyway, so I might as well try something new in the process, right?

I make quick work of applying my makeup, paying special attention to the dark circles under my eyes, and then I slip into my work clothes. Pulling open the door, I come face to face with Mia and Benny. They're both leaning against the wall opposite the bathroom and they're watching me expectantly.

"What the heck are you guys doing?"

"Were you crying?" Leave it to Mia to just put it out there. It's not like I value my privacy or anything.

"No." Scurrying past them, I keep my head down. Mia can tell if I'm lying from a mile away.

Benny's hand shoots out, stopping my bedroom door before I'm able to slam it shut. "Bullshit. We heard you."

"You heard my iPod. I wasn't crying. Why would I be crying?"

"Maybe because—" Mia trails off and looks at Benny. She's scared to say it.

"Because I had my first chemo treatment? Because I'm scared? Or maybe because I'm so exhausted I feel like I could crawl back into bed and hibernate for a week." She looks back at me and I hate the sadness I see in her eyes.

"Yes. Because of that," she whispers.

"Look . . ." Pulling them both into my room, I push them down on the bed so they're sitting in front of me. "I appreciate what you guys are doing, but you've got to stop hovering. I need you to stop treating me like I'm a vintage porcelain doll and I could break with the slightest touch."

"But we love you, and we want you to be okay."

"I know you do, Mia, and I'm going to be okay. But I'm also going to have bad days. There are going to be times when I cry, and there will probably be times when I get angry, but there's nothing you can do about it. One way or the other, it's going to happen. I've accepted it and you have to accept it." My eyes flit between Mia, who looks like she wants to hug me, and Benny, who looks about as uncomfortable as a nun in a strip joint.

Kneeling down, I drag my shoes out from under my bed and slip them on. "I'm tough, remember?" Hopping onto my feet, I flex my arms, giving my best 'strong man' impression. Benny reaches out and squeezes my bicep and immediately busts out laughing. I slap his arm then kiss both of them on the cheek and walk out, impressed with how well I handled that.

"Wait!" Mia's feet are slapping against the hardwood floor as she scurries after me. "Where are you going?"

"Work."

Benny strides up and stands behind Mia. "You don't have to be there for another couple of hours." I shrug, smiling at what I'm about to do.

"I've got something to take care of first." Grabbing my purse off the coffee table, I swing it over my shoulder and fling open the door. "See ya!"

"You haven't even done your hair," Mia hollers after me, and as I climb into my car, I swear I hear her tell Benny that I've lost my mind.

"Laney?" I turn around slowly to find Levi standing behind me. His eyes look like they're on fire, and I'm trying to gauge if that's a good thing or a bad thing. I'm hoping it's good.

"Yes?"

"She looks fucking hot, doesn't she?" Tatum smiles wickedly and props her elbows up on the bar. "I've been hittin' on her all day, but she's having no part of it." Today I had to work the lunch shift, which was crazy busy. The restaurant closes at three and then reopens at five for dinner. At the end of my shift, I made a plate of French fries and Toasted Ravioli and joined Tatum at the bar. I've been working on my bucket list and stuffing my face with food while she cleans and restocks the bar.

Levi flashes me a knowing smile and—holy mother of God—I think my panties just melted. He's probably remembering our kiss from the other night and knows exactly why I'm not giving Tatum the time of day—apart from the fact that she's attracted to women and I'm attracted to men.

"It looks good." He clarifies by pointing to my hair. "You look different."

"Different good or different bad?" I decided to go for a tapered stack. I've always loved that look on girls—the one where it's longer in the front and shorter in the back. I was just always too scared to do it.

"That's a trick question, dude. I'm a woman, I should know. Just tell her it looks hot." Levi and I both laugh at Tatum, who just shrugs her shoulder and continues restocking the bar.

Levi leans in close so only I can hear. "You look sexy." He pulls back all too soon when Mason walks into the room. He squeezes in between Levi and me, and I fight the urge to kick him in the shin.

Sitting down, he pops one of my French fries into his mouth. "What are you still doing here? You're off for the dinner shift."

I pull my plate from his grabby hands. "I'm just getting to know Tatum."

"And she's making her bucket list." Leaning across the bar, I throw a French fry at Tatum, who is squatting down on the floor.

"Bucket list?" Mason asks.

"Yeah. You know, a list of things you want to do before you die," I answer mirthlessly.

"Join the mile-high club. That's what I want to do." Mason tosses another fry into his mouth and smiles smugly. "And have sex in one of Levi's cages."

Tatum's head pops up over the bar and she's smiling wickedly. "That's a great one, Mase. I want to do that. Put that on your list, Laney."

"No," Levi snaps. "If anyone has sex in one of my cages, it's going to be me." All of our heads turn toward Levi. I can tell by the look on his face that he didn't mean to blurt that out, but it's too late . . . it's out there, and now all I can think about is Levi tying my wrists to the bars of the cage and having his naughty way with me. Tatum snaps her fingers, catching my attention, and when I look at her, she motions for me to close my mouth and wipe the drool off my face. Then she winks and dips back behind the bar.

Mason's hand pauses mid-air, hovering above my plate, and slowly he turns to Levi. "You mean, you haven't already done that?" Mason asks incredulously.

"Fuck you," Levi grumbles. Reaching past Mason, he grabs my notepad.

"Hey!" I try to snatch it back, but he's too quick and too tall, so I decide to just sit back and let him read it. I'm not ashamed of anything on my list anyway. His eyes roam across the page and when he gets to what must be the bottom, he looks up at me.

"Got any plans tonight?" I shake my head. "Meet me back here at eight then." My eyes are locked on Levi's, and the excitement bubbling up in my throat is making it hard to speak.

"What are we going to do?" I manage, swallowing past the gigantic lump in my throat. Levi holds out my list and I take it from him, wondering what the heck he's up to.

"We're going to hang out." My eyes drift to Mason and then to Tatum, who is now standing and grinning at me like an idiot, and then back to Levi again. "Okay?" he confirms.

"It's a date," Mason quips, looking between Levi and me. "You two are going on a date."

"It's not a date," Levi huffs, looking away sheepishly, effectively knocking my anticipation and excitement down a couple of notches.

"Whatever you say, bro." Mason claps Levi on the shoulder and grabs my now-empty plate. "Whatever you say."

Chapter 11

Laney

"IT'S A DATE," MIA SQUEALS, clapping her hands together.

"It's not a date," Benny grunts, rolling his eyes before grabbing a bottle of water from the refrigerator. "If the man said it's not a date, then it's not a date. Quit getting her hopes up."

"He's right, Mia. It's not a date," I agree.

Benny walks past me and stops long enough to kiss my forehead. "His loss," he whispers, walking into the living room.

"Please tell me you're trying to snag him." My words are directed at Mia, but my eyes are following the larger-than-life man walking through my house.

"No," she shakes her head, waving me off. "We're just friends. He made it perfectly clear that I'm not his type, and well, I'm not one to beg so . . ." She trails off and I know Mia well enough to know that it's more than likely bothering the hell out of her. She doesn't get shot down . . . ever.

"Wh—"

"So," she cuts me off, discontinuing any further discussion about Benny. "My dad wants me to come home." I shouldn't be surprised; I knew this was coming. I knew she couldn't stay here with me forever, although a small part of me had been hoping she would.

"Daddy can't run the place without you?"

"Riiiiight," she drags out with a dramatic roll of her eyes. "That place probably runs better when I'm not there. Hell, I'm not even sure what it is that I actually do other than fetch his coffee."

"Stop it." I push away from the table and she follows suit. "You run his life. He would fall apart if you weren't there."

"One of these days, Lane," she sighs, following me down the hall toward the bedroom. "One of these days I'll get to do what I want to do."

"Do what you want to do now. Don't wait, Mia. Who cares what your dad says? Do what makes you happy."

She plops down on my bed and throws an arm over her forehead. "You're right," she relents. "I know you're right, but it's just scary. Daddy said he'd cut me off and then I'll have nothing."

"No, then you'll have your freedom. Remember that fancy little teaching degree you worked really hard on?" She nods. "You can put it to use. Pay your own way through life."

"You make it sound so easy."

Grabbing onto her arm, I pull her up and into my arms, hugging her tight. "It is easy," I whisper. "You just have to want it badly enough."

"As hot as this is," Benny says as he saunters into the bedroom, "and it is hot—please feel free to rub all over each other any time—Laney has to get going or she's going to be late."

Mia and I bust up laughing. Then she pulls away, runs a hand over my hair, grips my chin and turns my face toward her, inspecting my makeup. Smacking my butt, she says, "You look perfect! Let's get you to your man."

I glance at my watch. "Shoot." I have ten minutes and I hate being late. "Benny's right, I have to go." Scurrying down the hall, I slide to a stop in the living room and slip on my Tom's. I grab my purse and then a minute later, I'm out of the house.

The drive to Flame is short and the parking lot is already filling up for the dinner rush. I pull around back, throw Ivy into park and take one last look at my makeup before making my way into the restaurant. Riley waves at me from behind the bar and I scan the room for Levi. "Hey, Riley. Have you seen Levi?" Just then, my phone vibrates. I pull it out of my pocket to find a text from Tatum.

Tatum: *Levi says to meet him over here at Blue.*
Me: *K. Headed over now.*

"I'm guessing by the smile on your face that you just found him."

"Actually, it was Tatum, but he's over at Blue. Have a good night."

"You too," she hollers after me.

I turn my back on her and weave my way through the restaurant and over to Blue. It's too early for the bar to be packed—the drinking crowd hasn't really shown up yet—but there are a few patrons scattered around, eating appetizers. My eyes immediately land on Levi. He's sitting at the bar, back to me, talking animatedly with Tatum. Wearing a black Henley, the arms bunched up around his elbows, faded jeans and Chuck T's, he looks absolutely amazing. My heart stutters at the thought of getting to spend the evening with him. In fact, this will be the first time we've been truly alone since I moved home.

Tatum must say something funny because Levi tosses his head back. His deep, throaty laugh floats through the room, eliciting a shiver through my entire body. *That sound.* I've missed that sound. An excited flutter tickles my belly and my breathing slows as a memory takes over.

"Let's spoon." Snuggling up to Levi, I tuck my head into his neck and wait for him to wrap his arm around me. I love that he has his own apartment. I don't stay over too often, because I hate leaving Luke at home alone with Dad, but every once in a while I let myself indulge. Levi's eyes are trained on the TV and I nudge him in the side. "Spoon. Now."

"How about we knife," he says without looking at me. What?

"Knife?" I clarify, pushing up onto my elbow so I'm looking down at him.

He glances at me and smiles, and if I wasn't currently annoyed at him for suggesting we 'knife,' then I might smile back. "Yeah, knife." He straightens his body, relaxing his arms at his sides. "Look, we're already doing it. No need to even move."

"Knife," I repeat, exaggerating the word with a slow nod of my head.

"Great, huh? Plus, you're a hotbox."

"I'm a hotbox," I mutter, looking at the TV. Saturday Night Live *is on, but I don't register what's being said because I'm pissed that my boyfriend wants to 'knife.' How the heck do you deny someone who wants to spoon? Most of the time, it leads to sexy times anyway!*

Flinging the covers off, I scramble out of bed and hightail it for the bathroom. Unfortunately for me, Levi's legs are a mile long and he snags my elbow before I'm able to get too far.

"Where the hell do you think you're going?" He pulls me against him, my back to his chest, and wraps an arm around my stomach. His fingers play with the hem of my underwear as he nuzzles his face into the side of my neck.

"I'm a hotbox, remember?" I push on his arm and try to pull away, but he's too strong. He chuckles at my pathetic attempt to struggle and tightens his grip on me. I huff out a heavy breath and let my legs and arms go limp, refusing to hold him back.

"I was kidding, baby. Lighten up, it was a joke."

"Well, I hope you still think it's a joke when you're sleeping in this big ol' bed all by yourself tonight." I'm trying really hard to stand my ground and keep my voice firm and steady, but his fingers have somehow managed to make their way up the planes of my stomach and are currently stroking the underside of my breast. Christ, his hands are heaven. *He places a gentle kiss at the base of my neck and nips lightly with his teeth. A low moan starts deep in my throat, but I push it back down, insistent on standing my ground.*

"Come on . . ." He turns me in his arms and moves in to kiss me, but I turn my head and his lips land on my cheek. I would have much preferred his pouty lips on mine, but the boy needs to be taught a lesson, and that lesson is that when Laney wants to cuddle, you cuddle! He chuckles again, this time sliding his hand down my back and under my panties. He squeezes my ass, his fingers digging into my flesh, and my eyes nearly roll back into my head. "Let's spoon."

My hand—on its own accord, because I sure as hell didn't authorize it—slides up his arm, over his shoulder and cups the back of his neck. Damn it. NO.

"Go fork yourself, Levi," I snap, making one last attempt at pushing him away. He throws his head back and laughs—a full belly laugh—and that sound alone single-handedly melts every inch of my soul. I love his laugh, and this particular laugh is saved only for me. It's deep and throaty, and it makes my toes tingle. All of my resolve fades away and I start laughing with him as I wind my arms around his neck. Like an old dance that we've done a million times, he lifts and places me in the center of the bed. My eyes linger on his hands, and I watch as he rips off his shirt, pushes his pants and boxers down his thighs, and slowly crawls his way—

"EARTH TO LANEY!"

I shake my head and blink my eyes several times to regain focus. When I do, I find Levi and Tatum at the bar staring at me. Tatum is smiling—apparently, all the girl can do is smile—and Levi is watching me with such intensity that I would almost swear he knew exactly what I'd been thinking about.

With languid movements, I make my way across the bar, never taking my eyes off of Levi. He has a magnetic pull on me that I can't explain; it's intense and, at times, overwhelming, but I wouldn't give it up for the world.

"Let me have your phone." I stick my hand out, waiting for him to hand it over. Levi narrows his eyes as he digs his phone out of his pocket and hands it over. "Next time you have a message for me, let me know yourself. Don't have Tatum message me," I say, making quick work of adding my contact information into his phone before handing it back.

"I didn't have your number."

"Well, now you do, so no more excuses." He cocks an eyebrow, the side of his mouth ticking up in a smile. "So, where are you taking me?" That must be Tatum's cue because she reaches under the bar and grabs a large brown paper bag that appears to be stuffed.

"Have fun, you two." Her grin is wide . . . too wide. I scrunch my brows at her, wondering what in the heck she knows that I don't.

Levi grabs onto my elbow and tugs me forward. "Are you coming?"

"Oh, I'm sure I'll be coming at some point, but probably not tonight. It's a little too soon, don't you think?" Levi stumbles in front of me and I slam into his back. Then he keeps walking right out of the bar and across the parking lot. "Did you trip back there, or did my witty commentary cause you to lose your balance?"

He chuckles, shooting me a quick glance out of the corner of his eye. "Since when are you the witty one out of the two of us?"

"Since I've got your panties in a bunch."

"What?" He laughs, continuing down the path that leads to the riverfront. "Where the hell did that come from?"

I shrug my shoulders, looking down at the sidewalk. "Mason said your panties have been in a bunch since I came home." I look up to find Levi watching me.

"Is that so?"

I nod emphatically. "Yup. I think you need to pick that wedgie so we can get on with things."

"Damn, you're feisty tonight," he says, stopping in a grassy spot. He looks up at the sky and then takes a few more steps forward. "This'll do."

I look up, trying to figure out what he was looking at, but all I see is the top of the Arch and a blanket of brightly lit stars against a black canvas. Street lights are scattered haphazardly along the walking path, but it's the soft glow of the moon that gives the evening a dreamy feel. A warm breeze floats through the air and I catch a familiar scent.

"Is that what I think it is?" Levi is sitting on the ground, pulling containers out of the bag. When he has them all situated, he pats the grass next to him and I take a seat, folding my legs underneath me.

"It is," he says, handing me one of the Styrofoam containers and a fork. "It's still your favorite, right?" he asks, and there's a cloud of doubt slipping across his face.

I think about telling him 'no' just to get a rise out of him, but I can't. He's obviously gone through a lot of trouble putting this all together—whatever this is—and I don't want to ruin it. Things felt good last night when we parted ways, and then again today, but I wasn't sure how they would be tonight once we were alone. I had hoped that we could move past the wall between us, and I think we finally have. Why else would he bring me out here for a picnic featuring my all-time favorite food?

"Are you kidding? Of course it's my favorite." Popping off the lid, I close my eyes and inhale the scent of the delicious food. Beef Pepper Steak has always been my favorite, and no one—and I mean, *no one*—can make it the way Levi does. I grab a fork, stab the sauced meat and then pause before the juicy goodness hits my mouth. "Wait. You made this, right?"

Levi's face shines brightly, a wide grin splitting his lips. "What would you say if I told you Mason made it?"

I scowl, dropping the fork into the container. "Levi Beckford, that is not funny," I pout, staring at my food like it's growing mold. "Did Mason make this?"

Shrugging his shoulder, Levi stabs a pepper and pops it into his mouth. "Guess you're going to have to try it to find out." Putting the container down, I grab another one and peek inside. Mashed potatoes. Okay, there is no way Mason could've screwed up mashed potatoes. Right?

Just as I'm about to dig into the potatoes, they're ripped from my hand. "What are you doing? Try the damn Pepper Steak." Levi scoops up a heap from his bowl and lifts it to my mouth. I stare at him numbly, unable to move because the memories are crashing into me like waves on a rocky shore. Levi used to feed me all the time. To anyone else we probably looked like idiots, but it was nothing for the two of us to feed each other an entire meal. And here he is, feeding me. "Lane?"

"Yeah?"

"Are you going to try it?" I mentally snap myself back to reality and lean forward as Levi raises the fork a little more. My lips slip around the plastic cutlery and my eyes instantly roll back in my head. *Hea-ven!*

"Oh my god, that's amazing," I mumble around the food in mouth, desperately trying to ignore the growing wave of nausea in the pit of my stomach. I close my eyes and attempt to savor the flavor, knowing full well that Levi was the one who made me this meal. "Mmmmm," I groan, slowly opening my eyes as I swallow. Levi's watching me, lips parted, eyes glossed over, and if I'm not mistaken, his breathing is a little faster and a tad bit heavier.

I take a deep breath in through my nose, willing the churning in my stomach to stop. I have my nausea medicine in my purse, but I'm not sure Levi and I are ready for that conversation quite yet. My hope is that he can get to know me again, that he will trust me again and maybe even love me again. But I don't want any of that to be out of pity; I want it to happen naturally. "Levi?"

"Yeah?"

"Do I have some food on my mouth?"

"No. Why?" he asks, his eyes still trained on my mouth. My tongue darts out, licking a slow path across my bottom lip, and he swallows hard.

"Because you're staring at my mouth."

"Sorry. I, uh . . ." He shakes his head and looks away sheepishly.

"It's okay." I wave him off nonchalantly, taking another small bite despite the uneasy feeling in my stomach. "My lips are plump and juicy, and most guys stare at them, so don't even think twice about it."

A laugh rips from his throat as he tears a chunk off of his bun, tossing it at my head. I don't react in time and it smacks me in the forehead. "That wasn't nice," I pout. Levi pulls a napkin out of the bag and I playfully yank it from his hand, causing him to chuckle. I wipe the garlic butter off and Levi goes back to eating his food.

There is nothing more that I want than to devour the rest of my dinner, but my stomach disagrees wholeheartedly "Can you hand me a water?" Slipping my hand into my purse, I twist the cap of the pill bottle, slide one out and grab the opened bottle of water that Levi has waiting for me.

"What's that?" he asks, nodding at my purse.

I should probably tell him—put it all out there and let things fall where they may. But I can't. I want to see where tonight goes, and I need to tell him when I feel the time is right.

"Tylenol," I answer, tossing the tiny white pill into my mouth, I chase it with a swig of water and hope that it takes effect quick enough for me to eat a few more bites.

"Headache?"

"Just a little one." Levi nods and we fall I watch as he devours everything in his container, along with half of the mashed potatoes and two of the rolls. I manage to eat a little more of my Pepper Steak and half a roll, but it's not nearly as much as I usually eat.

"Aren't you going to finish that?" He looks confused, peering down at my container. Shaking my head, I hand it to him.

"Nope. I'm full. It was absolutely delicious. Please, finish it." I take a long drink of my water and nod for him to eat.

He frowns but shoves the delicious food into his mouth. Lying back on the grass, I tuck my hands behind my head and look up at the stars. It's a clear night. No fog, no smog, and a million stars in the sky.

"So, how have things been since you've been home?" How the hell do I answer that? I can't very well say, '*To tell you the truth, with all the chemo and everything, it's majorly sucked.*' Instead, I go with the response I've gotten used to telling people.

"Good. Things have been good. Luke is happy I'm home, and Benny spends so much time at my house that I'm not sure he even knows what his house looks like anymore." I can hear Levi cleaning up our mess, but I don't move to help him, deciding to stay here in my bubble of perfection—a blanket of darkness above me with the man I love beside me.

"I always thought he had a thing for you."

Say what? I prop myself up on my elbows and look at Levi curiously. "You're kidding, right?" He shakes his head, eyebrows raised. "You're crazy. Benny has always been like another brother to me, and he'd probably break your neck just for thinking that."

"You're probably right," he laughs, jumping up to toss our trash into a nearby can. My eyes linger on his butt and when he turns around to walk back, I look back up at the stars.

"How is the job going? Do you enjoy working here?" Levi plops down next to me and I watch as he leans back casually, looking up at the sky.

"What are you doing?" I certainly wasn't expecting stargazing to be on the evening's menu.

He points to the stars and draws a line. "I'm finding constellations. Look, just found Orion's belt."

"That one doesn't count," I laugh, lying back down beside him. "It's the easiest one up there. You have to go for the tougher ones."

"Okay, first one to find Corona Borealis wins."

"Challenge accepted. Wait"—I look over at him—"what does the winner get?"

"What would you want?" He looks at me skeptically, and I can only imagine what's running through his head.

"I don't know. I'd have to think about it."

"Alright," he says with a nod, turning back toward the sky. "Winner gets whatever they want . . . within reason." He stresses the 'within reason' with a cock of the eyebrow and I wink at him.

"Deal. Are you ready?"

"Already started, darlin'."

"What?" I gasp. "You got a head start. That's not fair!" Levi laughs and I can't help but laugh right along with him. The minutes pass by, or maybe hours . . . hell, I don't know. All I know is that this is the happiest I've been in as long as I can remember, and I'd lie here forever if I could somehow get away with it.

I've peeked over at Levi a couple of times and each time he's got a big ol' grin on his face. He has one arm tucked behind his head and the other draped across his stomach. My hand itches to reach across and touch him—hold his hand, maybe—but in no way do I want to risk setting us back. "I missed this," I whisper, my gaze shifting back to the stars. I don't see Levi look over at me, but I know he is. The weight of his eyes is heavy. "And not just the clear skies. I missed being here . . . I missed home." I pause. "I missed you. You're what I missed most." I feel his body move beside me and when I look over, he's lying on his side, facing me, with his hand propping up his head.

"Was California everything you wanted it to be?" he asks. He doesn't look or sound angry, and I wonder momentarily if he's been able to let go of the past or if he's simply choosing to move on. I'm not really sure there is a difference between the two, but I'd like to think there is. I'd like to think that any person, if the will is there, could let go of something, even if it was something that impacted their life the way that my leaving impacted Levi.

"At first, it was horrible. I hated it. I wanted nothing more than to come home, and not just because of you. Although you were a big part of it. I missed Luke and I missed working at the restaurant. I missed my friends, the few that I had. I just missed everything."

"Then what changed?" he asked.

"I'm not sure," I sigh. "A lot of things, I guess. I knew I didn't have you anymore. I'd made sure of that with our last phone conversation. And then I met Mia. That's probably what changed. I met Mia."

"Tell me about her."

Looking over at him, I smile, genuinely happy that he's interested in what I've been doing. "She's amazing. The best friend a girl could ever ask for. She's loyal and strong and she's funny as all get out. She's feisty and brave, and I think that's what drew me to her the most—her bravery. She challenged me to try new things and meet new people. She pushed me out of my comfort zone."

"She sounds great," he replies. I can feel his warm breath fanning across the side of my face when I look back to the sky. "She seemed nice when I met her."

I nod. "She's fantastic. I'm a little bummed she's going home soon."

"How soon? I thought maybe she moved here with you."

"I'm not sure." I shrug. "She just told me tonight that her dad wants her back home. She works for him, so this was only temporary." My eyes start to gloss over just thinking about Mia leaving. She's been my rock for the past several years, and now I'll only have her via phone and e-mail. "It's all good though. I've got lots to keep me busy."

"Oh yeah, like what?"

My eyes catch on a formation and I sit up, squinting, trying to figure out if I found it. I look at Levi and smile. "There, it's right there." Closing one eye—because everyone knows that helps you see better—I point to the stars and trace my finger around Corona Borealis.

"No way." Levi sits up and leans toward me so the sides of our heads are touching. "Well, I'll be damned." We both turn to look at each other at the same time and our noses nearly touch. His smile slowly fades as his eyes drop to my mouth. The air around us grows thick and my heart hammers inside my chest. I want so badly to grab the back of his neck and yank him to me, but I refrain, knowing this is a step that he needs to take.

To my dismay, he clears his throat and backs up, putting space between the two of us. "Um . . . so . . . what do you want?"

"What do you mean, what do I want?" I ask, still too caught up in the moment to fully comprehend what he's talking about.

"You won. So you get to pick your prize."

"Hmmm." I flop back down on the ground and tap my bottom lip with my finger. What do I want? "Nothing. I don't want anything." I look to the sky and then back to Levi. He lowers himself to the ground and looks over at me.

"Nothing?"

"Nope. This is perfect." Our eyes stay locked for several seconds, but the connection is too intense and I have to look away or I'll physically melt. "I'm just glad we got to spend some time together, just you and me. It's been really nice, Levi. So this is it. You've already given me what I want." I take a deep satisfying breath, chancing a quick glance back at him. He's grinning from ear to ear, and I swear that his smile alone could light up the darkest of nights. His features have softened, his eyes are sparkling with happiness, and I'm glad it's directed at me.

"Okay." His warm voice evaporates into the evening air and I sigh, knowing that right now, in this very second, everything has changed. We seem to have found our footing again and some sort of peace, and I can only hope that it will grow from here.

Time slips away as we talk about the past several years. Levi tells me about finishing up his degree and about how Blue came to be. I laugh hysterically when he describes his dad's face the day he had the cages installed, and I nearly cry when he talks about the pride he felt the day it officially opened.

My education means the world to me, and I love what I do, but I would give it all up if I could rewind time and be there with him for those precious moments that he'll remember for the rest of his life—moments that I'll only ever be told about. But that's why I'm here now, I remind myself, not wanting to get caught up in the 'should-haves.'

Out of nowhere, a shooting star darts across the sky. "Did you see that?" I gasp at the same time Levi's hand shoots in the air, pointing to where it flew through the night. "Make a wish," he says, glancing over at me. I squeeze my eyes shut and wish for the exact same thing I wish for every time I see a shooting star. "What are you wishing for, Laney?"

I open my eyes and look over at him. He looks raw and vulnerable, which is exactly how I'm feeling right now. Regardless, there is nothing I can say but the absolute truth. "The same thing I always wish for—you."

Levi's eyes widen just a fraction and he sucks in a deep breath, holding it for a few seconds before blowing it out. I feel like I should say something else, but I don't want to ruin the moment. He asked what I wished for and I told him.

"We should probably get going." Sitting up, I finger comb my hair, knocking loose any grass or leaves to the ground. Levi follows suit, stretching his arms up to the sky with a big yawn. The moment is broken, but that's okay because more than anything, at least he knows how I feel.

"You're right. It's probably getting late." He looks down at his watch. "Nah, not too bad. Only ten thirty."

"Way past my bedtime," I yawn, picking up my purse. Levi stands up and offers me his hand, which I graciously accept, because there is no way I'm going to pass up the opportunity to touch him. He pulls me to my feet and we walk unhurriedly back to the restaurant, enjoying each other's company. When we reach my car, I click the button to automatically unlock the doors and he reaches for the handle, opening the door for me. I toss my purse into the front seat and then turn back to Levi. "Thank you for this. I had a great time."

"Me too," he says softly.

"Okay, well"—I look down at the keys in my hand and then back at him—"I should go." Sliding into my car, I move to pull the door closed but Levi stops it.

"Wait, I need your list."

"My list?"

"Your bucket list. Can I have it?" he asks, his hand outstretched and waiting.

"Um, sure." I dig around in my purse, looking for the folded piece of paper. When I find it, I reluctantly give it to him. "What do you need that for?"

"Do you have a pen?" he asks, ignoring my question. I dig one out of my purse and hand it over, then he walks to the back of my car and unfolds the piece of paper before laying it on the trunk. His eyes travel down the page until he finds whatever it is he's looking for. He scratches the pen across the paper, neatly folds it up and brings it back to me. "Do you have any plans next Friday?"

I get ready to tell him 'no' and then remember that's my day for chemo. Chewing on my bottom lip, I hesitate before answering his question. Although my treatment won't last all day, I'm not sure how I'll feel afterward and I don't want to make any plans just in case I end up feeling like a zombie. "I do, actually. I took off work every other Friday, remember?"

His brows furrow and then quickly soften out. "Yeah, I forgot. No biggie. How about that following Monday?"

"I'll have to check my schedule to see if I work the day or evening shift, but I'd be free at some point."

"Okay. Let me know and then I'll tell you where to meet me." He looks hopeful, and it takes everything I have not to jump up and start squealing for joy. This is even better than I could have imagined. A date—well, semi-date—ending with a request for another non-date. This night couldn't have possibly ended any better. Well, it could have, but I'm not going to go there.

"Night, Laney."

"Goodnight, Levi." He pushes my door shut and I watch him walk back into the restaurant. Once he is completely out of sight, I unfold my list. When I see what he's done, tears well up in my eyes.

Laney's Bucket List
1. Go Skydiving
2. ~~Get a tattoo~~
3. Make love on a beach in Bora Bora
4. Kiss my husband under the Eiffel Tower
5. Make a significant positive impact on a stranger's life
6. Dance in Levi's cage
7. ~~Have a picnic under the stars~~
8. Go skinny dipping
9. Go cliff diving
10. Visit the Grand Canyon
11. Go to New York
12. Get married
13. Have children

He checked something off my bucket list.

I'm not even sure what to think about that. It has to mean something that he wants to do this, right? Surely he wouldn't go out of his way to check something off my bucket list if he didn't still care. I take a deep breath. It's ironic, really, that the man I love is helping with my bucket list, but he doesn't know why I started the list in the first place. I squeeze my eyes closed, pushing away that thought. I have to stay strong. I have to fight.

For my life.

For Levi.

I take the pen that Levi just used and I open my list back up to scribble down another item.

14. Make Levi fall in love with me again

Chapter 12

Levi

"IT WAS GREAT SEEING YOU, Brady. Please tell Mark we're sorry he couldn't make it." Brady takes my outreached hand in a firm shake and slaps my back with the other. "Let Mason and I discuss things, and we'll be getting back with you soon."

"Absolutely," Brady says, letting go of my hand and stepping over to Mason to shake his hand. "As soon as you guys make a decision, let me know so we can get the ball rolling."

"Are you headed back home today?"

"Nah, man. I'm going to stay tonight and head home tomorrow." Brady slips on his jacket and checks his phone as he's walking out the door. "See you two later."

Mason shuts the door behind Brady and turns to me, eyes wide and full of excitement. "We are doing this, right? Please tell me we're doing this."

I laugh at him, mostly because he's close to pissing his pants. "Hell yeah, we're doing this," I answer, pulling my baby brother in for a hug. "We've worked hard and we're not passing up this opportunity. We'd be stupid to walk away from this."

"That's what I'm talking about, brother. Let's go celebrate," Mason says, loosening the tie around his neck.

"You go. I'll be there in a few." Pulling out my desk chair, I drop into it with a content sigh. "I've got a few things to do first."

"Like what?" he asks incredulously, eyebrows arched, hands out to his sides. "What could be more important than celebrating right now? This time next year, we'll have restaurants in Chicago and Nashville. How fucking awesome is that?"

"It's fucking fantastic, and I promise I'll be down there in a few minutes to celebrate with you. I just have to do a couple of things first." Slipping my phone out of my pocket, I check for any missed calls then toss it on my desk.

"Don't be long." Mason opens the door and narrows his gaze on me, finger pointed in my direction. I flip him off and then hear him laugh as he walks down the hall. Leaning back in my chair, I run my fingers through my hair.

I can't believe this is happening. We've worked so hard for this, and it's fucking unreal that it's actually going to happen. My hands itch to pick up my phone and call Laney. My first instinct when I knew this was going to happen was to call her.

After our picnic a few weeks ago, things have been crazy. I've been busy at work, and she's been busy with work and whatever else it is she does. We haven't really gotten to see each other so we've resorted to phone calls and texting, and I'd be lying if I said it hasn't been fun. We've slowly gotten to know each other again, one call and text at a time. I told her about what Mason and I have been working on with Mark and Brady, and she told me about how she used to volunteer at a homeless shelter in California.

I've started letting my guard down around her, a little bit more each day, but it doesn't take away that uneasy feeling I get in the pit of my stomach—the one that says she still has the same power over me that she had eight years ago. She has the power to walk away, and I'm not sure I'm up for going through that shit again.

I'm not going to lie, I've become borderline obsessed with her. I find myself fantasizing about her tight little body and her husky voice talking dirty to me. There have even been a few times that I've gone out of my way to see her at the restaurant, just because I needed to satisfy the craving. And that's what it is. It's a craving that I've had since the day she came back home—a craving that's also a fucking thorn in my side because the god-damn thing grows every time I see her.

"Fuck it," I mumble, grabbing my phone off my desk. I scroll through my contacts, find Laney's name and hit 'talk.' The phone rings several times, and I'm about to hang up when her voice comes through the line.

"Well, well, well, if it isn't Levi. To what do I owe the pleasure, kind sir?"

"You're fucking crazy, you know that?" Her tinkling laughter rings loudly and a shiver runs down my spine.

"What's up?" she asks, still laughing.

"I—" I have no fucking clue why I called her. Okay, that's a lie. "Brady just left."

"Oh my gosh!" she gasps. "What did he say? Is it going to happen? Oh, Levi, please tell me it's going to happen."

"It's going to happen," I answer excitedly with a stupid-ass smile on my face. She squeals through the line and I hold the phone away from my ear, picturing her dancing around her house.

"Levi, that's amazing. I'm so happy for you. You guys deserve this so much."

"Thanks. We're pretty keyed up about it. In fact, Mase is already down at the bar waiting for me to celebrate with him."

"Well, what the heck are you waiting for? Get your butt down there and celebrate with your brother." Her enthusiasm floors me. She sounds genuinely excited, and I can't help but wonder if she's considered the fact that I might have to move. Well, son of a bitch. I haven't even considered the fact that I might have to move.

"I'm heading down there." I pause, picturing her beautiful face, wanting to see it again. "Are we still on for tomorrow?"

"We're still on. I'll meet you at Flame at five o'clock tomorrow evening." I hear laughing in the background and I wonder who the hell she is with. Mia left last week so I know it isn't her.

"What are you doing this evening?" I ask, because I'm fucking nosy and I want to know who's there. "You can come celebrate with Mason and me if you're bored."

"Thank you, but Benny and Luke are here and we're about to watch a movie." Benny is over there all the damn time. I know it shouldn't bother me; it's not like I've laid claim to Laney. But it still pisses me off. "I just hope I can stay awake for the darn thing."

"Are you tired?" I ask, looking down at my watch—it's only seven o'clock. "You've been tired a lot lately . . . is everything okay?"

"Yeah, everything is fine," she says dismissively. "I'm good, you just go and have fun, okay?"

"Alright, well, I'm going to go meet up with Mason. Enjoy your movie, and tell Luke I said hi."

"I will." She pauses and I'm about to say goodbye when she says my name. "Levi?"

"Yeah?"

"Congratulations. I'm so proud of you."

"Thanks, Lane. That means a lot." And it does. Probably more than it should, but I'm not in the mood to dive into that right now. "Have a good night and I'll see you tomorrow."

"Night, Levi."

I hang up the phone, stuff it in my suit pocket and make my way over to Blue, where I'm certain Mason is already celebrating enough for the both of us. And sure enough, I walk in to find him sitting at the bar, surrounded by a group of women. Mason is a ladies' man, through and through. The girls fucking flock to him, and although I've never had problems getting laid, I've used him as my wingman once or twice. Too bad the bastard is still hung up on Quinn, and she sure as hell isn't giving him the time of day . . . at least not that I'm aware of.

"Levi," Mason calls, spotting me from his seat at the bar. "Get your ass over here." I walk across the wooden floor toward the bar, and Tatum comes flying around the corner and straight into my arms.

"Congratulations," she squeals, tightening her grip around my neck. "I'm so happy for you guys."

"Thanks, Tatum."

"Can I transfer to the one in Chicago?" she asks, pulling away from me.

"Are you serious?" My brows dip low. "You don't like it here?"

"It's not that. I'm just ready for a change, and I've heard Chicago is fantastic."

"We'll see. We haven't even officially agreed to the deal yet."

"Just promise you'll think about it."

"I promise. Now get back to work." She skips away as I yell, "Crown and Coke."

"Coming your way," she hollers back. When I make it to Mason, he already has two empty glasses in front of him and one in his hand.

"Balls to the wall tonight, huh?" I nod at his empty glasses and he grins.

"Hell yeah. This is fucking fantastic. I can't wait to get the fuck out of here. I'm thinking Nashville sounds about perfect." Tatum must have been watching him because when she brings me my drink, she has another for Mase. His words catch me off guard. I push past a busty blonde with a quick 'excuse me' and take the seat next to my brother.

"Could you girls give us a few minutes?" It's been nice having our fair share of women, but sometimes it's just plain annoying. I've had a hard-and-fast rule for the past several years—no fucking the same woman twice. It seems Mason and I have made a name for ourselves in the area. Flame and Blue have become hotspots for several professional sports players, and that alone will bring in the crowds. We've also hosted several parties for various celebrities that have been in town. Of course, the women see that and they want a piece of it. So once is it for me. The few times I've bent my rule, I've ended up with a clingy female who apparently thought 'this is just sex' actually meant 'he's going to propose.'

The women at the bar do eventually take off, but not until after a few last attempts at flirting. I've gotten good at ignoring them or politely declining, especially in recent years. I'm thirty years old now and the majority of these girls are barely twenty-one.

Mason nods at a sexy brunette when she whispers something in his ear, and he must have agreed to something good because she walks away with a huge smile on her face. I shake my head at him, but he just chuckles and shrugs. "What can I say?"

"You finally over Quinn?" That must sober him up a bit because the happy-go-lucky look on his face quickly transforms into something resembling annoyance.

"We're not talking about Quinn," he says, bringing his glass to his mouth.

"Okay. Let's talk about you wanting to get the hell out of Dodge. What's up with that? I had no idea you were looking to leave."

"I don't know." He swivels his chair toward the bar and props his arms up on the sleek wood. "I didn't really think about it until I walked out of your office. I hadn't even considered it as an option, but now that I know it is, I want out." He glances at me but I school my features, doing my best to appear impassive. No way do I want to see Mason move, but if that's what he needs to be happy in life, I sure as hell wouldn't stop him. "Doesn't a small part of you want out too?"

I take a swig of my drink and the warm liquid slides down my throat, igniting a fiery burn that instantly soothes me. "I honestly don't know. If you'd asked me five years ago, I would've jumped all over the idea. But now, I'm not so sure."

"Is it because Laney is back?" He keeps his eyes locked on me as he asks the question.

"No," I deny. "Not at all. She doesn't factor into this at all."

Mason keeps staring at me, and suddenly I feel the need to defend myself. "She doesn't. Not even a little bit. I wouldn't think twice about leaving."

"You're a horrible fucking liar."

"Whatever," I scoff, signaling Tatum for another drink. "Laney has nothing to do with it." At least, I don't think she does, but no way am I telling Mason that. "I just think that one of us should stay here with Dad. He isn't getting any younger, you know. If we both leave and hire management for Flame and Blue, then you know as well as I do that Dad would be here every day."

Mason snorts with laughter. "That's for sure. The old man would probably drive everyone insane, and he'd sure as hell have your cages ripped down before you passed the city limit sign."

"So . . . Nashville. Are you going to start wearing cowboy hats and saying y'all?" I quip with my best Southern drawl.

"Of course I am. That's my whole reason for going. Have you seen those girls in their short dresses and cowboy boots?"

"You're twenty-seven, Mase. You do realize that one of these days you're going to have to stop talking about all of these women and actually settle down with one." To be honest, I'm not even sure what Mason does with his hordes of women. I've never seen him kiss one. Sure, I've seen him flirt and touch but never kiss, and I've never seen one at his house taking the walk of shame.

"Don't worry about me, big brother. I'll settle down when the time is right. For now, I think you need to be worrying about *you*." He gives me a pointed look and waves his glass in my direction.

"Oh yeah? Why's that?" He's determined to have this talk, and I need to just let him so that he'll get off my fucking back.

"Because there is a certain dark-haired pixie that you've been spending a lot of time with, and I completely disagree that she doesn't factor into you wanting to stay here."

"We haven't been spending time together. We've only been alone once, which hardly constitutes us spending *a lot of time* with one another."

"Technicalities," he says, waving me off. "You've been coming to the kitchen a lot more than usual, and when you do come, the only person you talk to is Laney. And don't think I haven't noticed how much time you've been spending on the phone. Funny how those times just happen to be when Laney isn't here. Coincidence? I think not." He gives me a cocky smirk and takes another drink.

"Fine," I concede. "We've been getting to know each other again, but that's it. Just two old friends getting reacquainted."

"Levi. I'm your brother. You think I don't know you inside and out, and you think I can't read you like a fucking book? Newsflash, I can!" I take a deep breath and close my eyes . . . this is the only way I can keep from my connecting my fist to his face.

"You're a prick."

"Yes"—he nods—"that may be true. But I'm your brother and I want you happy."

"I am happy."

"I know. But it's only been since Laney has come home." I thought I'd done a good job at feigning happiness over the years, but obviously I was wrong. "It's cool, dude. Nothing to be ashamed of. The girl is a fucking dream, both inside and out, and no one would think twice about you giving her a second chance. Lord knows that's what she wants. Plus," he adds, sliding me a shot glass that mysteriously appeared, "you're different around her."

Damn it, Mason.

"Of course I'm different around her. I'm a fucking idiot around her! All this stupid shit starts floating around in my head, and I start acting like a pussy. Well, I'm not a pussy," I declare, squaring my shoulders.

"Hell no, you're not." Mason gives a firm shake of his head. "You are not a pussy."

"I'm Levi Fucking Beckford," I proclaim, lifting up the shot glass.

"That's right." Mason raises his shot glass and taps it to mine, but when I tip my glass back to swallow the clear liquid, he says, "You're Levi Fucking Beckford, and you're still in love with Laney Fucking Jacobs."

Tequila spews from my mouth. Tatum glares at the mess in front of me while Mason rolls with laughter in his chair.

Chapter 13

Laney

LEVI IS WAITING FOR ME when Benny drops me off at the restaurant. I can tell the exact moment that he registers who is behind the wheel of my car because he stands a little bit taller and puffs out his chest, which totally cracks me up. Benny notices it too because he's smiling like a fucking clown. "That boy would shit his pants if I hauled off and kissed you right now." He puts the car in park and turns to me, his eyes sparkling with mischief.

"Please don't," I laugh, not putting it past him. I don't know why, but Levi and Benny never quite got along. If I had to guess, I'd say it was because Benny was too protective of me for Levi's liking. Levi felt like that was his job and Benny was infringing on something that wasn't his. I think after a while it became a joke to Benny, and he started to do things to piss Levi off . . . like what he's thinking about doing now.

"He's lucky that you're like my sister and the thought of kissing you sort of grosses me out." He turns his nose up as though he has a bad taste in his mouth. I scowl, slapping him on the arm, which just makes him laugh harder.

"Get out of here. And be good to Ivy; she's all I've got left." I start to climb out of the car when Benny catches my hand.

"Do you have your pills?" I cock my head to the side adoringly. This man is going to make some woman very happy one of these days.

"Yup, I've got them in my purse." This last chemotherapy treatment was little bit harder on me than the first. I actually threw up a few times during my treatment, and they ended up giving me extra fluids so I wouldn't get dehydrated, along with some anti-nausea medicine. The nausea has been coming in waves for the past few days, but it's the fatigue that's bothering me the most. I'm tired all of the freaking time.

Some days it takes absolutely everything I have to get myself out of bed. The other night, Luke came over at five o'clock for dinner and I had already passed out on the couch. I've tried drinking some energy drinks, but all they do is make me feel jittery and I've got enough crap going on—I don't need to feel like that too.

"Good girl. Call me later and I'll come pick you back up."

"That won't be necessary." Levi's voice is thick and raw, causing goose bumps to break out along the back of my neck. He steps up behind me, a hand planted firmly on the small of my back, and leans down so he's eye to eye with Benny. "I'll bring her home when we're done. If I'd known she needed a ride, I would have come and gotten her."

Benny cocks an eyebrow at Levi and I clear my throat, catching both of their attentions. Benny shakes his head and puts my car in reverse. "Lane, call me if you need me."

"Sure thing. Thanks, Benny." I shut the door and he drives off, leaving me in the middle of the parking lot with a brooding Levi, which is never a good thing.

"Why does he have your car?" Levi's face is red and his thumb is toying with his bottom lip.

"Why, Levi"—I chuckle—"are you jealous?"

"No," he answers quickly. "Why the hell would I be jealous of Benny?"

I offer him a bemused smile but decide to drop it. I can tell he isn't in a joking mood, and I want to have fun today. I can't wait to see what he has planned for us.

"Benny is changing the oil in my car, that's all." Turning around, I walk in the direction of Levi's truck and he falls in step beside me. "It's not a big deal."

His fingers run through his hair, mussing it up, and I nearly trip over my own feet. He's too sexy for his own good. It should be a crime to look as hot as he does. "I know," he huffs. "Let's get out of here." He opens the door of his truck, offering a hand to help lift me up. Once I'm in and buckled, he shuts the door and jogs over to his side before climbing in.

"Where are we going?" He looks over at me with a smile, his cerulean eyes dancing with happiness . . . much different from how they looked just moments ago. I smile back, simply because there isn't any other choice.

"You'll have to wait and see." Levi fishes his keys out of his pocket and starts his truck. Then he makes one last check in his rearview mirror and off we go.

"I love surprises." Rolling the window down, I stick my arm out and lean back in my seat.

"I know you do," he says quietly, sparing me a quick glance. I cringe, internally berating myself for bringing up the last time the two of us talked about surprises. That was a horrible night, and the last thing in the world I want is for him to be thinking about *that.*

"Well, it hasn't changed. Plus, you're starting a trend here. This is two surprises in two weeks. If you keep this up, I'm going to start expecting it."

Like a good boy, he keeps his eyes on the road, but a soft smile splits his face. "Duly noted."

Leaning forward, I flick on the radio and Chris Daughtry's sultry voice floats through the speakers. "I love this song." Relaxing in my seat, I close my eyes and let the lyrics from "Home" seep inside of me. Levi is humming, and if I thought lying next to him and looking up at the stars was heaven, then I was sorely mistaken—*this* is heaven.

"Laney—" Someone touches my shoulder and I startle awake.

"Hey. Sorry," I say when I see it's just Levi. "I guess I fell asleep. How long have you been driving?"

His brows furrow. "Not long. Fifteen minutes. Are you okay?"

"Yeah, I'm fine. I'm just tired."

"You're always tired. And you don't look that well." I cock my eyebrow and he quickly continues, "You just look tired and you have dark circles under your eyes. If you're not up for this, I can take you home. We can do it another time." His words are laced with genuine concern and that warms my heart.

"No." I shake my head. There is no way I'm going home. I'm not letting this monster stop me from doing whatever Levi has planned. "Where are we anyway?" Sitting up in my seat, I look out the window, effectively dismissing any further talk about being tired or going home. SENIOR CENTER is written in large black letters across the front of a building and I look at Levi. "You brought me to a senior center?" I ask dryly, giving him a curious glance.

"Don't judge a book by its cover, Laney." He smirks at me as he turns off the truck. Then he hops down and walks over to my door, opening it for me. I take his outstretched hand and when I jump out of the truck, my body slides down the front of his, and he sucks in a sharp breath.

"Sorry," I murmur, stepping away. He grabs my arm and I stop. I expect him to whip me around like it happens in all those romance novels I read, but he doesn't. He tugs gently on my arm, and I turn around and look at him. I'd give anything to know what he's thinking. The air around us buzzes with electricity, and butterflies have taken flight in my stomach. I have no idea how I affect him, but he sure as heck does something crazy to me.

I'd give anything to have the freedom to touch him or kiss him again anytime I want, but I lost that privilege. His hand drops from my arm and I close my eyes in defeat, vowing to hold myself together. When I feel his fingers slip between mine, goose bumps scatter up my arm and my eyes flutter open. I look down at our joined hands and hope starts churning deep inside of me.

"Laney?" His voice is hoarse with raw emotion. I glance up and he steps into me, our fronts molding together. My heart is beating so fast that I'm certain it's going to fly right out of my chest. His free hand makes its way to my hip and I take a deep breath, relishing the way his long fingers curl around me.

This is happening, and he's orchestrating it. All of it. I've given him complete control. My body is his puppet. His touch is controlling everything from the rate of my heartbeat to the depth of my breath to the tingle in my toes. Right this second, I'm breathing for him, not with him, and I will only move when he moves.

His large hand sits at the base of my waist and he gives it a light squeeze. His eyes are two pools of swirling water, and I want nothing more than to dive inside and drown in his soul. Resurfacing is not an option because I need him more than I need my next breath.

When his head lowers, my stomach flutters in the best possible way. His nose brushes against mine, our warm breath mingling in the evening air. His chin drops and his lips land lightly on mine. It's perfect. This moment with Levi is absolutely perfect.

"Levi! Get your ass—" Levi pulls back and looks up, clearing his throat as his hand falls from my hip. My body is instantly cold, and I turn around to see Harley standing outside the door. "Sorry," she says sheepishly, looking away. "We, um . . . we need to get started." She looks at the door and then back at us. "But if you need a few more—"

"We'll be right in." Levi's voice is clipped but not rude, and I wonder if it's because he wanted that kiss as badly as I did or because he's glad she interrupted before he could make a monumental mistake. He looks confused when his gaze meets mine again, and he runs a hand through his hair. "I, uh . . . about that . . . can we just . . . ." His stuttering is cute, but I decide to put him out of his misery. I hate that he feels uncomfortable.

"It's fine, Levi. Let's just go inside. We can talk later, okay?" I walk past him toward the door and when he doesn't follow, I turn around. His chest rises on a deep breath, and for a split second I think he's going to say something . . . but he doesn't. He nods his head and then walks toward me.

We head inside and I stop dead in my tracks. The room is filled with people of all ages, from tiny babies to the elderly and every stage in between. But that's not what catches my attention. It's obvious that they're all either homeless or severely poor and malnourished.

My head whips around to Levi and he shrugs. "You said that one of the greatest things you ever did was volunteer—oomph." His words are cut off when I throw myself at his chest, my arms wrapping tightly around his shoulders.

"Thank you," I whisper into his neck. "Thank you so much."

Levi's arms wrap around me, and with one of his hands he cups the back of my head. "You're welcome."

"As much I enjoy seeing you two all cuddly, it's really starting to creep me out. Are we going to feed these people or what?" Harley asks, hands on hips.

Levi laughs and I untangle myself from his arms. "We're going to feed these people." Rubbing my hands together excitedly, I walk away from Levi and Harley and make my way over to the kitchen.

Several people are wearing aprons, busying themselves around the room. I walk up to an elderly woman and tap her on the shoulder. She turns to me with the sweetest smile and I ask, "Where do you want me?"

Her smile gets just a little bit bigger and she points toward the stove. "Over there would be great, dear." She hands me an apron, and I slip it over my head and tie the string around my back. Stepping up to the stove, I look around to see what still needs to be done. A gentleman next to me hands me a wooden spoon and then startles the heck out of me when he kisses my cheek. I look at him with wide, amused eyes and he winks, pointing to my apron. I look down and sure enough, written in large red letters across my chest, it says 'Kiss The Cook.'

"You're the cook," he mutters, patting me gently on the cheek before turning away.

I sense him before I feel him, the hairs on the back of my neck standing up, and within seconds, the front of Levi's body is resting against my back. "No fraternizing with the other workers, especially of the male variety." He leans over my shoulder to look at what I'm stirring and I throw my head back, laughing. Levi's eyes find mine when my head lands on his chest, and awareness simmers beneath my skin. His warm breath fans the side of my face, causing our almost-kiss from the parking lot to pop into my head. My laugh softens to a light purr and Levi's eyes spark with lust. "I'm still thinking about it too," he whispers, giving me a devilish smile before pushing past me to grab a spoon out of the drawer.

The next several hours fly by in a joyous flurry. We cooked, served and mingled, and I laughed more than I've laughed in the past several months. These people are absolutely amazing, and it reminds me so much of the place in California where I used to volunteer. Levi doesn't know it yet, but I plan to come back here as often as I can. This is where I'm most happy. Helping people that actually need it and appreciate it. This brings me peace. I imagine it's because I didn't grow up in the best conditions, and if I can make someone's life a little bit better or put some food in their empty bellies, then, by gosh, I'll do it.

"Honey—" I look up and a frail-looking woman, probably in her eighties if I had to guess, is standing in front of me. "Is there any of that food left over?" She puts a fist to her mouth and coughs several times.

"Are you okay?" My hand rests on her shoulder, and she shakes her head as she breaks out into another coughing fit. Gripping her elbow in one hand and wrapping an arm around her back, I lead her over to a nearby table and help her sit down. Her coughing fit dies down once again and she apologizes.

"Don't be sorry. Please don't be sorry. Are you okay?" I ask again, concerned that something might be seriously wrong with her.

"I'll be fine, dear. It's just a cold. Nothing a little cough medicine won't cure." She runs a withered hand over her forehead and swallows, her loose-fitting dentures shifting in the process. "What I could really use is some of that food if you've got some extra."

"You stay right here and I'm going to go see what I can come up with." She pats my hands and offers me a soft smile. Most of the food is gone, but I saw someone stuff a large bowl of spaghetti into the refrigerator earlier. Walking into the kitchen, I pull open the cabinets to look for something to put it in.

"What are you doing?" Levi asks.

I shut a set of doors and move to the next when I don't find what I'm looking for. "That woman out there needs to take some food home. I'm looking for a container." My eyes scan the shelf, but there's nothing except glass dishes and cups.

"Here." Levi walks to the refrigerator and pulls out the bowl. "Just give her all of it."

"Really?" I ask, turning toward him. "The Senior Center won't mind? I mean, I can make arrangements to get it from her and I'll make sure it gets back—"

"It's fine," Levi says, waving me off. "Laney, I provide the meals for this place to feed those from both the homeless shelter and women's shelter nearly every day of the week. I assure you, they won't mind if a bowl goes missing."

"Thank you." I don't give him time to respond. Moving past him, I take the bowl to the woman and her face lights up. That look slams into me something fierce. She looks so excited and it breaks my heart because I hate the thought of this woman ever not having enough food. She reaches for the glass bowl and I shake my head.

"I'll carry it for you. Let me walk you out." Her tiny feet shuffle along the floor next to me. When we make it outside, she turns to me, her hands outstretched and waiting.

"Where's your car?" This woman can barely hold her purse; there is no way I'm going to let her carry this glass bowl. I look around the empty lot but come up short when only Levi's truck remains.

"Oh, I don't have a car, honey. But it's okay, I don't live far."

"Well, where do you live?"

She points to a small blue house across the street. "Right there. See, no need for a car," she says with a laugh, which once again turns into a coughing fit.

"Let me walk you over there."

"Really?" Her surprised look absolutely floors me. Has no one ever done anything nice for this woman?

"Absolutely." The door behind us opens, and I peek over my shoulder to find Levi walking out.

"What's up?" he asks, stepping up behind us.

"Mrs. . . ." I realize then that I haven't even gotten her name. When I look at her, she catches on quickly.

"Mary. It's just Mary."

"Mary lives right across the street. I'm going to walk this over there with her real quick, if that's okay."

"Sure. I can drive you—"

"Nope," Mary says, shaking her head. "I need the exercise. It's good for the ticker." She pats her hand over her heart and Levi laughs.

"Then by all means—" He waves for us to proceed and I mouth 'be right back' to him.

"He's a handsome little devil," Mary remarks as we make our way across the street.

"He is, isn't he?" She nods her head and pulls a single key from the pocket of her cotton pants as we stroll up her sidewalk. After she unlocks the door, we walk in and she directs me to the kitchen. Her house is small with narrow walkways, torn rugs and stained furniture, but the dozens of pictures hanging on the walls somehow make it feel cozy. I stand in front of one of the walls that is peppered with pictures, and my eyes hone in on the picture in the center. It's an old black-and-white photo of a couple on their wedding day. The woman looks absolutely stunning wearing a white lace gown. "Is this you?"

"It is." I look over at Mary and watch as she kicks off her shoes and plops down on the couch, a haze of dust floating up around her. "That's my Ronald. He died twelve years ago last month, and there isn't a day that goes by I don't wish he was still here." My heart sinks at the thought that I might never have this—a wall full of photos depicting all the best times in my life.

I want the wall. I want the wedding photo and pictures of my kids and grandkids. My hands tremble at the thought that I might never have all this. But I want it . . . and I want it with Levi.

"He's very handsome," I say, swallowing past the lump that has settled in my throat.

"Much like your fella over there," she says, motioning toward the Senior Center.

"He's not mine." I shake my head, wishing that it were true. "We're just friends."

"Nonsense," she scoffs. "I see the way he looks at you. That's the look of love." I open my mouth to insist that she's wrong, but she keeps talking. "Why don't you put that bowl in the refrigerator?" She points to the kitchen yet again and I follow her directions, taking note of the empty bottle of cough syrup on her counter. Sliding the spaghetti inside the fridge, I also notice the lack of food on the shelves.

When I walk back into the living room, Mary has her head tilted back on the couch and her eyes are bobbing heavily. I'm sure it's quite a feat for her to make that little walk every day. She looks too tiny and frail, and I imagine that it wears her out.

"It was a pleasure meeting you, Mary," I say, probably a little too loud because I never know if older people can hear or not.

"You, too. What was your name again? I don't think I caught it."

"It's Laney." I offer her my hand, but instead she pushes up from the couch and wraps me in a hug.

"Thank you, Laney. It was a pleasure meeting you as well. Now you get back to that hunky man of yours." She winks and drops back to the couch.

"Yes, ma'am," I reply, wanting nothing more than to get back to that 'hunky man'—mine or otherwise—and thank him for this amazing day. He gave something back to me that I love and something I've missed, and for that I'm extremely grateful.

Chapter 14

Levi

I'M ABOUT TWO SECONDS FROM walking over there and seeing what in the hell is taking so damn long. Laney has been in that house for ten minutes and now I'm feeling like I shouldn't have let her go alone. We don't know this woman, and for all I know she could have some psycho grandson living there. Mind made up, I jump from my truck and make my way across the road. Just as my feet hit the front porch, Laney comes barreling out of the door and straight into my arms.

"Are you okay?" Gripping her shoulders, I pull her back to inspect her body, needing to make sure she's alright.

"I'm fine." She swats away my wandering hands and throws herself back into my arms. "I want a wall."

"You what?"

"I want a wall of my life," she mumbles into my chest.

"Laney, you're not making sense." She unravels her arms from around my neck and takes my hand in hers, which is cold despite the warm weather. I bring her hand to my mouth, cupping it so that I can blow hot air over her fingers to warm them up.

"She has a wall full of photos. Everything from her wedding day to the day each of her kids were born to her grandkids' soccer games. I want that." Her eyes are misty and I can tell that this really matters to her.

"You'll have that. Why is this bothering you?" I ask, dropping her hand so I can warm up the other one.

"You don't know that I'll have that. It's not guaranteed. I'm almost thirty, Levi." Her words are frantic and I can't help but laugh. She's worrying about things she shouldn't be worrying about.

"Laney, I know it's not guaranteed, but you can't think like that. Anyone could die at any time from anything and lose out on a lifetime full of happy memories. But you can't live your life worrying." She takes a deep breath and nods. "You will have all of those things. I just know it."

"Thanks," she says, straightening her back and shoulders as though pulling herself back together. She looks at her hand that's cupped against my mouth, and she furrows her brow as though she didn't even realize it was there. "What are you doing?"

"Your hands are freezing. Which is totally odd, by the way, considering it's nearly eighty degrees."

"Hmmm. I didn't notice."

"Let's get out of here." Keeping her hand locked in mine, we walk to the end of the sidewalk, looking both ways before running across the road.

"Can we stop somewhere before you take me home?"

"Sure." I open the passenger door and help her in before climbing in myself. "Where do you need to go?" I crank the key in the ignition and put the truck in drive.

"Just the grocery store down the road. I won't be long." I'm already pulling out of the parking lot by the time she finishes what she's saying. I drive the three blocks to the closest market, and we both hop out of the truck when we arrive. "You don't have to come with me."

"I know I don't," I say with a shrug. But I want to. There was something about watching her today that I found extremely sexy. It wasn't like at work where she is doing a job. No, today I could tell that she was doing something she loved. Her happiness shone through with every meal that she served, and it amazed me how she took the time to talk with nearly every single person there.

We walk into the grocery store and she snags a cart before taking off through the store like she's a woman on a mission. She grabs a few gallons of milk, some orange juice, canned soup, canned vegetables and enough frozen meals to feed a grown man for a year. "You do realize you're a chef, right?"

"Yes," she laughs. She pushes up on her toes to reach for a bag of chips and her shirt rides up, exposing the curve of her waist. Her skin looks silky smooth and my cock stirs. Just thinking about her tight body writhing under me is enough to get me rock fucking solid. I've touched a lot of women over the years—women of all shapes and sizes—but no one's body has ever compared to Laney's. And as much as I've tried over the years, I have never been able to forget the way she felt under the palm of my hand.

"Can you reach that?" She whips around to look at me, and I clear my throat and step forward, hoping to God she doesn't see my dick throbbing against my jeans.

"Umm . . . sure," I stutter, mentally bitch-slapping myself for nearly getting caught ogling her—again. Flinging the bag of chips in the cart, I take the handle and follow her through the aisles. She throws in a box of granola bars and a couple boxes of cereal and then makes her way over to the medicine section, tossing in a box of cough syrup before telling me she's ready to go. We head to the front of the store and get everything loaded on the conveyer belt. "Mind if I throw in some gum?"

"Not at all." She stretches across the cart, grabbing a pack of my favorite cinnamon gum and throwing it in with the rest of the food.

"You remember that?"

She looks at me like I've grown two heads. "Of course I remember. It's ingrained in my senses." A look of determination falls across her face. "I've thought about that taste—your taste—for years."

My throat grows thick with emotion. Laney is staring at me, her heart one hundred percent on her sleeve, and I have absolutely no words for her.

"That'll be seventy-six dollars and thirty-one cents." Laney blinks and twists to face the cashier. Digging in her purse, she pulls out a credit card and slides it through the machine.

"That can't be right," she mumbles, sliding it again.

"What's wrong?"

"Do you have a different card you could try, ma'am?" the cashier asks, glancing at the growing line behind us. Laney swipes her card one last time and I lean forward to look at the screen. DECLINED. As Laney scrambles through her purse, I remember her making a comment at Blue that one night about how she couldn't afford the wine because it was too expensive. Has she gotten herself into credit card debt? The thought that she could be struggling tugs at my heart. I whip my wallet out and slide my card through the reader before she's able to find another form of payment.

"Levi," she scolds. "You didn't have to do that. I have another card. This has to be a mistake. There is no way my card could be declined." She looks away sheepishly.

I've got to find out what's going on with her.

"It's not a big deal," I tell her as she loads up the cart with our bags of food. We walk out to the truck and she doesn't say a word. I almost feel guilty for embarrassing her, but that wasn't my intention. I just hated that look on her face and wanted to step in and help.

She climbs in the truck before I can assist her and when I slide behind the wheel, she has her arms crossed over her chest. "I'll pay you back."

"Laney," I turn toward her, propping my leg up on the seat. "I'm not worried about you paying me back. But I'm not going to lie, I am concerned about you. Is everything okay?"

She takes a deep breath and looks up. I can't tell if she's trying to fight back tears or gain some strength or maybe a little bit of both. For a split second, I get the feeling that she's keeping something from me—something big—and my stomach sinks. But then she swallows hard, runs a hand over her face and smiles. "I'm sure it's just a mistake. I'll call tomorrow and get it straightened out."

I should push her, but right now she looks stressed out and I'm a little terrified at what a push would do. So I bite my tongue and vow to revisit this later.

"Alright. Back to your house?"

"Oh, no. I'm taking these to Mary." The weight of her words slams into me. Just the thought of her not having enough money for herself, and yet she's willing to spend whatever she does have on someone else who needs it more? I'm completely floored. Laney has always been extremely giving; I think I just forgot that about her for a little while.

"You got all of this for Mary?" I question, needing to make sure I heard her right. "Or just some of it?"

"All of it." Her eyes are wide with concern. "Her refrigerator was bare, Levi. She had nothing. I think she might be living off the meals she gets at the Senior Center."

Everything inside of me shifts. I feel as though I'd been teetering on the edge of my feelings for Laney and this just tips me over.

"You're doing a really great thing, Lane. You're going to make her day." Signaling a right-hand turn, I pull out onto the road and make the three-block trip back to Mary's house. "I'll help you carry everything." We hop from the truck, gather all of the groceries and walk to the front door.

"I hope she's still up. She looked like she was about to fall asleep earlier," Laney says, pounding on the door. Within minutes, it's being pulled open. At first Mary looks at us, trying to figure out why we're here, and then she looks down and sees all of the bags we're carrying. "Can we come in Mary?"

The frail woman nods her head and steps back to let us pass. Laney walks right into the kitchen and starts unloading bags like she owns the place. When we get everything put away, we both turn back toward the living room but find Mary standing in the doorway. She doesn't say a word; she just walks right into Laney's arms and holds her like she hasn't been held in years. Laney looks at me with eyebrows raised and I just smile. Mary pulls back, wipes the wetness from under her eyes and squeezes Laney's hand.

"Thank you," Mary whispers with a watery voice. "No one has ever done anything like this for me before." I watch as Laney's bottom lip trembles. Tears build up in her eyes and she swallows hard.

"You don't have to thank me, Mary. Trust me, it was my pleasure." And apparently, that's all it takes. My heart explodes inside my chest and suddenly the only thing I need is to get her alone.

"Laney," I interrupt with a hand on her shoulder. "We should probably get going." She looks at me and nods and then gives Mary one last quick hug. Mary walks us to the door, thanks us again and shuts it softly behind us.

Laney bounces excitedly down the sidewalk and I follow her to my truck. "Wasn't that fantastic? Did you see her face, Levi?" she asks, flinging open the door. "That was probably one of—"

Stepping up behind her, I push the door shut, spin her around and press her back against my truck. My hands cup her face, and my mouth on hers stops everything. Her words melt away as her lips mold to mine, and all of the regret and pain I've been holding onto dissipate as I lose myself in this kiss. Her hands find their way to my hair and she grips it tightly, pulling me to her. My tongue pushes into her mouth and she opens for me instantly. At first I kiss her hard and rough, my mouth desperate to get as close to her as it can possibly get. Her lithe body rubs against mine and, in turn, my body hums with approval. She's trembling beneath me and I pull back, resting my forehead against hers, both of us panting and out of breath.

But she obviously isn't done because, within seconds, she has her sweet little mouth back on mine—only this time she takes control. The kiss is slow and passionate, and so much like our kisses from nearly a decade ago. Our tongues are no longer dueling for power but reveling in the simplicity of being reunited. I slip my hands into her hair and grip the back of her neck. She whimpers, her body relaxing into mine, her touch igniting a fire deep in my gut.

Even though I kissed her a few weeks ago, this is different. This time *I* initiated it, this time *she* was the one taken by surprise . . . this time it's *my* heart that's involved. I'm not sure at what point I realized that fighting this was a losing battle. It could've been when she made my grandmother's pie or when she kissed me in the kitchen. It could've also been when we had dinner under the stars, but most likely it was the very moment I saw her in my parking lot. I think I knew then that I was still hers.

Her hands slide down my chest and I groan, drawing back. I know that if I don't stop now I'll likely lay her out in the cab of my truck and fuck her . . . and that's not how I want our second first time to be. Laney's eyes are closed, her lips swollen and wet, and her chest is heaving as if it's fighting for air. She smiles, and then her hooded eyes peek up at me. All it takes is this one look—this one kiss—and I'm owned. Every piece of my broken soul belongs to this angel . . . I just pray to God that she can find a way to put it back together. And more than that, I pray to God she doesn't break it again.

Chapter 15

Laney

MY FINGER RUNS A SLOW path along my bottom lip, and if I close my eyes, I can still feel his mouth on mine. That kiss was fantastic, but the best part about it was that I didn't even see it coming. I thought I had memorized everything about Levi, but now I see how faded my memories had become because they were *nothing* compared to the real thing. I had forgotten how soft his lips are and the way he takes complete control when he kisses me. I'd also forgotten how he ends nearly every kiss by lightly sucking and nipping my bottom lip. I don't ever want to forget those things again.

Neither one of us said a word after our kiss, but as soon as we climbed into the truck, he reached across the seat, slid his hand into mine and left it there, resting against my inner thigh. I'm now watching his thumb as it swipes lazily across my knuckles and it's hypnotizing. I'd like it sweeping across other parts of my body, but now is probably not the time to shove his hand in between my legs and demand that he show me what he can do. Right?

"You're awfully quiet over there."

"I'm afraid that this isn't real." He squeezes my hand and I look up at him.

"It's real. I promise, it's real." He brings our joined hands to his mouth and kisses my knuckles.

I can't help the smile that sweeps over my face. That smile quickly turns into a curious glare when he pulls onto my street. "How did you know my address?"

"Your employment paperwork you filled out for Flame," he says, pulling into my driveway. "I might have taken a peek at it." Levi flashes me a grin. "I hope you don't mind." My eyes roam across the front of my house, and although I'm extremely proud of my little nest, I can't help but wonder what kind of home Levi has. Is it a sleek condo overlooking the city, or a ranch-style house on the outskirts of town? He probably doesn't live in a rundown neighborhood where the houses are all a foot apart and you have to walk past homeless people to get to your front door.

He must sense my insecurity because he drags me across the seat and pulls me onto his lap. "What's wrong?" he whispers, his hands gliding up and down my back.

"Nothing." I look away, but he grips my chin and pulls my face back to his. "It's not much," I shrug, nodding toward my house. "It's probably nothing like where you live, but—"

"It's perfect." His lips find mine in a feather-light kiss. "You amaze me, Laney."

"What? Why?" I frown, having absolutely no idea why he would be amazed by me.

"Look at you. You've never been afraid to go after what you want, even if it means leaving a man in the dust . . ." I punch him lightly in the gut, and he grabs his stomach and laughs. "Too soon for the break-up jokes?" I nod, laughing along with him, and he continues. "What I'm getting at is that you're courageous and strong and so incredibly kind. I'm in awe of you."

"Thank you," I mouth, my heart creeping its way into my throat.

"Can I see your bucket list again?" he asks.

My brows dip low. "For what? We didn't do anything for you to cross off." Reaching for my purse, I dig out the list and hand it over.

"I disagree." I hand him a pen and he opens the list against my chest, then scratches the pen against the rumpled paper. "I think today you made a significant positive impact on a stranger's life, and I think Mary would agree with me."

"Levi," I exhale, at a complete loss for words. Strong, callused hands grip my face, and I stare into his sapphire eyes that are open and raw and so full of emotion. "I promise that I'll never let you down again," I say with as much conviction as I have within me. "Just tell me this is real. Tell me this is happening. I've thought about this . . . about you, for so long. I've hoped for a second chance, and if you give it to me, I swear you won't regret it. You won't regret me."

"I've never regretted you, Lane. Even when I was mad as hell at you, I never regretted you." His thumb darts out and catches the first tear that manages to escape my eye, and then it catches many more because I simply can't keep them in. This feeling is indescribable, knowing that after all these years, I'm finally getting my chance to make things right—a chance at the happiness I took from us.

"Laney?"

"Yes," I answer, my eyes trained on his mouth, silently begging him to kiss me one more time.

"You're thinking way too much." My eyes snap to his and he's wearing an amused grin. "You're thinking so hard that I can practically hear your thoughts. This is happening. I told myself that it would never happen again, but I can't stay away from you. Hell, I can't even stop thinking about you long enough to take a piss." I laugh and drop my forehead to his. "Let's try this, Laney. Let's see where it goes."

I nod, mostly because my wildest dreams are coming true, and I'm mildly terrified that if I try to talk, I'll burst into tears. It's like a package of fireworks was just set off in my soul and now they're exploding through me in a million different directions, lighting my life with a rainbow of colors. I don't ever want this feeling to end.

"Will you kiss me now?" My voice cracks on the last word, but Levi's mouth is on me so fast that I don't even have time to think about how pathetic I just sounded. His lips slam against mine, our tongues colliding, twisting and pushing in the most beautiful dance. My hands are fisted in the front of his shirt, because right now I need an anchor—an anchor to this moment, to these feelings . . . to this man.

He pulls back far too soon but keeps his face close to mine. Our noses brushing and breaths mingling, I peek up and see that his eyes are closed and a faint smile touches his gorgeous mouth. "Let's do that again soon, okay?"

His faint smile twists into a wry grin and he looks at me. "Count on it," he whispers.

I smack one last kiss on his mouth. Then I pick up my purse and reach for the door, but he grabs my arm, stopping me.

"No." His voice is clipped and firm. "I'll walk you to your door, Laney. It's dark out and I need to make sure you get in safely." He leans forward and peers out the window. "Is this neighborhood safe?" His worried eyes find mine and when my lips purse, he sighs. "I didn't mean anything by that. It just looks a little run down, that's all."

"It's safe. It looks worse than it is, but I assure you, I'm safe. Plus, Benny lives next door so it's like I have a live-in bodyguard."

"Great," Levi huffs, causing me to laugh. "Well, I'm still walking you in."

"Levi, you do realize the door is five feet away? I'm a big girl, and this night has been perfect. That kiss"—I run the pad of my thumb across his bottom lip—"was the perfect way to end the night. Now I want to go inside, change into my pajamas and crawl in bed so I can relive it, over and over."

His expression softens and he nods. "Goodnight, Laney."

"Goodnight." A goofy grin is plastered to my face as I jump out of his truck and hightail it to my front door, making quick work of unlocking it. I slip inside and give him one last wave before shutting the door behind me.

I can't believe this has happened. I'm still in shock and I desperately need to tell somebody. Pulling my phone out of my purse, I pull up Mia's number and hit 'talk.' In true Mia fashion, she answers on the first ring.

"Are you okay?" Her voice is high and frantic.

"No, I'm not okay." It's a good thing she can't see me smiling, because she'd surely slap it right off my face for messing with her like this.

"Oh my god. Okay. I'm packing a bag. I'll have Daddy get the plane ready and I'll be there by morn—"

"Don't you want to know what's wrong?" I ask, interrupting her before she really gets on a plane and flies here.

"Yes. Please tell me. What's going on?"

"I'm dying, Mia."

"Laney, we've talked about this. You can't think like that. You have to stay positive, and I know it's hard but—"

"I'm dying of happiness, Mia. Seriously, I'm so deliriously happy that I think I might explode. That, and this goofy grin might become a permanent fixture on my face." I toss my purse on the floor and walk into the living room.

"I'm lost. What do you mean you're dying of happiness? You just told me you weren't okay."

"Levi took me out today. We volunteered at the Senior Center and then we kissed. He kissed me, Mia," I squeal, falling onto the couch. "He kissed me, and it was perfect and amazing and earth shattering, and if I die now, I would die a happy woman."

"I'm going to kill you, Laney Jacobs," she scolds. "Do you realize what you just did to me? You took ten years off my life. You can't call me and tell me that you're not okay . . . that's not fair." My smile quickly fades and my stomach drops as her words sink in. She sounds mad and scared, which wasn't at all my intention.

"Mia—"

"No," she cuts me off. "It's not fair. I'm not there with you,

Laney. I'm thousands of miles away and I worry about you constantly. I almost walked out on my dad the other day because I miss you so damn much. My life isn't the same without you in it every day, so no, you can't call me and make jokes about your health."

"I'm so sorry, Mia." My head is shaking despite the fact that she can't see me. "I wasn't thinking and you're right, that wasn't fair of me. I just had a really good day, and I was feeling silly and"—I sigh—"there is no good excuse. I'm sorry, it won't happen again."

"Good. And just so you know, next time you do something like that to me, I'm going to kick your ass."

"Noted."

"Now tell me about that sexy-as-hell man of yours, and I want all the details. Don't leave anything out." And I do. I tell her all about our time together and Mary and our kiss . . . and our second kiss, and that Levi wants to start things up with me again. We spend the next hour laughing, talking and reminiscing, and—like I knew she would—she tells me that she's happy for me and that I deserve it. Then she asks the one question that nearly ruins it all. "When are you going to tell him?"

Pushing up from the couch, I walk into the kitchen and pour myself a glass of water. "I don't know. I haven't thought about it."

"Well, you better think about it. This is your life for the foreseeable future, and he *will* find out some way or another. It'll be easier if it comes from you."

"Christ, Mia"—I take a sip of water—"how the hell do I tell him? 'Oh yeah, by the way, I have Stage 3 cancer and I had my boob cut off and I'm getting chemotherapy, and if I'm really lucky, I'll survive.'"

"Well, I think you could say it a little bit nicer than that," she quips, nearly making me choke on my water.

"I was joking. Geez." I take another drink and then dump what's left in the sink and walk back to my bedroom. "It's going to be hard, Mia. How do you tell someone that? And not just anyone, but someone that means so much to you. Someone that you have a history with. Someone that you love."

"The same way you told me," she says. "You just come out and say it, because there will never be a perfect time to tell him or a painless way to ease the blow. It's a punch in the gut, Laney, but there's no way around it. Rip that Band-Aid off, sister, so the two of you can heal these wounds together."

"You're right," I concede. "You're absolutely right. I need to tell him."

"I'm always right, Lane. Never doubt me. Ever. Now get some beauty sleep and text me tomorrow."

"Love you, Mia."

"Love you too, doll."

Chapter 16

Laney

HE RIGHT TIME STILL HASN'T come. I've had plenty of chances to tell him, I just haven't been able to get the words out. But it *needs* to happen. Things are moving too fast and he's getting too close, and a couple of nights ago he almost found out that his girlfriend—if that's what I am—is of the one-breast species.

I'm not going to lie, I'm scared for him to find out. What if he doesn't find me attractive? I feel deformed, almost like a monster. My scar is jagged and puckered and I hate looking at it, so I would never expect a man to look at it, let alone touch it. Someday, way far in the future when I have extra money lying around, I may try and get an implant, but right now it's just not a luxury I can afford.

I close my eyes and rest my head back on the seat, trying to get comfortable—well, as comfortable as I can be sitting for hours on end while chemicals are being pumped into my body. My mind wanders to the other night, and as the memories start flooding in, my heart fills with deep warmth.

Levi's eyes are locked on mine and they're swirling with passion. Our make-out sessions have gotten intense lately, but I can tell by the look on his face they're about to kick up a notch. We've been playing it safe, stopping before we let things get too far. I know why I'm stopping, I'm just not sure why he is. If I had to guess, I'd say it's because he's still a little gun-shy. Which is okay, I get it. He has to learn to trust me again . . . and he will. I'll make sure of it.

He starts walking, pushing me backward toward the desk. "Thank you for wearing a dress." I glance down at my outfit. It's nothing special, just a pink halter dress with white sandals. I didn't even wear it for him, I wore it for me. I've been feeling a little depressed lately, which according to my oncologist is normal, and Benny swears that if I stop wearing mesh sports shorts and t-shirts and start dressing up a little more, it might make me feel a bit better.

Well, it's doing something alright. I'm not sure I'm feeling less depressed, but if Levi wanting to have his way with me in his office is what happens when I get dolled up, then I'll dress to the nines every day. "I appreciate it, Lane, you taking me into consideration when you pick out your clothes. The downfall here is that I have a shit-ton of work to do and easy fucking access to all the parts of you that I've been dying to get my hands on."

"Oh, you have, have you?"

"You have no idea, baby." He crowds against me until my thighs hit the cool wood of his desk, and then he wraps an arm around my waist and hoists me up. "Don't get me wrong, kissing you is by far one of the greatest things in the world. But I want to touch you. I need to touch you, Lane."

"Oh, shit," I moan when his thick hands slide up my bare thighs, pushing under the skirt of my dress. I forgot how primal Levi can be. He's been quite mild since we've started whatever it is that we've started, but today I'm seeing a glimpse of the old Levi—the Levi that used to take and not ask . . . the Levi that was in control and demanding and possessive in the very best possible way.

It's been eight years since I've had a man inside of me and my body is aching for it—it's aching for Levi. My head tips back at the same time his drops forward, and his mouth, hot and needy, descends on my neck. One hand is braced firmly on my thigh, while the other one is inching up higher and higher on the opposite leg until his fingers find the edge of my panties.

"I tried to block this out—how good you felt under my hands— but I couldn't. You feel amazing, Lane." My hands are behind me on the desk, keeping me propped up, but I risk the fall by lifting one and bringing it to his face.

"Touch me, Levi." My voice is husky and thick, but I must have said exactly what he wanted to hear because in a matter of seconds, his hand slips into my panties and two thick fingers find my entrance. My sandals fall to the floor with a soft thud when I lift my legs to wrap them around his hips. Levi moves his free hand to the small of my back, holding me to him as his fingers work their way inside of me.

"Christ, Laney," he moans as his hand pulls back and then thrusts forward again. His lips slam over mine in a kiss that is both needy and full of passion. My arms wrap around his neck, my fingers curling into his hair, and only because he knows me so darn well, he wraps his hand in my hair and he tugs. Heat explodes deep in my gut and slowly seeps through my veins. His mouth leaves mine as he begins to trail open-mouthed kisses across my jaw. His lips wrap around my earlobe and he sucks gently before nipping it lightly. A guttural moan floats through the air, but I'm so wrapped up in the movement of his fingers deep inside me and his hot breath on my ear that I have no idea who actually made the noise. Frankly, I don't care either.

I can feel Levi smile against the side of my face and I revel in the fact that I'm the one who put it there. As much as I love Levi's smile, however, I know one sure-fire way to wipe it off his face. My hands make their way down his back and I slip one in between us, skimming down his stomach, stopping to toy with the button of his jeans. I pop the button, yank down the zipper and Levi falls hot and heavy into my hand. Good Lord, I forgot what this man is made of.

"Commando, huh?"

His answer is nothing but a grunt into the base of my neck when I wrap my hand around his cock and start working him up and down. My finger swirls over the tip before I repeat the movements, over and over. "Laney," he says gruffly as his lips pass over the top of my shoulder and then move back toward my jaw. "I don't want to come in your hand, baby. The first time I get off with you, I will get off inside of you."

"Then you better work your magic. If you want me to stop, then you better get me off." Levi's eyes narrow but a grin tugs at the side of his mouth—he's always loved a good challenge.

"You forget how well I know you," he pants, his fingers pushing and twisting. "I know that you like your hair pulled." His mouth finds mine in a quick, hot kiss. "And I know that you like when I talk dirty. Don't you, Laney?" I nod my head, desperately trying to keep my movements going despite the tingling at the base of my spine. "You like it when I tell you how hot and wet and tight you are. And you are tight, Laney. So fucking tight." Those tingles turn into vibrations that start making their way up my body. "But I know that what you like most is this—"

"Holy shi—" His mouth sears mine, swallowing my words, at the same time he twists his hand and curls his fingers, hitting that one spot deep inside of me that only he has touched. His thumb finds my clit, hard and throbbing, and I have absolutely no idea how he's doing what he's doing but it's absolutely amazing and I don't want him to stop. His fingers slide and pump, his thumb swirling around me, and all of those little vibrations that have been building shatter into a million shards shooting through every inch of my body. My hand drops and I clutch the side of his shirt as he works me over the edge and then slowly guides me back down to earth.

"I love it when you challenge me, Laney." His wicked words are whispered in my ear and my head drops to his shoulder. He chuckles, pulling his hand from between my legs. He smoothes out the skirt of my dress and drops a gentle kiss to the side of my

head.

"Give me two minutes and I promise I'll make up for losing the challenge." I nuzzle my face into the side of his neck, inhaling long and deep. He smells so good. As his hands move to my waist, his thumb grazes the underside of where my right breast should be and I jerk back. I quickly lace my fingers with his, hoping that he didn't notice my hasty retreat.

"What's wrong?" he asks, bringing our joined hands to his mouth. Well, so much for hoping.

"Nothing. Sorry. That just tick—"

"Hi, Laney." The soft voice interrupts my memory from the other night . . . and why does that voice sound so familiar? My eyes pop open to find Levi's friend Harley sitting in a chair next to my recliner. She's wearing the normal 'chemo' nurses' attire—blue scrubs and a light blue lab coat—and she looks confused and maybe a little shocked . . . or scared.

"Harley." I sit up a little straighter in my seat and run an anxious hand down my arm, which is stupid because I can't hide the IV and pole that I'm currently attached to. Her eyes bounce around my body, and when they land back on me I expect to see pity . . . but I'm wrong. She's looking at me with empathy.

My heart starts beating fast as I realize what seeing her here could mean. Before I even think, I blurt, "Please don't tell Levi." My eyes fill with tears and I grab her hand. "I'm going to tell him. I swear, I'm going to tell him. I know you're best friends and you probably think I'm a horrible person for not telling him, but I will. I swear."

"Laney"—she squeezes my hand and scoots her chair a little bit closer to mine—"I would never tell him. First, because I can't." She points to her scrubs and badge. "It's against the rules . . . Privacy Acts and all that fun stuff. But even if I could, I would never tell him." She looks down at my trembling hand wrapped firmly around hers. "*You* need to though. It won't be long and you won't be able to hide it. I'm a little shocked you've been able to hide it this long." Her eyes find mine again and she offers me a tiny smile.

I know what she's talking about. I'm going to lose my hair, and then I'll have no choice but to tell him. And it's already started. Every morning when I brush my hair, more and more seems to be coming out. I hate it. This has to be the worst part . . . well, other than getting my breast removed.

"I know." I'm thankful that she wouldn't tell him even if she could. "This is all just so . . ." I pause, blinking several times to push back the tears. "It's just hard. If I don't talk about it, then sometimes—even if it's only for a couple of minutes—I'm able to forget about it." She nods her head in understanding, and I can't help but wonder what she's gone through in her life that would make her understand that feeling. "I want to tell him, I do. I just want to do it when the time is right. And things have been going so well between us, I don't want to screw anything up."

"Well, for the record, I don't think you could screw anything up. He's smitten, Laney. Absolutely smitten." She shakes her head, almost as if she can't believe it, and laughs.

"He's talked about me?" I ask, curious as to what he's said and hoping that it's nothing horrible.

"Don't worry, that boy won't give me any juicy details, but it's not for lack of trying. I'm going to be honest, I'm dying to know everything about you. Levi has been my best friend for the past several years, and only once did he allude to ever being in love. But based on what he did tell me, I knew that she had to be special. And then when I saw you that day at Flame"—I nod my head, remembering my jealous fit—"I knew you must be the girl he told me about."

"Did he tell you we've been—" I hesitate, trying to decide what exactly it is that we've been doing. *Are we dating?*

"He told me that you two have been spending time together," she says, saving me from my thoughts. "He told me that he's been happier these past several weeks than he has been in a long time."

"What else did he say?" I ask hopefully, loving what I'm

hearing so far. "I mean . . . if you can tell me. If you can't, I understand."

"Are you kidding? Hell yeah, I'll tell you. This stuff is important, and we women need to know these things." We both laugh and I look down, noticing that we're still holding hands . . . and I like it. I like having someone here with me—someone that's close to Levi. It almost makes me feel like he's here with me.

"Laney, Levi has been different than most single men that I've known. I've never seen him with a girl more than once, and he was never in a relationship. Now I know why. It's because he couldn't get over you." Her words slam into me and my heart bursts with the news that he couldn't get over me. It's a little unsettling to hear that he's been with other women, but I'm not going to let myself dwell on something I can't change. "Levi came over for dinner the other night, and he just looked so light and free . . . completely different from the Levi I usually have over for dinner. The clouds in his eyes were gone, and I love that you were able to do that for him."

Admittedly, I'm a little jealous that he went over to her house for dinner. I know she has a fiancé and I probably shouldn't care, but Levi and I have been talking every single day and he hasn't once mentioned it. "The sad thing is that I'm the one who put those clouds in his eyes. And I hate myself for that."

"Oh no. We're not doing this. No regrets, darling. The past is in the past, and what matters is that you're here now and you've found each other again," Harley says, looking like she might know a thing or two about what's she's saying. "Laney, I don't think you get it. The boy can't stop talking about you. He drove Tyson and me nuts. Not that we don't love hearing about you," she clarifies, "because we do. But seriously, for like two hours it was Laney this and Laney that."

If a soul could smile, then I think that mine just did. It not only smiled, but it sighed and it laughed. Knowing that I'm making Levi happy again makes my soul happy. "Thank you," I whisper.

"I needed to hear that. I see the happiness in him and the change from when I first got home, but it's nice hearing the words."

"That's because men are stupid," she says, puckering her lips. I laugh at her and she smiles. "It's true. They just have no idea about anything, and that's why we girls have to stick together. So trust me. When you do find the right time to tell him, which should probably be sooner rather than later, he's not going to be mad. Sure, he might be upset that you didn't tell him sooner, but that's something he has to get over. This is your life, Laney. It's your journey and I can tell that it's been a rough one, and you still have so far to go."

"I know," I sigh, leaning back in my seat.

"I read your chart because you're my patient today," she says with a hesitant look, "but I'd love to hear it from you. Will you tell me about it?"

"There isn't much to tell. I was taking a shower, found a lump, and within the blink of an eye, I was having a mammogram and then an ultrasound followed by a biopsy. Honestly, I don't really remember the visit where the doctor told me it was malignant. By that point, I was numb. It was like my mind had just shut down in an attempt to preserve my sanity. But I'm lucky enough to have a really great friend who stepped up and took notes and made sure I was where I needed to be. I decided to have the whole breast removed rather than just the lump, and now here I am"—I frown, looking at the tubes and wires that are attached to me—"getting chemo every other week in hopes that if there is any cancer left after the surgery, this will kill it off."

"Wow," she says, eyes wide. "You just seem so strong and un-affected by it all. When I saw you at Flame, and then again at the Senior Center, you appeared to be full of so much fire and life, and right now you look really great too. What's your secret?"

"Trust me," I laugh mirthlessly, "I am far from unaffected. I hate this. I just choose to deal with it privately. Sometimes I feel like if I can look like I'm holding it together, then it will make it easier for everyone around me." A lump forms in the back of my throat and the tears I pushed away just moments ago are starting to reappear. "But it's hard. It's so hard. There are days that I don't even want to move, and I'm not sure if it's because my body is worn out or because I'm depressed. And that . . . that's a whole other ball game."

"What do you mean?" The machine attached to my IV beeps, and Harley stands up and messes with a few knobs and buttons, making the machine quiet back down.

"I'm so happy right now with Levi, and when I'm with him, I'm able to forget all of this." I lift the tubing attached to my arm. "But when I'm by myself, my mind takes control and it starts running in a thousand different directions, most of which aren't good."

"I'm so sorry, Laney," Harley says and exhales deeply. "I hate this for you. No one should have to go through it. For what it's worth, you should tell Levi. Especially if you plan to keep seeing him. He wouldn't want you to go through this alone."

"But that's the thing. I don't want him to do it out of pity." I rub my hands over my face. "I want him with me because he wants to be with me. Not because he feels bad for me or thinks I might d—"

"Don't! Don't say it. That is not going to happen, and I don't even want to hear it come out of your mouth. Plus, he's already with you and he doesn't know. So when he does find out, I swear to you that he's going to want to support you one hundred percent."

"I'll tell him. I promise."

"Good," Harley says, giving my hand a gentle squeeze. "And although I hate that we're getting to know each other under these circumstances, I'm really glad we got the chance to talk." She rises from the chair. "So, my lunch break is over. I got pulled down here because someone left sick, so hello"—she reaches out her hand playfully to me—"my name is Harley, and I'm going to be your nurse for the rest of the day."

I shake her hand firmly and we both laugh. "It's been a pleasure meeting you, Harley. I'll be your patient for the day, and don't mind me . . . I'm not going anywhere for the next couple of hours."

"Hey," she says, dropping my hand. "Do you have someone here with you? A family member or friend? I can go get them for you, if you want."

"Nope. Today it's just me."

"Okay, well now you have me." She smiles and I smile back, knowing deep down inside of me that she really means that.

Chapter 17

Laney

"HOW WAS YOUR DAY?" LEVI steps up to my back, nuzzling his face into my neck. I'm sure he would wrap his arms around me if he could, but the burning stove and scalding hot pan in front of me might be a bit of an issue right now.

"Good," I laugh, scrunching up my shoulders because the scruff on his jaw is tickling me. "Now go. Stop harassing me. I'm trying to work here."

"No way." His soft lips pepper kisses up and down the length of my neck, and he stops to suck on the soft spot just below my ear. "It turns me on to watch you cook."

"It does?" I spin in his arms, spoon held high, and smack a kiss right on his mouth. "Then I should cook for you more often." He nods his head in agreement and brings his mouth back down on mine. As much as I love Levi's kisses, I don't have time right now—I need to finish this food. I pull away from him, nipping his bottom lip as I do, and he growls in response. Then I twirl back around to check the pasta.

"Is it ready?" he asks, peering over my shoulder.

"Yup. Would you mind getting some plates out?" Tonight we are at Levi's house, and it was my first time seeing it. I was pleasantly surprised that he didn't live in some bachelor pad condo, although he told me he used to but recently sold it. He lives in a ranch-style brick home on the outskirts of town and it's stunningly beautiful. The entire living room is nothing but ceiling to floor windows. What little wall is visible, is painted a bold red, which offsets the light oak hardwood floors perfectly.

And let's not forget about this kitchen. It's a chef's dream, and I practically drooled the second I walked in here. Black granite countertops practically go on for miles and there's more room to move than I've ever had in a kitchen of my own. So, of course, I had to cook here.

"Not at all," he says against my temple, kissing it softly before moving to get the plates and silverware. I made chicken alfredo, mostly because I know how much Levi loves it, but also because it's super easy to make and the quicker we eat, the quicker I can tell him. Harley's words have stuck with me this past week, but every time I opened my mouth to tell him, I froze. Well, not tonight. Nope, tonight, come hell or high water, I am telling him. My palms start to sweat just thinking about it, but I know it has to be done.

I drop the alfredo into a serving dish, then walk it over to the table and take a seat. Levi surprises me when he plops into a chair right next to me rather than across from me, and I give him a curious glance. "What?" He scoops out a helping for himself and then fills my plate as well. "This way I can touch you if I want."

"Okay." I smile around my mouthful of pasta, loving when he drops his hand to my thigh. We spend the next half-hour eating and laughing, sharing stories about our day, and throughout the entire time, Levi's hand stays locked on my leg. It's possessive and extremely sexy, and every time he moves a finger or swipes his thumb, I want to just say screw dinner so I can maul him.

After he's cleared his plate and I've eaten as much as my stomach could tolerate, I stand up and head toward the sink with our dishes. Setting them down gently, I turn on the hot water.

"The dishes can wait." Levi flicks the water off and turns me in his arms. "I've got other things I'd like to do first."

"Oh yeah?" He kisses my nose and I giggle when his fingers skim up my sides until they rest at the base of my neck, where he gently holds onto me and brings my face to his.

"Yes, and they don't involve dishes." His mouth fuses with mine and his hands slide down my shoulders, stopping to play with my bra strap that is peeking out from under my shirt. He slowly starts to tug, moving the strap and shirt out of the way, exposing more of my shoulder. That's when my brain kicks in.

"Wait, Levi. Please wait." His fingers stop, but he doesn't move; he just pulls back enough to look me in the eye.

"Is everything okay?" Well, if that's not a loaded question, I don't know what is. I push gently on his chest and he steps back, his head cocked to the side. My eyes dart to the floor and I suck my bottom lip into my mouth as I try to figure out the best way to say this. I've practiced these words hundreds of times, but funny how right now they are nowhere to be found. My legs feel restless, so I brush past Levi and walk into the living room. His feet pad behind me on the floor and when I stop, he stops. "Laney, what's going on?"

Every worst-case scenario starts flashing through my head, especially the one where Levi gets upset that I didn't tell him sooner and walks out on me. I'm just not sure I'll survive that.

I take a ragged breath and meet his gaze. He runs a hand along the back of his neck and cocks an eyebrow. "Okay . . ." I rub my hands down my thighs as I move over to the couch. "I think you should sit down for this."

"I don't want to sit down."

"Okay, well, I would like for you to sit down because I'm already nervous and you pacing around me isn't going to make things better." He growls in frustration and tosses himself onto the couch.

"Just tell me what's going on, Laney." He props his elbows on his knees, his hands fisted between his legs. His eyes are watching me intently, and he's no doubt trying to figure out exactly what I'm about to say. I'd bet anything that every last guess he has is so far off the mark it isn't even funny.

"I, uh . . . wow." I rub my hands down the front of my face. "This isn't easy. I didn't think it would be, but it's even harder than I thought. So—"

"You know what? Forget it. I can't believe I let myself do this again." Levi pushes up from the couch and paces around the coffee table.

"What?" I stammer, not sure what he's talking about.

"This. *Us.*" He waves a hand between us and then rubs his hands down the front of his pants. "I knew this would happen. I knew you'd find a way to fuck it up again, but I convinced myself that you were different . . . that you wouldn't hurt me again."

"Levi, no—" I shake my head firmly, tears burning the back of my eyes. *How could he think that?*

"Then what is it, Laney?" he yells, his hands out to his sides. "What do you have to tell me, and why is it so damn hard for you spit the words out?"

"I have cancer!" I blurt, plastering a shaky hand across my mouth as soon as the words are out. Adrenaline is pumping through my veins and my entire body is trembling. Tears start slipping from my eyes, but I can't move. My body is completely numb as I wait for him to say something.

Levi's mouth falls open and a cold knot forms in my stomach. "What?" he gasps. "What did you say?" He isn't moving either. He's just standing there staring at me like I just told him pigs fly.

Very slowly, I let my hand fall. "I have breast cancer," I whisper, my voice cracking on that hideous word.

"Laney." My name falls from his mouth in a desperate plea, and in three strides he's standing in front of me, gathering me in his arms. A strangled cry rips from my throat and I wrap my arms around him. My fingers curl inward, gripping the back of his shirt tightly in my fists. My body heaves on a deep sob as I finally let myself grieve in front of someone else. My tears are blinding, falling from my eyes in waves, but I don't make a move to wipe them. I need to let them fall. I need to rid them from my body.

Levi nuzzles his face in the side of my neck and whispers sweet words to try and comfort me.

It's going to be okay.

We'll get through this together.

You're not alone.

I can't lose you.

I'm not sure how long we stood in that embrace, and I don't remember how or when we moved to the couch, but when I look up, I'm cradled in his lap and he has a death grip on my body.

"I—I don't want t-to die, Levi," I hiccup, my face buried in his chest. "I'm not r-ready."

"Shhh . . ." His strong hand is soothingly stroking up and down my back in a hypnotizing rhythm. "You're not going anywhere, Lane. I won't let you. I'll hold onto you and I'll never let go."

"But that's the thing—" I pull back frantically, tilting my tear-streaked face up to his. "You d-don't know th-that. What if the s-surgery didn't work? What if the ch-chemo doesn't work?"

"Surgery?" His face falls and his voice is desperate. "What kind of surgery did you have, Lane?"

"Mastectomy."

"So that means they removed the whole breast?" he clarifies. I nod and look down. "How long have you been getting chemotherapy?"

My head snaps up, my eyes pleading with him not to be mad at me. "It's why I'm off every other Friday." My tears start to slow but my breathing picks up pace, along with my heart as I wait for his reaction.

"This whole time . . ." He breaks eye contact and looks off to the side. "This whole time that's where you've been going, and I didn't even know. I would've been there with you, Laney." His eyes find mine again. Sadness and frustration are warring for a spot on his beautiful face, and I curl myself into his chest.

"I should have told you—I know I should have told you—but I wanted you to pick me again for the right reasons." I watch as regret, defeat, sadness, and pain flash across his face. I wait to see anger and disgust, but they never come.

"The fatigue—"

"Chemo," I mumble.

"You've lost weight and you haven't been hungry." He isn't asking a question. He already knows.

"And nausea—"

"Because of the chemo," he says dryly, finishing my sentence. I nod feebly. Levi slips his arm under my legs and lifts me from his lap. With gentle ease, he places me on the couch and then stands up.

"I, uh . . ." He spares me a quick glance and then looks away. "I need a minute." He walks out of the living room and into the kitchen. I hear the faint sound of a door opening and shutting, the noise signaling the exact moment when my heart breaks into a million little pieces.

He left me.

Bending my knees, I pull my legs to my chest, my arms clutching at them for dear life. I can't believe this happening. I'm numb. Completely numb. Levi was the reason I was fighting. He was the one thing I wanted if I survived . . . and I just lost him.

Chapter 18

Levi

MY HANDS CURL INTO MY hair and I tug forcefully, desperately needing to feel something other than this sharp pain that is stabbing through the left side of my chest. I tilt my face up to the sky, blinking several times, but it doesn't help because a tear still floats carelessly down the side of my face. And then another and another. I brush them away angrily, but they just keep coming. A guttural moan tears from my throat as I let the weight of her words settle inside of me.

Cancer.

Laney has cancer. *My* Laney has cancer.

This can't be happening. She can't come back to me and then be ripped out of my arms—the world wouldn't be so cruel, would it? Anger seeps through my veins, slowly taking over the sadness and grief that I was feeling just moments ago. Anger at God for letting this happen to such a wonderful person . . . *my* wonderful person. Anger at Laney for not telling me sooner so that I could be there for her, because—damn it—I want to be there for her. And anger at myself for not asking more questions. Not once did I bother to ask what she was doing on those Fridays off. I didn't push for more answers when she was always yawning or falling asleep in the middle of a conversation. Her pale face and dark circles were unmistakable, but I was so wrapped up in our new little world that I didn't even bother to try and figure out what was going on.

I sit on the ground, leaning against the side of my house. The bricks are still hot from the midday sun, but I don't move because I feel numb. I'm at a loss for where to go from here. But I guess, in all honesty, there isn't really a choice. Laney has to have this chemo. She has to fight for her life, and I'm going to be there with her every step of the way. There's no way I'm letting her go now, and I can't lose her. *I just can't.* She deserves to have someone fight this battle with her, so that's exactly what I'm going to do.

And then it hits me like a ton of bricks—I'm not in there with her now. She just dumped a load of information and insecurities in my lap, leaving herself open and vulnerable, and I just left her there in my living room, crying. I'm a fucking dick.

Pushing up from the ground, I stalk back into the house, determined to show her how much she means to me. I want her to know, without a shadow of a doubt, that her scars don't scare me and that I want her, just the way she is.

Laney is exactly where I left her, only now she's curled into a ball and her shoulders are bobbing as she cries into her arms. Wasting no time, I walk over to her and scoop her into my arms. Her head snaps up and I inwardly cringe at her wide eyes—fuck me, she's shocked I actually came back.

"Levi?" Her voice is scratchy and raw. I don't answer her because I need to show her, and if I talk right now I'll probably lose my shit. When I don't speak, she tucks her hands under her chin and cuddles into my chest. *This is where she belongs.*

I walk quickly through the house and kick my bedroom door open with my foot, then set her gently on my bed. "Will you scoot back for me, sweetheart?"

She moves herself to the center of the bed and watches me with naked vulnerability . . . and that look alone splinters my heart in two. I kick off my shoes and then slip her sandals off of her tiny feet. Leaning back on her hands, her eyes follow every move I make. When I reach for the button on her shorts, she sucks in a sharp breath but lifts her hips without question. I drag her shorts down her legs then make quick work of taking off my clothes, leaving only my boxers. I crawl onto the bed and she starts to move back, but I shake my head and she stops. Her eyes are searing through me, taking me in the same way I'm taking her in. When I grip the bottom of her shirt, her body stills and I can practically see the breath hitching in her throat. Maybe she isn't ready for this.

I pause, giving her the chance to stop me, but she inhales deeply before raising her arms so I can slip the shirt over her head. My mouth waters and my eyes greedily roam every inch of her nearly naked body in an attempt to sate my eight-year craving. She's wearing a white lace bra and matching white cotton panties, and it doesn't matter that it's not blood red or black or barely there, it's sexy as hell because it's wrapped around her delectable body.

She's an angel.

My eyes land on the right side of her chest, where I can't help but notice that the cup of her bra is full and round. She glances down to see what I'm looking at. "It's a mastectomy bra." Blinking rapidly, she bites down on her lower lip before adjusting the underwire. "It isn't comfortable, but it looks almost normal when I wear a shirt . . ." Her words trail off and I watch a subtle flush creep up her neck, infusing her cheeks.

"You look sexy as hell, Lane." I crawl up her body and toy with the front clasp of her bra. "May I?"

She peeks up at me and nods. With a quick flick, the bra falls open. Laney's body is trembling under my hands and I hate that she's this nervous about me seeing her. Cradling her face, I rub my thumbs along her jaw. With my eyes locked on hers, I bring her face to mine and when our lips meet, she lets out a soft sigh. "I want to make love to you, Laney."

Her eyes are glistening and there's a slight quiver in her bot-

175

tom lip. Releasing her face, I trail my fingers down the length of her neck then sneak them under the straps of her loosened bra, tugging it down her shoulders. After I toss it aside, I bring my hands back to her neck, my thumbs tracing her jaw. "Are you okay?"

She offers me a tremulous smile and nods jerkily. "I'm just scared."

"There's nothing to be scared of. We've done this a thousand times before. You haven't forgotten about all those times, have you?" I ask playfully, trying to get her to loosen up a tad.

She chuckles and shakes her head. I scatter kisses across her beautiful face and tuck a strand of her silky hair behind her ear. Laney takes a deep breath, a look of resolve flashing across her face. Pulling back from me, she lies against the pillows at the head of my bed.

Laney is showing me her scars. With graceful beauty, she's presenting me with her body.

Her left breast is perky and plump, but where her right breast should be, there's a serrated scar. That side of her chest looks like it's sunken in, and the skin looks stretched and mildly uncomfortable.

"Please touch me," she pleads. I look up at her to find her eyes frantically searching my face. I'm not sure what she's looking for, but if she's wondering if her scars are turning me off, she sure as hell won't find that. Reaching up, I tenderly stroke a hand down the center of her chest. When my fingers draw a line across the puckered skin where her breast used to be, she squeezes her eyes shut.

"Open your eyes, sweetheart." She follows my gentle command. Her heart is pounding so hard that I can feel it through her chest. "Your scars don't bother me, Laney. They're a part of you. They're your battle scars. If anything, they make me insanely proud of you."

My lips trace a slow path along her scar and then progress to the puckered skin around it. Her fingers tangle in my hair and her body relaxes. My mouth moves to the other side of her chest, where I find her nipple tightened and hard. My lips wrap around the swollen bud, and her body jerks beneath me.

"Levi," she moans, her head tilting back on the pillow, and I work my tongue faster, sucking harder. My free hand skims down her body and dips into her underwear. She's wet and throbbing, and I can't wait any longer to claim her and make her mine.

"Are you on birth control?" She probably is. I'm sure there's some rule about not getting pregnant while you're undergoing chemotherapy.

"No," she whispers. My eyes flash to hers and I smile at the look of horror on her face.

"It's okay," I chuckle, grabbing a condom from the top drawer of my nightstand. I peel off my boxers then tear open the wrapper, but Laney stops me before I can slide the latex on.

"Let me." She grabs the condom and with incredible ease, she rolls it down my hardened length. My cock jerks under her touch, and she looks up at me and smiles. "I think you're forgetting something."

"Oh baby, I'm not forgetting anything. I'm just saving the best for last." Her face lights up, her eyes flashing hot with passion, as I slip my fingers into the top of her panties and slide them off.

Chapter 19

Laney

" I 'VE BEEN WAITING FOR THIS." Levi's breath is warm on my skin as he settles himself between my legs. The weight of his body pushes me into the mattress, and he props his elbows up on either side of my head and cradles my face in his hands.

"Me, too," I whisper, breathless with anticipation. His eyes burn with desire and I push my hips into his, urging him to take me, despite the fact that I'm terrified how he's going to fit. Levi is well endowed, and although I'm not a virgin, I haven't been this intimate with a man since I was last with *this man.*

Levi uses his legs to nudge mine open further and I let them drop to the side, opening myself up to him. He positions his cock at my entrance and my body arches, seeking his touch, then he pushes into me slowly, inch by delicious inch. My eyes drift shut, and I roll my head back on the pillow at the feel of him inside me.

"Look at me, Laney," he growls, and my eyes snap open. With a devilish grin on his face, he rocks his hips, pulling out a fraction before pushing back in. "Christ, you're tight." And I am. I can feel every inch of him as he works his way in further.

My body is humming with energy and I need him to move faster. I need to feel all of him. My legs wrap around his back, my heels digging into his ass as I pull him to me. He buries himself to the hilt and drops his head to my shoulder at the same time a string of incoherent words fall from his mouth.

Emotion builds thick in my throat, my eyes clogging with tears. This was the one thing I wanted more than anything else— to be with Levi and have his love again. I know he hasn't said the words, but I can feel it deep inside. It's in the way his fingers skim across my body, the way he smiles after he kisses me, and the way his eyes shine after I tell him how much he means to me. It's in everything he does and everything he says, and when I'm wrapped in his arms, I feel safe and loved.

Right here, in this moment, I'm not consumed by thoughts of cancer or dying or losing my hair. I'm consumed by him . . . this wonderful man that I will love every day for the rest of my life, no matter how long that may be.

A couple of tears slip from my eyes, disappearing into my hair, and I take a deep cleansing breath. I want him to make love to me so I tilt my hips upward, silently begging him to move. Levi gets the hint and starts to move slowly, effectively driving me out of my mind. Our mouths meet in a frenzy, our tongues pushing and sliding, taking and teasing. I'm meeting him thrust for thrust, but it's not enough—I need more. I groan, writhing underneath him, trying to get him to pick up the pace, and he actually has the nerve to chuckle.

"You can push all you want, baby, but I'm the one in control." His words cause a shiver to run through my body. Levi runs his hand down my bare thigh and grips it tightly in his hand. His primal touch ignites a small-show fireworks low in my belly. "Does this feel good, Laney? Did you miss having me inside of you?"

"Yes." My head thrashes from side to side as he slowly works my body into a frenzy.

"I've thought about this—about you—nearly every day." He pulls out of me slowly and then slams back in. His hips continue this torturous rhythm as his words seduce me. "Do you feel it, our connection? Your body was made for me, Laney. It was made for me and no one else."

"No one else," I confirm, bringing my hand to my breast. My fingers pinch and twist, and when Levi's lust-filled eyes see what I'm doing, he pushes my hand out of the way.

"That's my job, sweetheart, so you just wrap those sexy arms around my neck and let me do the work." I do as I'm told, but now my body is teetering on the edge. With each stroke, he's hitting that sweet spot deep inside of me, and every time he pushes in, his pelvis grinds against my clit. The steady rhythm is driving me mad, and I can't keep my arms around his neck. My hands drop to the bed, fisting the sheet, and I moan.

Levi's head drops and his swollen lips encircle my aching breast. His teeth nip and tug on my nipple, shooting sparks straight down my spine, causing me to squirm beneath him. My hands move to his shoulders and skate down his back, and when they reach the globes of his ass, I squeeze, pulling him close to me.

His mouth leaves my nipple with a wet pop and he makes a soft *tsk tsk* sound. "You just don't listen, do you?" If me not listening puts *that* look on his face, then heck no I don't listen. He looks like he wants to devour me and spank me and fuck me, and really, any of that sounds good. In fact, if he could just combine all three, I think I'd be perfect.

Levi sits up, still lodged deep inside of me, and my eyes rake hungrily over his sculpted chest. The warmth from his body is gone, and when a warm breeze passes over my chest, I stiffen beneath him. It doesn't matter that he's already seen it; just the fact that I'm open and bare makes me want to wrap my arms around my chest to cover myself up. Levi must sense my discomfort because he catches my hands in his and brings them to his lips. "No, baby. We aren't going backward, only forward. From now on, you and me, we only go forward. Got it?" I blow out a long, slow breath and nod my head.

"Good." Levi wraps both of my wrists in his left hand and leaning back over me, he pins my arms above my head. His right hand brushes down the side of my cheek as he begins to pick up his pace once again. "I still have your body memorized, Laney." He places an open-mouth kiss along my jaw. "Every last inch of it. And we're not stopping tonight until I've explored"—his hand skims slowly down my chest—"and reunited myself with all of the amazing beauty that is your bo—"

I feel his fingers rub gently over my mastectomy scar and then his words cut off. His face goes slack and a look of wonderment flashes in his eyes, which quickly dart to my face and then back down to my body. "Laney?"

"Yes," I moan, slightly perturbed that he has stopped . . . yet again. Doesn't he understand what we're trying to accomplish he—?

"Your tattoo." Oh yeah. *That.* His lips are parted and he blinks several times before leaning toward the right side of my body to get a closer look. "Laney?"

"Yeah?" I'm watching him for a reaction. This could either be really good or really bad, and I'm still trying to figure out which way it's going to go.

"What's it say, Laney?"

"You can't read it?" I ask with a hesitant smile, but he doesn't look up at me. His eyes are still trained on the script that's indelibly inked along my ribs.

"I want you to tell me what it says." His voice is hoarse and finally his eyes shift to mine.

"Levi," I answer softly. His entire face transforms—lust and passion are quickly replaced by astonishment and admiration. "It says *Levi.*"

"That's my name, tattooed on your body." His eyes are glassy, his voice thick and raw. My fingers itch to touch him, but my arms are still pinned above my head and I'm not sure now is the right time to move them. "Why? Why is my name there . . . on your body . . . in permanent ink?" His words are slow and concise as though he's trying to make sure I understand what he's asking.

"Because I want to take you with me," I whisper.

"Where?"

I swallow hard past my heart that is now sitting firmly in the middle of my throat. "To heaven." Levi's breath rushes from his lungs as the weight of my words sink in. My stomach tenses as I wait to see what he's going to say or do, and when he just continues to stare at me, I keep going. "You're a part of me, Levi . . . you've always been a part of me. I know we haven't been together for the past eight years, but *that* never changed. I never stopped loving you. You don't just have my heart, but my soul belongs to you too. I just . . ." I avert my gaze, trying to find my words before bringing my eyes back to his. "I just wanted to know that no matter what, whether I'm here on earth or soaring through heaven, I'll always have a piece of you with me. Because my life isn't complete without you, and it's not much of a life anyway if you're not in it."

Levi releases my hands, a look of determination written on his face, and without dislodging himself from my body, he some-how manages to flip us over so I'm sitting astride his hips. His fingers rake through my hair as he grips the back of my head and pulls me to him. "I *am* with you. There isn't anywhere else in this world I'd rather be. I'm not going anywhere—and neither are you, for that matter, because I won't let you. I'll fight enough for the both of us. Just let go, Laney . . . let me be your rock. Let me help you get through this." The tears that have been building for the past several minutes leak from my eyes and spill over my lashes, but Levi catches them with his thumb. And as they keep coming, he keeps catching them, the entire time assuring me that we're in this together.

"Please make love to me. Please," I beg, hating the way my voice cracks. Levi doesn't say a word but cradles my face in his big warm hands, then makes love to my mouth as his body fol-lows suit. My hips are rolling in rhythm with his in a dance so perfect and so passionate that I feel he's somehow touched my soul. I moan, digging my fingers into his chest.

My body and soul are overwhelmed with sensations, and all

it takes is one perfectly timed thrust to send me toppling over the proverbial edge. My entire body goes up in flames before it explodes into a million colorful little pieces. Levi grunts, his body continuing to pound into mine as I convulse around him.

"Laney." My name leaves his mouth on a deep growl as he buries his face in the side of my neck and lets go. His body rocks into mine several more times before coming to a leisurely stop.

I feel like I'm bursting at the seams with emotions—love, peace, contentment, happiness, anticipation, and gratitude, to name a few. And I'm feeling them all in enormous doses. I want nothing more than to shout it out to all the world, but for now I'll have to settle with these words: "I love you so much, Levi."

He shifts his head from the crook of my neck and kisses me softly several times, infusing his own amount of emotion into each gentle peck. "You're amazing, Laney. I'm so glad you came back to me."

I bite down hard on the inside of my cheek, desperate to stay on the cloud that I've just started floating on. I know I can't expect him to say those three little words quite yet, but hey, a girl can hope, can't she? One of these days . . . one of these days when he's ready, he'll say the words.

Chapter 20

Laney

LEVI RETURNS FROM THE BATHROOM and crawls under the covers. He lays himself across my chest and peppers kisses along his name that is forever etched on my skin. "I love this, by the way." He gives me a devilish grin. "I didn't get the chance to tell you earlier, but I love it. Thank you."

"What are you thanking me for?"

"For your words . . . and for this." His fingers trace over each intricate line. "For never forgetting about me, and for loving me enough to want me with you forever." My mind drifts to the story he told me about his mother, and I realize that maybe—just maybe—I've proven to him that he can trust me again.

"Did it hurt?" he asks.

"Like a bitch." He laughs and kisses his name one more time before propping himself up on the pillows. He tucks me under his arms and pulls the covers up to my chin.

"That's because you're a pussy."

"I am not," I scoff, ramming my elbow into his side when I push myself up to glare at him. "I'm tough as nails."

"Sure you are, babe." He pats my arm like I'm a petulant child then tugs me back down. His eyes drift shut and I nuzzle into his chest with a sigh of contentment, relishing the fact that I'm here—in Levi's arms—and this isn't a dream. I'm not sure how long we lie here, but Levi's steady breathing and the strong beat of his heart are quickly lulling me to sleep. Right when I feel myself dozing off, Levi whispers my name.

"Yeah?" I yawn, stretching my arm across his chest.

"That night I first saw you again, you told me you came back here for me and another reason." I nod my head; I remember that night all too well. "You said I wasn't ready to hear the other reason. Was it because of the cancer?"

"Yeah," I sigh, rubbing my hand down his toned stomach. "I wanted to come home for my chemotherapy. This is where Luke and Benny are"—my fingers lazily trace around each defined muscle—"and this is where you are. I wanted so badly to tell you sooner, but I needed us to be in a better place. Does that make sense?"

"It does." He pauses for several beats and then takes a deep breath. "How did you find it . . . the cancer?"

"I was taking a shower, washing my body, and there it was. It felt like a rock under my skin, and I freaked out because I remembered my dad telling me that when mom found her cancer, she'd said the same thing." I squeeze my eyes shut and push out the rest of the story. "I called the doctor and within the hour I was at the hospital having an ultrasound and mammogram. I remember sitting in that cold room all by myself—"

"Mia wasn't with you?" he asks.

"Nope." I shake my head. Then I spend the next hour telling him every little detail about my diagnosis, all my options and everything leading up to the surgery.

"Why did you choose the mastectomy over the lumpectomy?"

"I wanted it gone. I was so scared, and all I could think about was getting whatever was growing inside of me out. So I had the surgery, went through six weeks of recovery, and moved home."

"Are you scared now?" he asks. I'm sure it wasn't easy for him to ask me that. Hell, it's not easy for me to answer that, but

I'll try. Because keeping anything at all from him, even my fears, is no longer an option. When it comes to Levi Beckford, I am an open book.

"Terrified." His arm tightens around my shoulders and his chin drops to the top of my head. "I'm terrified of what I might miss out on."

"Does it hurt?" he asks softly.

"The cancer?"

"No . . . yes. I don't know. The chemo, your scar—all of it. Are you in pain?" I love that he's asking these questions because it shows me that he cares.

"No, no pain. There are certainly other things going on with me, but right now pain isn't one of them."

"Will you tell me about it?"

"It's weird," I start off, trying to put my feelings into words. "There are days when the cancer is all I think about. It consumes me to the point of exhaustion, and I feel like I'm going to go insane from worry. And then there are days when I'm able to forget and my life seems completely normal."

"When it consumes you—what's that like?" Levi's hand is tracing circles on my arm, but when he asks the question, his fingers stop.

"Keep doing that—with your fingers," I demand, wriggling my arm. He chuckles and starts tracing again. "I just get a jumbled mess of thoughts that I can't seem to work through, and I'm constantly battling to stay strong and not feel sorry for myself. A lot of times I find myself thinking about things I want to do before I die . . . just in case."

"Your bucket list."

"Yes," I nod. "But more than anything, it scares me to think that at any given time I could be gone from this world—forever—and never be able to come back. I'll never get to hug Mia again or fight with Luke and Benny or make love to you. Essentially, I would be like a face in the background of a forgotten photo. A blip on the radar. And that scares the hell out of me."

My voice gets scratchier with each word and tears well up in my eyes. "I've never said that out loud to someone before. It's much harder to say than it is to think." Tears drip from my eyes, landing on Levi's chest, and he wipes them away tenderly. Then he pulls me up his body so we're face to face.

"I didn't mean to upset you, Lane. I just need to know what we're up against."

"What *we're* up against?" I clarify. Levi brushes his nose against mine and then kisses me softly.

"Yes, *we*. Us. Me and you," he mumbles, his lips brushing over mine with each word. "You're not doing this alone, not any of it. Absolutely everything you go through, I will go through with you." My heart flops over in my chest as I soak in his words.

"That's a lot, and I would never ask you to do that."

"That's the thing, you don't have to ask me. Because that's just what you do when you care about someone." Levi's thumb runs a slow path across my bottom lip before brushing my bangs out of my eyes. "I couldn't imagine not doing this with you."

"I'll warn you, it's not pretty. There are days when I get so depressed just thinking about things that I can barely get out of bed. And eating? Not happenin.'"

"That's why you didn't eat much when I took you on the picnic."

"That night it was the nausea. But my appetite, in general, is fading. I'm just not hungry, and most of the time when I do eat, it's so that you, Luke and Benny don't ask questions."

"I won't push you to eat, baby, but you have to keep yourself fed so that you can stay strong and fight this," he says with conviction. "I'll start cooking for you."

"I'd love for you to cook for me." I kiss him gently and smile. "I just don't want you to get your feelings hurt if I don't eat much."

He purses his lips and nods, his eyes searching mine. "Stay with me tonight." That's Levi . . . never one to ask, only tell.

"I was already planning on it." I slink down on the bed and

wrap my naked body around his, and it's the single best feeling in the world.

As it turns out, Levi makes one hell of a pillow. I don't think I've ever fallen asleep as quickly as I did last night. Unfortunately, as per usual lately, I woke up way before I wanted to, so I've spent the past several hours watching Levi sleep. I can't count the number of times I've wanted to touch him or kiss him, but he just looks so peaceful and I've missed being with him like this. Awake or asleep, he has a calm presence that somehow soothes my soul.

My bladder finally forces me to sneak out of bed and pad down the hall to the bathroom. I glance around the room as I take care of business, noticing that somehow my clothes made their way from being strewn across Levi's bedroom to being folded and stacked neatly on the bathroom counter. I smile, wondering when he did this.

Right before I jump in the shower, I spot a clock on the wall. It's only eight a.m. and I recall Levi saying he doesn't have to be up at any certain time today. As I wash up, I think about what I'll make him for breakfast and I find myself smiling again.

In and out quickly, I grab a towel from the bathroom pantry to pat myself dry. I slip on my shorts from yesterday, hating that I don't have a clean change of clothes and forgoing underwear altogether, and I walk back into Levi's room to rummage through his closet. Grabbing the first t-shirt I find, I pull it over my head and return to the bathroom. I rinse my mouth out with some mouthwash and then run my fingers through my hair.

I'm standing in front of the mirror when it happens. A chunk of hair is tangled around my fingers, and the sight of it makes my stomach drop. Panic sets in and I reach up, running another hand through my hair, only to come up with more chunks. "No, *no no no,*" I whisper, frantically pulling the stray hairs from my hands. "This isn't happening. It's too soon." I shake my head furiously and, without warning, tears start falling down my face. My hand comes to mouth and I hold back a sob.

I can't do this here; I need to be at home. I *want* to be at home. All the articles and pamphlets in the world can't prepare you for what it's like to actually lose your hair. They can tell you it's going to happen and when it's going to happen, but in the grand scheme of things, there's no way to prepare for the way it rips you apart.

I tiptoe quietly into Levi's room, dig an old receipt out of my purse and scribble a quick note to him.

Levi,
I hate not being here when you open your eyes, but I have some errands I have to run. Thank you for last night; it was better than I imagined.
Call me when you wake up.
                                    Love, Laney

I lay the note on the pillow next to him so he won't miss it, then walk out of his bedroom, quietly shutting the door behind me. I'm barely holding on by a thread, and I just need to be alone right now.

Chapter 21

Laney

*J*DON'T REMEMBER THE DRIVE HOME or walking in the house, and I certainly don't remember how I ended up standing in my bathroom in front of the mirror with a pair of clippers. But here I am, staring at my reflection, daring myself to get it over with.

I look like hell. My eyes have dark circles under them and my cheekbones are prominent, a product of the weight I've slowly been losing. I rub a chunk of hair between my fingers and watch as several loose strands fall to the floor. *Who in their right mind would find this attractive?*

My lip quivers, followed by my chin, and I squeeze my eyes shut, vowing that I can do this. Not that there are many options. I could let my hair fall out slowly, but that's not how I want this to happen. My plan was to do this gracefully, and I had always told myself that when my hair started to fall out, I'd simply shave it. Well, I'd been fooling myself because that is much easier said than done.

I don't want to lose my hair.

I don't want to be bald.

"Fuck," I cry, throwing the clippers on the counter. I sink to the floor, a pile of loose limbs and tears. A deep sob rips from my throat and I bury my face in my hands. My mind is racing, battling itself at every turn, one minute telling me to stay strong, and the next telling me to let it all out. My cheeks are flushed and my body starts trembling as self-pity washes through me. My sobs turn into gasps as my lungs fight against the screams that have been clawing to get out.

This isn't fair. This isn't fair. This isn't fair.

Those three words cycle in my head over and over again, until I get so fed up with my own damn brain that I grip my hair in my fists and pull . . . hard. I growl, pushing up from the floor. A chunk of hair falls from my hand and I look down to see dozens of strands scattered across the tile floor. I'm yanking on my hair and reminding myself how unfair life is when the doorknob to my bathroom starts rattling. I stop dead in my tracks, hands in hair, eyes red and puffy, hot tears streaking down my cheeks, and I stare at the wood, waiting to see what's going to happen.

"Open the door, Laney." I sigh in relief when I hear Benny's voice through the door instead of Luke's. My little brother doesn't need to see this. No one needs to see this.

"Go away, Benny." My hands drop from my hair and I turn around, propping them up on the sink. My head dips low and I draw in a ragged breath.

"Laney Jacobs." My head snaps up at Levi's firm voice. "You have three seconds to open this goddamn door or I will kick the fucker down." I close my swollen eyes and wipe angrily at the tears that are still racing down my face. "One . . ."

I look up at the door, then at the mess on the floor. I don't want them to see me break down. I don't want them to see me like this.

I drop to the toilet seat. "Levi, please—"

"Two," he yells. His strong voice sends shivers down my spine. Damn him, and damn Benny because I'm sure he had something to do with Levi showing up at my house only minutes after I left his. Well, let them kick the stupid door in; it'll be their problem to fix, not mine. Although this is my only bathroom and I'd prefer not to be without a door.

I can hear faint whispering, but I can't make out what they're saying. "Three." My eyes pinch shut and I tense up, waiting for the door to fly open. Several seconds pass and I chance a peek to find that the door is now wide open and there are two brooding men standing in front of me. "Turns out, I just needed a coin." Levi holds up said penny and shrugs. *Stupid child lock doors.*

Benny pushes past Levi. "Your boyfriend is a fucking Neanderthal." He squats down in front of me and takes in our surroundings before his eyes fly to mine. His face is awash with kindness and compassion, but I'm still too raw and I can't do this right now.

I shove myself off the toilet seat, brushing past Benny and Levi, taking extra precaution not to touch either one of them or look them in the eye. If I do, I'm afraid of what I'll find, and I'm not ready to see pity. I can hear two sets of feet bound after me. They're not going to stop . . . and if I'm being honest, I don't want them to. I keep trying to remind myself that they love me and they're worried about me, so I leave my door open when I walk in my room, silently inviting them in. Even facing the other direction, I know they're both standing there because their presence in a room is demanding. Not to mention, the hairs on the back of my neck are standing up, and that's usually a good indicator that Levi is within close proximity.

I spin around to face them at the same time my front door opens and then slams shut. "Laney?!" Luke comes barreling down the hall, pushes past Benny and Levi, and doesn't stop until he's toe to toe with me. His golden eyes bounce around my body, and I can tell the moment that he notices my hair. "Oh, Laney." He yanks me into his arms, and for several seconds I just stand there, unable to move. Then something inside of me crumbles, and I wrap my arms around my brother.

"I'm losing my hair, Luke," I cry, squishing my face into his chest. "I don't want to lose my hair. This isn't fair. I don't want to be bald and I don't want to wear a wig, and I don't want people to stare at me and wonder what's wrong. I just want to be normal and have hair and boobs. Is that too much to ask for?" I sniff. "Hair and boobs. That's all I need." The words sound funny when I say them aloud, and I choke back a laugh because it just doesn't seem appropriate to go from bawling like a baby to cracking up in a matter of seconds.

"Your hair will grow back, Lane." I can't see Benny because I still have my face buried in Luke's shirt, but his voice is laced with sympathy.

"Plus, you still have one breast, and it's a really great breast." My head snaps up and I stare at Levi in horror, shocked that he would say that in front of Luke and Benny. "What? It's true." I keep staring and he keeps shoving his foot further and further into his mouth. "I don't care if you only have one breast. You could have no breasts and I'd still find you insanely attractive. It would be a little bit harder to get you off—"

"Stop." Luke's voice booms through air. Still clutching me tightly in his arms, he spins around and glares at Levi. "I do *not* need to know about my sister's breasts. Please, for the love of God, don't *ever* talk about her boobs or lack thereof again if it in any way pertains to anything unrelated to her cancer. There is only so much a brother can handle, and that's just pushing the limits."

We all stand in stunned silence for a solid minute before Benny and Levi start to bust up laughing. Levi's head falls back and a deep throaty laugh erupts from his mouth that does nothing but send tingly sensations to all my fun parts. Benny slaps Levi on the back and they do one of those weird man-hug things.

"So . . ." Luke says, stepping away from me. "You and Levi, huh?"

"Yup."

"You never told me." He looks hurt, and I instantly regret not sharing that with my brother. He's been busy with work but we text or talk nearly every day, and I should've told him.

"I'm sorry, Luke. Things have just been crazy, and it all sort of happened really fast."

"It's okay. Just tell him not to talk about your boobs in front of me again, okay?"

"You got it." I giggle, amazed at how quickly these three wonderful men were able to make me feel better.

"So . . ." Benny eyes me up and down, hands on hips. "Your hair looks like it could use a cut." Levi smacks him upside the back of the head and walks over to me. He wraps an arm around my shoulder and pulls me into his side.

"You're right," I say, pursing my lips, preparing myself for my next words. "I think it's time to shave my head." I haven't looked in a mirror, but I'm sure my little tirade in the bathroom did nothing but make me look like a cat with mange.

"Only when you're ready, baby." Levi kisses the side of my head and my brother rolls his eyes.

"So how did you guys all end up here, anyway?" I ask, shooting Benny an accusatory glance.

He raises his hands innocently, but before I can call him out on it, Luke speaks up. "Benny called me," he confesses.

"What the fuck, dude?" Levi shoots Benny a glare. "You called him and not me?"

"Wait . . . who called you?" I ask Levi.

"No one. I woke up and you were gone—"

"Wait a second," Luke interjects. "Woke up? Are you sleeping over there?"

"Butt out, Luke," I say, keeping an eye on Levi. "Keep going."

"I got your note, but it didn't make sense because last night you told me you didn't have any plans until this evening." Levi runs a hand along the back of his neck. "Then I went into the bathroom to take a piss and your hair was all over the sink. I knew something had happened so I came straight here."

His words melt my heart. "Thank you." I push up on my tiptoes and kiss him. My mouth traces the seam of his lips until he grants me access, and I sink my fingers into his hair, angling my head to the side. Levi's arms wrap around my back and he picks me up, my legs dangling beneath me.

"Fuck," Luke hisses from across the room. "This shit is going to drive me crazy." Levi laughs, breaking the kiss, and looks over my shoulder.

"Get out, Luke. You're cock-blocking me," Levi quips, a wide smile gracing his gorgeous face. Luke mumbles a string of curse words and Benny laughs, pushing him out of my bedroom, leaving Levi and me alone.

"Are you okay?" he asks, his brows dipped low. "I was really worried about you."

"I'm okay." I rub my eyes with the heels of my hands and take a deep breath. "I'll be okay. I just freaked out. I was ready for it, but I wasn't, ya know?" Levi scoops me up and sits down on my bed, settling me in his lap.

"So what do you want to do?"

"I think I'm ready to shave it. I don't want to walk around looking like this," I say, lifting a strand of what's left of my hair.

"I've got an idea." Levi smirks, tapping my nose. "Get into an old shirt, get the clippers and meet me in the bathroom."

"Okay . . ." I say skeptically, giggling when he slaps my butt on the way out the door. I have absolutely no idea what he has planned; all I know is that when my head hits the pillow tonight, I'll be bald. Unlike earlier, I find that the thought of that doesn't make me panicky. Maybe I just needed to have a meltdown. Maybe I just needed a good old-fashioned cry. Or maybe I just needed these three men to remind me that losing my hair isn't the worst thing in the world. Losing my life would be, and if one of the side effects of the medicine that may save my life requires me to be bald, then I guess that's just something I'm going to have to learn to live with.

Chapter 22

Laney

TEN MINUTES LATER I'M STANDING in the bathroom, clippers in hand, wondering what in the heck is taking so long. "Are you coming?" I holler, not really sure who I'm hollering at.

"Christ, you're impatient," Benny says, walking into the bathroom followed by Luke and Levi. They're all holding beers and Luke puts a shot glass full of clear liquid in front of me.

"Water?" It better be water. I'm a lightweight, and the last thing I need is to get rip-roaring drunk right before I shave my head. On second thought . . . that might not be such a bad idea. I reach for the glass, tip my head back and cringe as the liquid burns my throat. With my nose scrunched, I hand him the glass.

"Atta girl," Levi says, popping the top on a bottle of beer and handing it to me.

"What was the shot for?" I ask, taking a swig.

"Just to loosen you up." Luke gently guides me down onto the side of the tub and peels his shirt off. Standing in front of the mirror, he says, "I'll go first." My eyes widen and I set my beer down.

"Luke, what are you doing?" Apparently what I say doesn't matter because no one answers me as Levi picks up the clippers and runs a straight line over the top of Luke's head.

"Oh my gosh!" I gasp, my hand covering my mouth. I wait for Luke to turn around and deck Levi, but he doesn't. He just stands there patiently as Levi keeps making swipe after swipe until my brother's hair is nothing but a short buzz. I watch in stunned silence as Luke brushes the stray hairs from his head into the sink and pulls his shirt back on. Before I can even form words, Benny yanks *his* shirt off and Levi makes a swipe down Benny's head.

"Benny," I sigh, at a complete loss for words. Levi gives Benny the same buzz cut and then immediately reaches behind his head to pull his own shirt off.

"No." I shake my head furiously, pushing up from the tub. "This is too much. You don't have to do this."

"This isn't up for discussion, pretty girl." Levi gives me a gentle kiss on the cheek and gestures for me to sit back down on the ledge of the tub.

"Do you want to do the honors?" Luke asks, holding out the clippers.

"No. You do it," I say, overwhelmed by how supportive and caring these men are. I expect it from Luke, because that's how I raised him, but never in a million years would I expect Benny and Levi to follow suit. It hits me all at once that these three wonderful men are doing this for me because they love me and don't want me to go through this alone. I just know that the women they end up with will be very lucky, and I pray to God I'm that woman for Levi.

A finger snaps in front of my face, and I shake the fog from my head and look up. Levi, Luke and Benny are all standing in front of me with completely shaved heads. The sight alone is enough to bring a grown woman to her knees. When I think of all that they could be doing today, a tingling warmth saturates my skin and my chest feels like it's expanded. I don't know what I did to deserve this, but I know that I'll never be able to repay the kindness and support they've shown me today.

I stand up and pull my brother into my arms. "Love you,

Luke." He whispers the words in return and kisses the side of my head. I slip out of his embrace and then squeeze Benny around the waist, smashing my face into his chest. "Thank you, Benny," I whisper, emotion finally starting to clog my throat. In true Benny form, he stays quiet, although his arms do find their way around me.

After a minute or two, Levi clears his throat and Benny chuckles. I move to pull away but Benny squeezes me tighter, refusing to let go, which is completely okay with me. Right now, I just need to show each of them how much I love them. Apparently, Levi isn't too happy with the extra show of affection because I soon find myself being ripped from Benny's arms and tucked firmly against Levi's hard chest.

"Come on, Benny." Luke slaps him on the back. "Let's leave these two lovebirds alone." He turns to us before he follows Benny out the door. "Don't take long, the pizza will be here any minute."

"Pizza?" I gaze curiously at Levi.

"We decided to have a party today," Levi says with a smile. "We've already got the beer, and Benny has more DVDs than he knows what to do with. All we needed was some pizza."

"A party," I say slowly. "For shaving my head."

"No," Levi retorts. "A party to celebrate your bravery."

"I like that." Pushing up on my toes, I fuse my mouth to Levi's in a sensual kiss. "I love you," I whisper, and his arms tighten around me. Waiting a couple of seconds, I give him the chance to say it back, but once again he doesn't. It's okay that he hasn't said it back, but I'll keep saying it to him anyway. In fact, he'll probably get sick of hearing it, because if there's one thing I've learned from this whole experience, it's that our time here on earth is limited so you have to tell people how you feel or you might never get the chance.

"Okay." I pull from Levi's warm embrace and clap my hands together with as much enthusiasm as I can muster. "Let's do this."

"You're so strong, baby." He picks up the clippers and I spin around to face the mirror. "Take your shirt off or you'll get hair everywhere." Stretching across the small space, Levi flicks the lock and I lift my shirt over my head then toss it to the floor. "Ready?"

I nod once and close my eyes as the soft buzz of the clippers gets closer to my head. At first contact, the vibrations tickle and I scrunch up my shoulders as Levi runs the shears over my scalp. I concentrate on breathing in and out, pretending that with each pass I'm letting go of my insecurities. It's cathartic really, and by the time Levi is done, my anxiety level is about as low as it can go.

Levi runs his knuckles down the back of my head and then twirls me around. His strong, warm hands cup my cheeks. "Open your eyes, beautiful girl." My heavy lids peel open and I come face to face with two deep pools of swirling water. He blinks twice, his eyes shining with a soft glow, and kisses me several times before whispering, "I'm so proud of you, Lane. So proud."

I reach up and grip his forearms in my hands. "You're amazing, you know that?"

"Not amazing," he counters, shaking his head. "Enamored. I'm in awe of your strength and perseverance. Not many women could do this with the grace that you have."

A quick laugh bursts out of me. "I wouldn't exactly call it grace. Did you see my meltdown earlier?"

"You had a moment," he shrugs, pulling my shirt over my head. "That's to be expected. It's the way you pulled yourself through and pushed on. You knew what had to be done and you accepted it, which is one of the many things I find so endearing about you. Now turn that gorgeous head of yours around and check out your new 'do."

Levi flicks the lock on the door and cracks it open, letting the boys know we're done. Slowly, I turn toward the mirror. I run my fingers along the top of my head, loving the way the peach fuzz feels against my skin. I'm aware that, in time, even the stubble will fall out, but for now, this isn't so bad. "What do you think?"

he asks.

My eyes snap to Levi's in the mirror. "I think you need to grow your hair back out."

He looks at me, brows bunched low and mouth tipped down. "Why's that?"

Turning back toward him, I rub my hand over his head. "You know how I feel about hair tugging," I say, waggling my eyebrows. "If you can't wrap your fist around mine when we make love, then I want to be able to grip yours."

Levi's face splits into a wide grin and I nip his bottom lip playfully. A loud groan comes from the hallway, and we both turn to see Luke walking away with his hands covering his ears.

"Good God," he yells. "Tits and hair pulling. Damn it, I do *not* need to hear this shit."

Levi smirks and I laugh as he wraps me in his arms. "Come on, let's go pick on your brother some more." He drops his hand to the small of my back and follows me into the kitchen, where we find Luke and Benny sitting at the table.

"Bald looks sexy on you, Lane," Benny says, earning himself a vicious growl from Levi and a slap against the back of the head from Luke. "What?" he asks innocently. "It's true. Not many women can pull off the bald look, but she can."

"Thank you," I answer, walking over to give him a kiss on the cheek. Luke kicks out a chair at the table for me and I sink into it, rubbing my hand across my face. My eyes land on the pile of bills in the center of the table, and I cringe at the thought of opening them. Screw it, I say to myself. A girl can only handle so much in one day—I think losing my hair is my limit for today. Bills can wait until tomorrow, especially since it's not like they're going anywhere.

There's a soft knock on the door. "I got it." Benny jumps up. "It's probably the pizza."

"Where on earth did you guys find a pizza joint that would deliver at ten a.m.?" I ask.

"Ask your boyfriend," Luke says, gesturing in Levi's direction. "He's the one that pulled it off."

"I called in a favor." Levi gives me a cheeky grin and plops down in Benny's vacant chair.

Faint bickering filters through the air. Levi gives Luke a knowing look as I stand from the table to go investigate. My feet don't even make it into the living room before I'm bombarded. "Mia," I gasp, catching her tiny frame in my arms. "Oh my God. Mia!" Her arms wrap around my neck tightly and she squeals, bouncing around on her toes.

"Holy shit, did I miss you," she says, pulling back to look at me. "You've lost weight." She yanks me back into her arms. "I'll fatten you up, I promise."

"What are you doing here?" I ask, gasping for air when she squeezes me too tight.

"Sorry," she giggles, untangling herself from me. "I couldn't do it. I couldn't be away from you when you were going through this, and I couldn't work for Daddy anymore. This is where I need to be."

"But Mia, what about—?" She waves a hand, cutting me off, and I know there's more to the story than what she's telling me. She gives a subtle shake of her head, which I recognize as the I'll-tell-you-later sign, and I nod my head to let her know the message was received. "I'm so glad you're home. I've missed you so much."

She squeezes my hand and offers me a soft smile. "Not near as much as I missed you, doll. Nice hair, by the way," she says, rubbing a hand over the top of my head. "All I did was think about you and worry about you. You were texting me so much right after I left, and then it started to die off and I couldn't help but worry."

"I'll take the blame for that one," Levi says, raising his hand in the air as he walks into the living room. He steps up to me and places his arm around my shoulders. "I've been occupying most of her free time." He offers Mia a cheeky grin and then winks at me.

"I know," Mia says, winking back. She pushes past the two of us and into the kitchen, and we follow behind her.

"She knows?" Levi whispers.

"Of course she knows," I whisper back. "She's my best friend. I tell her everything."

He stops walking and looks at me with his eyebrows raised. "Everything?"

"Not the juicy stuff, babe." I pat him on the back. "Don't worry, I only tell her enough to make her drool over you. The rest is between us."

"She drools over me?" His eyes twinkle—literally freaking twinkle—and I can't help but roll mine.

Chapter 23

Laney

SUMMER IS OFFICIALLY GONE AND in its place is the beauty of fall. Crisp red leaves are sprinkled across my yard, and I watch as a light breeze picks several of them up and tosses them around. I close my eyes, listening to the rustling sound, rocking back in my swing. It's the little things like this that I've been trying to absorb . . . to memorize. I've never been a morning person, but now I enjoy sitting on my porch and watching the sun rise. It's different each day, and I think that makes it even more exciting. You never know if you're going to get a bright orange glow highlighted with shades of red, or a pink sky sprinkled with purple clouds. But it doesn't matter which one you get; they're all beautiful because they all represent another day.

The front door creaks and I open my eyes to find Mia walking out, wrapped in a blanket, a cup of coffee clutched between her hands. Her hair is done and makeup is on, and she looks as gorgeous as ever. "What are you doing out here?" she asks, sitting down next to me, the tattered wood screeching with the weight of us both.

"Just thinking."

"About what?"

"Everything." I shrug, not wanting to burden her with the weight of my world. I feel like she gets the brunt of it as it is. She's been living with me since she officially moved to St. Louis a month ago, and although Levi is here the majority of the time, it's always when he's gone that I let myself break down. And unfortunately for Mia, she's usually the only one here.

Initially, she wanted to find her own apartment, but I asked her to stay because she's been my rock for so long and I feel like I need her close. It's been great having Levi around, but sometimes I just want Mia. She's been sleeping on the couch, and nights when Levi stays over she usually ends up sleeping on Benny's couch because she insists she can hear us 'bumping uglies,' as she puts it. Mia's had a hard time finding a job so she's been helping Benny with his small construction business by doing paperwork and ordering supplies. It isn't what she wants to do, but it's keeping her busy.

"Are you feeling okay?" she asks.

"As good as can be expected." I give her a sidelong glance and she sighs. That's the answer I give everyone these days because it's the easiest way to avert the question. As much as they all love me—and I know they do—I can't burden them with my endless amounts of fatigue and worry . . . and I worry a lot.

I've officially maxed out my credit cards paying off hospital bills. I met my deductible right after the surgery, but I still have to pay twenty percent of everything, and that adds up when 'everything' includes oncologists and chemotherapy. My checks from Flame provide enough to keep me afloat, but the anxiety of living paycheck to paycheck is starting to take its toll. Especially when you combine it with everything else I've got going on.

Levi is always the highlight of every day. His presence alone is usually enough to calm all of my fears. I have no doubt that he would help me out if I asked, but it isn't his place. It's my responsibility and I'll get through it, just like I get through everything else—one day at a time.

"I hate that answer." Mia looks away, taking a sip of her coffee. She blows across the top, and I watch as the steam rises and dissipates before she takes another sip.

"It's the only answer I've got."

She purses her lips. "So you say." We sit in the soft glow of the cool morning, neither of us saying a word, and for the first time in a long time, I feel peaceful. I've enjoyed having Mia around. Sometimes the triple dose of testosterone can get a little overwhelming, and she somehow manages to even it all out. "So," she says, breaking the silence. "Want me to go with you today?"

"You don't have to. I think Benny is supposed to come." I glance over at her, but her face is a blank mask. I have no idea what she's thinking. "I mean, you can if you want, but you don't have to."

"Why haven't you asked Levi to go?"

"I don't know," I say with a shrug. "I guess I just don't want him to see me like that."

"Like what?" she scoffs. "You're usually fine during your treatments, except for when they make you sick."

"I guess I just didn't want him to have to see me hooked up to the tubes. That part makes it more real, ya know?" Her face softens when she looks over at me and nods.

"Has he asked to come?"

"No," I sigh, tilting my head up to the sky. "And I figure if he isn't asking, then maybe there's a reason."

"Or maybe he's waiting for you to ask him. Maybe he's waiting for you to *need* him."

"Maybe." Digging my toes into the porch, I give us a push and the swing starts moving. "What are you up to today?" I ask, trying to avoid talking about this any further.

"I really need to go into Benny's office and work on his book-keeping. It's a fucking disaster." She rolls her eyes.

"How is working with Benny?"

"Okay, I guess." She takes another sip of her coffee and then sets the empty mug between us. "He's usually quiet and brooding, and when he does open his mouth, he somehow manages to piss me off."

I can't help but laugh. "What's he do to piss you off?"

"Oh, I don't know. He calls me *princess* for one, which he knows infuriates me. And he's always making little comments about how I look nice or that my hair looks pretty—"

"Wait," I interrupt, stopping the swing. "That's a bad thing, why?"

"Because, it confuses me," she huffs. "Ugh! I wasn't going to tell you, but right before I left to go back home, Benny kissed me."

"What!?" I screech as I fly out of the swing. "Are you serious? I can't believe you didn't tell me that!"

"It was nothing." Mia grabs my arm and yanks me back down. "Okay, well it was something . . . at least I thought it was. It was gentle and sweet, and I almost didn't leave because of it."

"But you did."

"But I did," she confirms. "He and I texted off and on while I was gone, but he was mostly keeping me up-to-date with you." She glances over and gives me an apologetic smile, and I roll my eyes. "So I mentioned to him that I wanted to move back, and I *may* have suggested that we pick back up where we left off . . . but he told me no."

"He told you *no?*" I ask incredulously. "What the hell?"

"Yeah, I have no idea. Of course, I was more than embarrassed and didn't talk to him again until the day I showed up at your door."

"Now that I think about it, you two have been acting sort of weird around each other. You're not near as friendly as you were before."

"Well, how the hell am I supposed to be friendly with him? Do you know how humiliating that was, to put myself out there like that and for him to just shut me down with absolutely no explanation at all?" Mia moans and drops her head to my shoulder.

"So why did you agree to work for him?" I ask, genuinely

curious.

"Because I'm an idiot. And even though I was embarrassed, I still enjoy being around the dumbass," she says with a slight shake of her head. "I usually just ignore him, which I think ticks him off, and every once in a while he'll shoot me a compliment, which he knows ticks *me* off. So it's become a mutual thing, us pushing each other's buttons."

"Interesting," I mumble.

"Okay." She slaps my leg and pushes up from the swing. "I better get going, and you should think about getting ready too. What time do you have to be there?"

"Nine." I follow her into the house with a yawn.

Mia walks into the living room and shrugs the blanket off her shoulders, letting it fall to the couch. She walks into the kitchen, drops her mug in the sink and then grabs her purse off the counter. "Call me if you need me, got it?"

"Got it," I respond with a mock salute. She rolls her eyes and smacks a kiss on my cheek before walking out the door. "Love you," she hollers over her shoulder.

"Love you too," I yell back, knowing she can't hear me because the door is already shut. I try to never let one of these amazing people walk out of a room without telling them how I feel. Luke and Mia always say it back, Benny responds with a grunt, and Levi . . . well, he usually gets this look on his face like I just leveled his entire world. I can tell he feels the same way, I just wish I knew why he hasn't said it back. 'In time,' Mia keeps telling me, and I know she's right. But when you tell someone over and over and over how much you love them and never hear the words back, that wears on a person.

I guess I can't complain too much because he always has some amazing words for me. He'll tell me that I'm his world and he can't imagine his life without me. And the other day after we made love, he told me that I meant everything to him. If that's the case and I mean everything to him, then he probably loves me, but I'm just aching to hear those three little words. I *need* to hear them.

A faint buzzing pulls me from my head. I dig my phone out of my pocket to see Benny's name lit up on the screen. Swiping the 'talk' button, I bring the phone up to my ear. "Good morning, sunshine."

"Don't ever call me that again."

"Oooh . . . Grouchy Benny. This should be fun," I quip, pulling a chair out from under the table and sitting down. "What's up?"

"I can't make it to your treatment today."

"Okay, did something come up?" I ask. It's not like Benny to cancel on me. Usually if something else comes up, he just cancels whatever it is since that's his way of 'showing support.' I don't mind that he can't come because, like I told Mia, I'm more than comfortable going on my own.

"Uh—" Benny's words cut off and his end of the phone becomes scratchy. I hear faint whispering, but I can't make out who he's talking to. "Yeah. Um . . . something came up. Look, I've got to run, but I'll check in later. Just call if you need me, okay?"

"Okay—" He hangs up before I even have a chance to respond, and I stare at my phone wondering what in the heck that was about. Tossing my cell on the table, I walk back to my room and get dressed, putting on nothing more than an old, ratty pair of sweat pants, a t-shirt and a light jacket. When you have to sit in those horribly bumpy chairs for hours on end, it's nice to at least be comfortable.

An hour later, I'm walking into the cancer treatment center and the secretary gives me a big wave. I've become a regular, yay for me! They all know me by name, and even though I hate coming in here, it's nice to see their friendly faces. You can tell they're all genuinely concerned about me because often times they'll come back to the treatment room to see how I'm doing. That alone is a nice feeling.

"How are you today, Laney?" Rose says from behind the counter.

"I'm good, Rose. How are the kiddos?" She hands me a clip-board, and I fill in my information like I do every other time I come in.

"They're rotten, like always." She takes my card and the clip-board and does whatever it is she does before returning my card. "Head on back to get your blood drawn, and then we'll get things started."

Getting my blood drawn is the easy part. Within minutes, I'm being escorted back into the waiting room.

"I'll let the girls know you're here and ready for them."

"Thank you, Rose." I tuck my purse under my arm and take a seat in the waiting room. Usually, there are all sorts of people in here and I look at them and wonder what they're here for, but today the waiting room is empty. I've talked to a few of the other patients from time to time, but I've yet to meet someone even close to my age.

"Laney." I look up when I hear the familiar voice and find Harley standing in the doorway. She has my chart in her hand and she's wearing a big, welcoming smile.

"Hey!" I walk over to her and she gives me a quick hug. "What are you doing down here?" I've only seen her here twice, and one of those times she'd just stopped by to check on me.

"I got pulled here, and when I saw your name on the schedule for today, I snagged you from another nurse," she says, leading me back in the direction of the exam rooms. "How have you been? And how is Levi?" She giggles. "I never see him anymore and I assume that's because of you."

"I've been alright, and yes, you're probably right," I laugh. "I'm not sure we've spent a night apart in the past month."

"That's good. You deserve to be happy." She opens the door to an exam room and ushers me in.

"Thank you. I feel like he's the one that deserves to be hap-py, and I just hope that all of this"—I motion to the sterile room around me—"isn't too much."

"It isn't." Her words are said easily and without any hesitation. "Trust me, Levi would speak up if it was."

"You're probably right," I agree, sitting down on the exam table.

"Okay, the doctor will be right in, and then I'll see you in the treatment room."

"Alright, see you soon." I pull my phone out of my purse and shoot Levi a quick text.

Me: Waiting for the doc. What are you doing?

It isn't at all surprising when my phone pings almost instantly. Levi is always quick to respond, especially when he knows I'm at the doctor.

Levi: Working. I hope it goes well. Who is there with you today?

Me: Don't work too hard. No one. Here by myself, but I brought Nate.

Levi: Another book boyfriend?

Me: LOL. You know me too well ;)

Levi: You read too much. I'm constantly competing with an alpha male that has perfect hair, a perfect body and a piercing in a place that I'll never get pierced.

Me: Never say never ;)

Levi: NEVER. Text me when you're done with the doc.

Me: Will do. Love you <3

I quickly tuck my phone back in my purse so I won't be disappointed when he doesn't respond. I picked the perfect time too, because Dr. Hopkins knocks twice and walks into the room. "Good morning, Laney." She gives me a tight hug and I return it effortlessly. The first time she hugged me, I was a little startled, but now I get it. My relationship with her is so much different than my relationship with my primary doctor—as it should be, since she's seeing me through what will most likely be the hardest time in my life.

"Good morning." I offer her an overly bright smile. She cocks an eyebrow and I wonder how in the world she always manages to see right through me.

"You've lost another five pounds." Her lips purse as she looks down at my chart and thumbs through a few pages. "And your counts are a little low."

"What does that mean?" I scoot forward on the table to try and peek at my chart, but it doesn't matter—I don't understand this stuff anyway.

"It's expected, because that's what chemo does, it kills off cells. But we pay particular attention to your white blood cells. Those are the ones that fight infection. If they drop too low, then I have to worry about you getting sick and we certainly don't want that." She keeps flipping through my chart and then looks up at me. "So you have a choice. Your numbers are low enough that I'm tempted to hold off on this treatment and hope they're up for the next one. But if you're feeling good and taking care of yourself, I wouldn't be opposed to moving forward with your treatment today."

"I've been doing well. My nausea isn't bad as long as I take the medicine, and even then it only lasts for a few days after the chemo. I will admit though that I'm finding myself getting weaker and more fatigued." My hands are clutched tightly in my lap, and I bite down on my bottom lip as I wait for her to respond.

"Chemotherapy is cumulative, so I expect your fatigue to get worse as your treatments progress. How have you been feeling otherwise?"

"Great." I shrug. "Well, as good as can be expected. I've actually felt really lucky that I haven't had more problems than I have."

She nods her head in agreement. "You have been lucky. Your body has been tolerating your treatments well." Dr. Hopkins closes my chart and sets it on the counter then turns back to me. "Okay, let's go ahead with your treatment today, as long as you promise to call me if you start to feel sick at all . . . and by sick, I mean a cough, runny nose, earache, fever, anything."

"Of course. I'll call right away."

"Okay then. Let's get you started." Dr. Hopkins opens the

door for me and follows me out, stopping at the nurses' station to hand them my chart. "I want you to come in next week and get your blood drawn, just so I can keep an eye on it, if that's okay."

"Absolutely. I'll schedule it on my way out." She pats me on the back and I head over to the treatment room. This entire process has become routine for me.

"Good morning, Laney." I smile at Jamie, and she waves and smiles back. Jamie is one of my favorite nurses, probably because, like Harley, she's the same age I am and therefore I can relate to her a little bit better.

"Mornin,' Jamie."

"Harley stole you from me today," she calls from across the room.

"I heard," I laugh, taking my usual seat in the back corner of the large room away from all the other patients. I'm not sure why I chose this spot. Maybe because it's tucked against a wall, or because it's the place I sat on my first day in this room. But it's become a source of control. I can't control what they put into my body and I can't control how my body reacts, but I sure as heck can control where I sit my tushy!

Harley scoots toward me on her seat and positions herself in front of me with her IV cart. "Ready?"

"As I'll ever be." Like every other time, I offer up my left hand and she starts my IV, then flushes it before hooking me up to my chemo.

"Alright, Laney. You're going." She pats my hand gently and packs up her IV cart. "Let me know if you need something, and I'll be by to check on you in a few."

"Perfect. Thank you, Harley." Reaching along the side of my chair, I pull my Kindle out of my purse and power it on, letting the words of the story carry me away. There is absolutely nothing better than getting wrapped up in a fictional world. It's an outlet, a way to forget about your own life and your own problems, and it's been a great means of escape these past few months.

"Laney?"

My head snaps up when Harley says my name. I take a quick glance at my watch, surprised to see her checking on me so soon. "What's up?"

Her green eyes are sparkling and her smile is so big that it's almost blinding. "Your visitor is here."

My brows furrow and lips purse, and I shake my head. "I don't have a visitor today," I say slowly.

"Yes, you do." She winks and then moves out of the way. My eyes instantly find Levi standing in the doorway. He looks absolutely gorgeous, and the sight of him alone brings tears to my eyes. My bottom lip trembles and I bite the inside of my cheek, determined to keep from crying. Levi's face is a blank canvas as he walks toward me, his eyes bouncing from my face to the bags of liquid to the IV in my hand, then back to me. I can't read him at all. There is nothing more that I want than to be able to know what he's thinking . . . what he's feeling.

"Hey." His hoarse voice makes my heart rate spike and I take a slow, deep breath.

"Hey," I sigh, shifting in my chair. "What are you doing here?"

Harley pushes a chair toward Levi and he grabs it, putting it as close to mine as he can get without disturbing the IV pole, and sits down. He reaches his hand out, lacing his fingers with mine, and I close my eyes, relieved that he's here. I knew I needed him here and I was a stubborn fool for not asking him to come.

"Laney, open your eyes." I peek up at him under my non-existent lashes and he cocks his head to the side. "That's a silly question, Lane. I'm here for *you.*" He leans forward, dropping a sweet kiss on my mouth. "I'm always here for you. I want to be here for you; you just have to let me."

Tears drip out of the corner of my eyes and Levi catches them with his thumb. "I do want you here. I just . . ." I look away and blink several times, trying to collect my thoughts, and Levi grips my chin to pull my face back to his.

"You just what?"

"I just didn't want to make things harder on you than I already have." His brows dip low and his lips thin into a flat line. "You already help me with so much, and I just—" I glance away, swallowing hard before looking back at him. "I guess I didn't want you to see me like this."

Levi runs his free hand down his face. "See you like this," he says, shaking his head. "Laney, that's not what it's about. It's about me *needing* to be here, me *wanting* to be here. Every single time that you've come, I've wanted to be here, and it has killed me to hear about Luke or Benny or Mia getting to sit with you."

"Why didn't you say anything?" My voice cracks and I squeeze his hand.

"I wanted *you* to want me here, Lane. I wanted *you* to ask me to come because you need me to be here as much as I need to be here."

"I'm sorry," I cry, wiping furiously at the tears that are once again tracking down my face. I yank him to me so I can bury my face in his chest. "I'm so sorry. I wanted you here so bad."

"Shhhh." He strokes a hand down the back of my head several times before dropping it to my back. "It's okay," he croons. "I'm not mad, but I couldn't stand the thought of going another day. So I texted Mia this morning and told her whoever was scheduled needed to come up with a reason to stay home, because I was going to be the one sitting with you from now on." I nod my head against his chest, still too caught up in my emotions to say anything.

"If this is too much . . . if it's *ever* too much—"

"You're my salvation, Laney, my miracle," he interrupts gently. "I told you I was doing this with you, and I meant it. If you cry, *I cry*. If you break, *I break*."

"If I die?" I whisper breathlessly.

"Then you'll take me with you because you've ruined me, Laney. I'm no good for anyone else because you *own* me. So if you go, I go." I know he's only speaking figuratively. Levi would never do anything to hurt himself, but it both breaks and warms my heart to know that he's going through this with me.

"But you're not going to die. You're going to survive this, because you're a fighter and that's what fighters do—they survive. Plus, you're too darn stubborn and I know that you won't let this take you down."

"I love you so much, Levi." I fist his shirt, anchoring myself to the one person that I need more than anyone else in this entire world. "I feel like the words aren't even enough . . . that they don't do justice to what I feel for you." Tears are still running down my face, but we've both stopped trying to catch them—there's just no use. At least they're happy tears, and right now, that's what matters. "I don't ever want to lose you," I stress, pulling him in as close as he can get. His hand wraps around the back of my head and he places three slow, chaste kisses to my lips before pulling back.

"You don't even have to worry about that. You're stuck with me, babe." He kisses me once more before sitting back in his seat. Then he links his hand with mine and looks up at the IV pole. "So, this is it? This is chemotherapy, huh?"

"Yup. Real exciting, isn't it?"

"And what do you do, just sit here and wait for it all to drip in?" he asks, looking around the room at everyone else who is hooked up as well.

"Pretty much. When that bag is empty," I say, pointing to the IV pole, "she comes over and pushes another drug straight into my IV . . . that's the one that usually makes me a little sick. And then I have one smaller bag and I'll be done."

"Wow, that sounds like a lot." His face looks strained and I'm sure that for someone who has never seen it or known someone with cancer, this is probably a lot to take in.

"It's not too bad." I give his hand a gentle squeeze. "It'll be much better for me since you're here."

His eyes soften and a smile tilts the side of his mouth. "Oh yeah?"

"Yeah," I reply.

And it was better—much better. Not to mention different than when one of the three stooges comes with me. Levi sat by my side the entire time, only getting up once to go to the bathroom. Harley talked to us a few times as she changed out my bags. I heard him whisper to her that he had a 'keeper' and that made me smile, even though I'm sure it wasn't meant for my ears.

As always, the second medication made me a little sick, but Harley quickly counteracted it with an anti-nausea medication. I could tell that made Levi a little uncomfortable. As soon as I started heaving, he was all over me, asking if I was okay and wondering what he could do. When I glanced at him, he looked so helpless and it literally split my heart in two to see that look on his face. I could tell he wanted to take all of this away for me, but unfortunately that isn't an option. So I did the only thing I could do—I told him I'd be fine and that this always happens . . . that he was doing exactly what I needed by being here with me.

By the end of the treatment, I think Levi was just as exhausted as I was. It took a toll on him in ways that I'll probably never understand. I've tried several times to look at the situation through the eyes of my loved ones, but I can't . . . it's just different. I know that if the roles were reversed, it would be incredibly hard and I would be devastated. But right now, I can't fully grasp the depth of what they're feeling.

Even after we finished at the treatment center, Levi didn't leave my side for the rest of the afternoon. He cooked me dinner, washed the dishes and then tucked me in bed, where he climbed right in behind me without saying a word. It was the first time in I-don't-know-how-many days that I fell asleep without worrying or crying. Being wrapped up in Levi's arms was so incredibly peaceful, and it was right then that I knew something without a shadow of a doubt. If I didn't make it through this—if this horrible disease did take me away from this wonderful man—then I would at least die happy.

Chapter 24

Laney

"WHAT THE HELL?" LUKE GROWLS when Levi saunters down the hall in nothing but a faded pair of his favorite blue jeans. "Did you stay the night again?"

"Luke," I scold, giving him my best stink eye. My lungs tighten and I cough several times, covering my mouth with my arm.

"You okay?" Luke's face instantly transforms from annoyance to concern, and I wave him off.

"I'm fine."

"They're horny humpers," Mia chimes in. I slap her on the arm and she giggles. "What?" she asks innocently. "It's true. Why do you think I've been sleeping on Benny's couch the past several weeks?"

"And you fucking snore. God, do you snore." Mia shoots Benny a death glare and he shrugs. "You do. It's very unladylike, Princess," he says. Mia rolls her eyes and pours herself a cup of coffee. Levi bends down and kisses my nose before walking over to make himself a cup.

My life feels so full right now. The four most important people in my world are all packed into a tiny kitchen, and despite the words that are being thrown around, I can feel the love. It's a feeling I wish I could bottle up and store on a shelf for a rainy day.

Levi brings his cup and sits down next to me. His hand finds my thigh under the table and he rubs it gently several times before settling it above my knee. I look over at him, smiling from behind my mug, and he winks. Luke makes a gagging noise, and I nearly spit my coffee across the table at his childish reaction. But it's all fun and games—I know he's happy for me and that he completely approves of Levi.

I feel like life has been flying by at warp speed ever since the day Levi showed up at my chemotherapy treatment. I've been working a ton, Levi and I have been volunteering regularly at the Senior Center, and there are some days that I feel like I barely have time to think, let alone remember what I'm going through.

Levi even managed to check another thing off my bucket list. He said he's not happy about it now that he knows the meaning behind it, but he's promised to keep working on it anyway.

"Bring a towel," he whispers into the phone and I smile, wondering who is standing near him that he feels like he has to whisper.

"Why do I need a towel?"

"Why do you have to ask so many damn questions?" he fires back, causing me to laugh.

"Fine, I'll bring a towel," I submit, knowing it'll be easier that way.

"Good girl," he answers. "I'll see you in an hour." Levi shows up fifteen minutes early, and I run out of my front door when I see his truck pull into the driveway. He hops out to open my door for me and swats me on the ass as he hoists me into my seat.

"Where are we going?"

"You have to wait and see," he says with a smirk, shutting my door and jogging around the front of the truck to climb in the driver's seat.

Twenty minutes later, we pull up to the old rock quarry where we used to go swimming after football games. "Levi?" He looks over at me, a shit-eating grin splitting his face. "What are we doing here?"

"Don't you trust me, Laney?" He hops out of the truck and comes around to open my door. When my feet are planted firmly on the ground, he reaches for the bottom of my Henley and pulls it over my head.

"Levi!" I shout, trying to wiggle my shirt back on. "What the heck are you doing?" Frantically, I look around to see if anyone is watching, which is stupid because we are literally in the middle of nowhere.

"Get naked, Laney." His demanding voice sends shivers up my spine, but I stand tall, determined to fight him on this.

"I will not get naked. It's freaking cold out here. If you want to have sex, we can do it in your truck." I cross my arms over my chest, covering up my white bra because I'm certain that my nipple is standing at attention.

"It's sixty degrees and you'll be fine . . . a little cold water won't hurt you."

"Cold water?" I screech, backing away from him. "You are out of your mind if you think I'm stepping foot in that quarry."

"Laney Jacobs, you have ten seconds to get naked or—so help me God—I will throw you in that water myself." He's not joking. I can tell by the look on his face, but I still jut out my chin and straighten my spine. There is no way I'm dipping any part of my body in there.

"One." He leans up against his truck and watches me, but I don't move. "Two." He cocks an eyebrow, and I fail miserably when I attempt to cock one back. "Three." I move slowly around the other side of his truck, but he sticks his hand in his pocket and clicks the automatic lock button, thwarting my attempt to seek shelter.

"Shit," I hiss.

"Four." Levi walks toward me, stopping when we're toe to toe. His fingers land on the button of my jeans and he pops it

*open, then lowers the zipper. "Five." His blue eyes are smolder-
ing.*

*"I am not taking my pants off." My hands disobey my words
because I push my jeans over my hips and let them pool on the
ground below. Levi's eyes flash with desire as he takes in my
white lace panties. I take several steps backward.*

*"Six." He stalks toward me, nudging me toward the water. I
kick off my shoes and rip off my socks. "Seven."*

*"Damn it, Levi. Stop counting. This isn't funny." My feet hit
the edge of the water and I squeal at how cold it is. "It's freezing
in there, Levi. You're nuts if you think—"*

*"Eight." He grips the collar of his shirt, lifting it over his
head. My eyes land on his toned stomach and my mouth instantly
waters. His fingers slide open the button of his pants then lower
his zipper before he slips out of his jeans, kicking them to the
side. I grumble, but tuck my thumbs into the sides of my panties
and shove them down my legs. Levi's eyes rake hungrily over my
nearly naked body and he bites on his lower lip, sucking it into
his mouth. I want to suck on that lip.*

*"Nine," he growls, sliding his boxers off. His thick cock
springs free and I squeeze my thighs together to suppress the
growing need that it is settling between my legs. I flick the front
clasp of my bra and let it fall to the ground with a quiet thud.
When Levi says "ten," I squeal and take off running in the opposite direction.*

"What are you thinking about?" Levi's hot breath against my
ear startles me and I jump, my hand flying to my chest.

"Crap. You scared me."

"Please tell me you were thinking about the same thing I was,"
he whispers, his teeth nipping my earlobe before he pulls back.

"I was thinking about the rock quarry," I whisper back. His
eyes sparkle with mischief and he cocks a brow. I smile at the
cute look on his face and watch his eyes widen with desire as his
mind drifts, presumably to the night in question.

"What were *you* thinking about?" I ask, poking a finger into his side. He grabs my hand and brings it to his mouth, nipping at the end of my finger.

"Last night."

"Fucking hell!" Luke's chair screeches against the tile, nearly toppling over, when he pushes out of it. "Add this to the category of things that I do not want to know, see or hear." He stalks out of the room and Mia clears her throat.

"Well, I don't know about you," she says, nudging Benny in the arm, "but I found it kind of hot."

"Wanna go to the rock quarry?" Benny asks with a smirk. Her jaw drops and she looks at me with a see-this-is-what-I-was-telling-you-about look. Then she turns to Benny, her shoulders back and spine straight.

"Not a chance in hell." Mia spins around quickly, flicking her hair over her shoulder, and follows in the direction Luke just left.

"That woman is more stubborn than a damn mule." Benny shakes his head and trails after Mia.

"What's going on between those two?" Levi asks, picking me up and settling me on his lap.

"I think they're throwing rocks." I giggle when Levi brings his lips to my neck and sucks at the soft spot under my ear.

"Throwing rocks?" he asks, looking up at me in confusion.

"Yeah. You know when you're in elementary school and you pick on the kid you have a crush on," I clarify, lifting my chin and tapping a finger to my neck, gesturing for him to put his mouth back on me.

"Gotcha." His soft lips sprinkle kisses up my neck, across my jaw and land firmly on my mouth. His tongue pushes between my lips for a searing kiss, and when he pulls back, my mouth follows his, begging for more. "Meet me at Blue in one hour." Levi lifts me off his lap, sits me in the chair and takes off down the hall.

"What? No." I scurry after him. "It's my day off. I don't want to go in on my day off." By the time I make it to my room, Levi has already pulled his shirt on and is tying his shoes.

"Okay. I guess you misunderstood because I wasn't *asking* you to meet me there, I was *telling* you."

I huff, my hands planted firmly on my hips. "You know your alpha tendencies aren't nearly as cute as they used to be."

Levi lets out a throaty laugh and then stands up, grips the back of my head and pulls me in for one last kiss.

"You love it, babe. I guarantee that if I dip my fingers into your panties, you'd be fucking soaked." He ends that declaration with a swat on the butt and then he's out the door. I fall back onto the bed just as Mia comes barreling into the room. She plops down next to me and stretches her arms above her.

"What are you doing today?" she asks.

"Well, according to Levi, I'm going to Blue." My chest heaves on the last word and I break into a coughing fit. When I stop coughing, I roll my head in Mia's direction to find her staring at me.

"What's with the cough?"

"Nothing. It's just a tickle in my throat. I'll be fine, keep going." She purses her lips at me but I raise my eyebrows, urging her to continue. She sighs and grins.

"You and Levi are so damn cute together." Her smile fades, and she looks at me with a longing in her eyes that I've never seen before. "I'm a little jealous. I want what you have."

"You'll get there, Mia." My hand wraps around hers and she laces our fingers together.

"I hope you're right." A soft smile plays at her lips. "I want a family. I want babies." Mia looks back over at me. "Don't you want babies?"

"Of course I do. And you will have babies, Mia. They'll be perfect and beautiful, just like their mama." I smack a kiss on her cheek and push up from the bed as Mia props herself up on her elbows. "Now, as much as I'd like to sit here and talk babies, I've got to get cleaned up or I'll never make it to Blue on time. And you know how Levi is about punctuality."

"By all means"—she waves a hand in the air—"go clean your

dirty self." I pull my t-shirt off and fling it at Mia, smacking her in the face. "Take it all off!" she calls after me, and I laugh all the way to the bathroom.

Forty-five minutes later, I'm pulling up to Blue to find that the parking lot is surprisingly empty. There are several vehicles in front of Flame, but not a single car in front of Blue. Glancing down at my watch, I look at the time. Noon. Hmmm . . . that's odd. *What in the world is Levi up to?*

Throwing my car in park, I open the door and slide out. When I get to the entrance, I push the door but it doesn't budge. *Weird.* Pulling my phone out of my purse, I shoot Levi a quick text.

Me: you have ten seconds to open this door or I'm breaking in ;)

I mentally count to seven when the door flies open and a strong arm shoots out, hooking around my waist and hauling me inside. Levi gathers me in close. "I missed you." He nudges my head to the side and his lips descend on my neck as he walks us backward. He's nipping and sucking, and it's driving me absolutely wild. My back bumps into the bar and Levi's fingers find the button of my pants. Before I'm able to comprehend what he's doing, he's divested me of both my jeans and panties.

"Levi—"

"No one's here, babe." He grips my hips firmly and hoists me up onto the cool wood. He plants his ass firmly on a stool, putting himself at eye level with my lady parts. I can't find it in me to be uncomfortable because the look on Levi's face is turning me inside out. His lips are parted, eyes clouded, and when I spread my legs, he sucks in a sharp breath through his gritted teeth. His large hands make their way up my thighs, and just when they get to where I want them most, he stops and turns his face up to mine. "Take your shirt off."

Holy shit. The intensity of his voice leaves me no option but to submit and obey . . . which I do. One by one, my fingers unbutton my blouse, and Levi's eyes swirl with lust as the front of my body becomes exposed. I shrug my shoulders and the flimsy material pools around my bottom on the bar. Then my fingers move to the clasp of my bra, and with my eyes locked firmly on his, I flick it open and toss it to the side. My body is now on full display and I'm finding it extremely erotic that Levi is still fully dressed. His hands slide under my thighs and he tugs me forward until my butt is nearly hanging off the edge of the bar. His fingers skate down my calves and then he props each foot on a barstool on either side of him.

"Gorgeous." His rough voice glides over my skin, infusing me with a need that I didn't even know existed. My body is humming with desire, and if he doesn't touch me soon, I may actually combust. Callused hands slowly make their way up my thighs, and when two fingers thrust inside of me, my head drops back between my shoulders, a soft moan falling from my lips. "Look at me, Laney." My head is heavy, but I manage to lift it. His fingers are pumping inside of me and with each pass he twists them, causing me to jerk off the bar. "How many men have you been with, Laney?"

"Wh-what?" I stammer, too engrossed in what his magical fingers are doing to my body to actually have a conversation.

"I asked how many men you've been with." The pads of his fingers hit a swollen spot deep inside of me and my eyes drift shut.

"Oh, God." Small bolts of electricity start sparking low in my spine when his thumb hits my clit. "Levi—" His name is an urgent plea, and just when his fingers should once again plunge inside of me, he completely removes his hands and my eyes jolt open. My chest is heaving and I lick a slow path along my bottom lip. "What's wrong?" I pant, tempted to put my foot down and demand that he give me back his fingers.

"I asked you a question. I expect an answer." His voice is

steady and strong, but I can see the uncertainty floating in his eyes. Whatever the question was, my answer matters.

"What was the question?" I ask, slightly out of breath.

"How many men have you been with?" His jaw clenches, his eyes bouncing between mine. I've been waiting for him to ask me this—or more importantly, I've been waiting to give him this answer.

"I've only been with one man," I state with a smile. His eyes light up and he tilts his head to the side.

"You've only been with one man since me? Wow." He rubs a hand over his shaven head.

"No," I correct him, shaking my head. "I've only been with one man . . . *ever*."

Chapter 25

Laney

"WHAT?" HE STANDS UP BETWEEN my legs and places a hand on each side of my neck. "You haven't been with another man . . . ever?" I wish he didn't sound so shocked. If I could somehow show him my soul and the imprint that he's made on it, then maybe he would understand why. I shake my head and he takes a deep breath, blowing it out, nice and slow.

"Just me," he clarifies. "You've only been with me?" The look of hope and longing in his eyes is almost too much to handle. I nod my head and Levi tugs my face in close to his and drops his forehead to mine. His thumbs glide along my jaw, and he's holding me and looking at me like I'm a fragile doll. The moment is intimate so I don't move because I'm trying memorize every last touch and sound and smell and—

"I love you, Laney," he chokes out, completely catching me by surprise.

"What?" I gasp, fisting my hand in the front of his shirt. A pained look overcomes his face and his lips find mine. This kiss isn't heated and passionate, and it isn't sweet and innocent. It's the kiss of a man and woman who are vowing to love each other; it's the kiss of two souls who have come together after a lifetime of searching. It's a kiss to end all other kisses.

Levi's lips are molded to mine, our tongues sliding and twirling and tasting, and tears are falling from my eyes at a rapid pace. "I love you so much," he mumbles in between kisses. His words are infused with passion, and I feel like my heart literally just lifted from my chest and laid itself in his lap. It may as well have because he owns it.

"I'm so sorry I didn't say it sooner, baby. Trust me, I wanted to." My hands grip his wrists on either side of my head and I give him a watery smile. "It has killed me to not say it back to you. Every time you said it and I made myself keep quiet, I was ripping my own heart out, and every time your face dropped when I didn't return the words, I knew I was slowly tearing you up inside. I didn't want you to think I was saying it because of the cancer or the chemo, because that doesn't even factor in. When I finally said it, I wanted you to know that I was saying it because I fell in love with you all over again. Every day I want you to know how much I love you. I don't want you to ever walk away from me or hang up the phone and think that I don't love you just as much—if not more—than you love me, because I do. You're my heart, Laney."

His words are like a soothing balm to my aching chest and warmth settles throughout my body. "I love you, too—so much. And please don't be sorry," I tell him as his hand darts out, wiping away my tears. "I knew you loved me. Even without the words, I knew it. I saw it every time you looked at me and felt it every time you touched me. There wasn't a doubt in my mind that you felt the same way, but it's still really great to finally hear." My lips meet his. "Say it again," I whisper, then bury my face into the side of his neck. His arms circle around me and he rubs a hand down my head.

"I love you." He kisses my temple. "I love you so much." He kisses my other temple. "I love you more." His fingers lift my face and he kisses my nose. "I love you always." He kisses my lips, and this time it's ravenous and full of possession. This time his mouth dominates mine, his tongue pushing and demanding. My hands make their way to his hair, and he swallows my growl when I realize there is no hair for me to grip.

"I need you, Levi." My voice is gravelly and sounds foreign to my own ears. He moves to unbutton his shirt and I stop his movements. "What are you doing?"

"I'm going to get naked and make love to you."

"No," I state firmly, cocking my head. "You're going to leave your clothes on and start where you left off."

"But I wasn't going to make love to you, Laney," he says with a touch of regret. "I was going to fuck you." My eyes light up and he laughs, seemingly dumbfounded by my reaction. "I'm not sure I can, baby. The moment shifted and I feel bad fucking you after I just told you I love you." Okay . . . well, that was sweet of him to say, but right now I need him to get over it and claim me.

"And I love you for that. But in my eyes, we've been making love every night, and right now I want you to—" My words drift off because I'm not a fan of the word, but it seems to be the only word that will fit. Levi laughs because he understands my hesitation.

"Fuck. You want me to fuck you." I smile and nod, and I'm sure I look like a darn bobble head, but I don't care. This is my man, and I want him. "Laney—"

Desperate times call for desperate measures. His words cut off when I plunge my hand between my legs, and he watches with rapt attention as my fingers swirl around my clit before diving inside. My eyes close and my head drifts back, and within seconds my hand is ripped from between my legs and replaced by Levi's hot mouth.

With his face buried between my legs, his tongue swirls and lips suck while his fingers torment me with their movements. My body is already strung so tight from earlier that it only takes him minutes before he has me spiraling off into the abyss. He nips the inside of my thigh, causing me to squirm, and then he lifts his face. His mouth is glistening, and all I can manage is a lazy smile because my bones have turned to liquid and my body is incapable of any other movements.

My legs are dangling as Levi steps back. Under lowered lashes, he watches me as his fingers swiftly unbutton his shirt. It falls behind him in a heap on the floor.

"Finish it," he demands, fighting back a smile.

"Finish what? You're doing a pretty good job as it is."

"Finish undressing me."

"Say please," I say in a sing-song voice. Levi furrows his brow as though he's thinking about his answer.

"Not gonna happen. Get down here and undress me."

"My pleasure," I giggle, hopping off the bar, not caring at all that he didn't use the magic word. I love this controlling side of Levi because I also know the softer side of him, and I know that he would never disrespect or debase me in any way.

Levi toes off his socks and shoes, pulls a condom out of his pocket and then I make quick work of removing his pants. When they tumble to the floor, his thick cock bobs heavily in front of me. "Since when do you go commando?"

"Since you. Get in the cage, Laney." His words stop me cold and I peek over his shoulder. The steel cage that normally hangs from the ceiling is sitting in the middle of the floor. *How did I not notice that earlier?*

My heart swells when I realize what he's doing, and I love him that much more for it. Without hesitation, I follow his command and make my way toward the cage. The heavy door is open and I step inside, instantly feeling like I've stepped into some sort of burlesque show.

My gaze roams the cage. There is nothing but steel bars and a red leather bench against the backside. Sexy. That's the only word that fits this cage . . . it looks sexy, and it makes me feel sexy.

Reaching out, I glide my fingers across the cool metal bars then grip the one above my head and arch my back. Levi's gaze rakes over the length of my body and he stalks toward me. "I want to tie you up in here."

"Okay," I reply, giving him a sensual smile. The thought of being tied up does nothing but turn me on more, if that's even possible.

"But not tonight. Tonight it's just us and this cage." He swallows hard. "Turn around, Laney." My body follows his command without question, and his chest presses into my back. His hands find mine and he guides my fingers to the bars in front of me. "Don't let go." I nod, the anticipation building so thick in my throat that I'm completely unable to speak. My heart is racing, but it's the kind of racing that makes me feel alive. "I don't care what happens," he says at the same time I hear the condom wrapper tear open. "You don't let go."

"I won't let go." My words come out scratchy from my dry throat, and I turn my face into my arm and cough several times before righting myself.

Levi kisses my shoulder. "Are you okay?"

"Better than ever." And isn't that the truth. It doesn't matter that toxic chemicals are swimming through my veins, or that I could have cells inside of my body trying to destroy everything that I am. All that matters is what's happening right here and right now, and that I know this man will own every part of me through this life and well into the next.

Levi is hot and throbbing against my lower back and I push against him, encouraging him to take me. But this is Levi, and we always do things in his way and in his time. His hands travel softly and slowly down both of my arms, skimming past the sides of my chest. His left hand grazes my left breast and I close my eyes, enjoying the sweet caress. Strong fingers wrap around the left side of my waist while his right hand travels down the outside of my thigh then makes its way up the inside. His long fingers stop to tease my entrance before they plunge inside of me.

"I love that you're always ready for me, Laney. It's fucking hot, knowing that I do this to you." My head drops forward as I suck in a breath, trying desperately to slow my body down, because if he keeps saying the things he's saying, I'm going to explode way too soon. "I want you, Laney. So fucking bad." Levi's fingers twist, rubbing the swollen spot that is sure to make me squirm.

"Oh God," I grunt, my eyes rolling back into my head. My hands want nothing more than to reach behind me and touch Levi, but I'm afraid that if I move, he'll stop—and I do *not* want him to stop. My body writhes against his. "Now, Levi," I pant, needing him inside of me.

A low rumble emanates from his throat as he removes his fingers and guides himself to my entrance. My body acts on its own accord as I thrust my hips back at the same time he slams into me, burying himself to the hilt.

"Fuck," he grunts, holding my hips still. My hands are gripped tightly around the bars, my knuckles turning white, and I use the grip for leverage. His body starts moving, pounding into me, and with each thrust he burrows himself deeper and deeper. I prop my foot up on the bench, opening myself up to him, and with one hand on my hip, he slides the other around to the front, rubbing tight circles around my clit. My breath hitches, and each time he slams into me, my body catapults closer to the edge. Levi wraps his hand around the front of my neck, cradling my chin in his fingers and tilting my head up. My neck and back are stretched about as far as they can go, but I don't fight it because I feel sexier now than I've ever felt in my entire life.

I hum low in my throat as Levi trails hot, wet kisses down the back of my neck, and I shiver when he blows over the damp skin. My body clenches, squeezing him tight, and he lets out a string of unintelligible words. My head drops back to his shoulder and his hand finds my breast, his fingers twisting and pinching my aching nipple. My lips part and I beg to let go of the cage, but Levi's answer is a firm slap to the ass that does nothing but ignite the fire that's already smoldering inside of me. My body tenses against his and when he spanks me again, that fire turns into a blazing inferno. His thrusts continue as my body quivers and jerks around his. His cock slides in and out of me, and I swear I can feel every single inch of him. "Levi." His name is nothing more than a hoarse plea.

"Hold on, baby. I've got you." A strong arm wraps around my stomach, holding me up. My legs are heavy and feel like limp noodles, and I'm certain that if Levi lets go of me, I'll fall flat on my ass. Within seconds, Levi is groaning out his own release. His body goes slack against mine, and I release my grip on the cage, draping my arms around the back of his neck. He nuzzles his face into me, peppering kisses anywhere he can get his mouth. "You mean everything to me, Lane," he murmurs. "I don't ever want to lose you."

Moving forward, I dislodge Levi from my body, instantly missing the feel of him inside of me. But right now, this is more important. Turning in his arms, I hold him close. "You're never going to lose me, Levi," I whisper. "Never. Do you hear me?"

His arms lock around my back, and the only response I receive is a trembling nod into the side of my neck. It's the only response I need because some moments are simply too big for words, and this is one of them.

Chapter 26

Levi

TWO HOURS AND FORTY-FIVE MINUTES . . . that's how long I've been watching her sleep. I'm worried sick about her, but she keeps playing it off, saying that she's okay. Laney has been coughing for the last three weeks. She's even missed several days of work, and despite the over-the-counter medications, she isn't getting any better. Her cough started out light and she said it was just a tickle, but I've noticed that it's progressively gotten worse.

Her coughing fit at four o'clock this morning startled the shit out of me. Surprisingly, it didn't wake her up, but I watched as her body curled in on itself, her lungs sputtering with hacks and wheezes. Thankfully, it only lasted a couple of minutes because I was seconds away from waking her. I hated to do that though, since she hasn't been sleeping well as it is and I knew that if I woke her up, she wouldn't fall back asleep.

So here I am, watching her like some sort of lunatic stalker because I'm nervous and I need to reassure myself that she's okay . . . that she's still here. My phone buzzes on the nightstand and I grab it, wondering who in their right mind would be calling me at nearly seven o'clock in the morning. Mason's name lights up my screen and almost instantly my heart starts pounding inside my chest. Mason doesn't get up this early—let alone call me this early—so I answer it, knowing that something must be wrong. "What's up, Mase?" As quietly as possible, I slip from the bed and walk into the kitchen, not wanting to disturb Laney.

"Brady called. Everything's a go." A rush of air pushes from my lungs and a stupid-ass smile overtakes my face.

"I seriously thought you were calling to tell me something bad happened, bro." I spin around in a circle, running my hand over the top of my head, anxiously wanting to tell someone the good news. With everything that's been going on, I forgot that Mason had called Brady and Mark to accept their offer to invest.

"I'm calling early because we have to head to Nashville to sign the contracts and okay the building they selected. We need to leave tomorrow."

"I can't, Mason. I can't go tomorrow." My mind starts racing as I think of everything I have to do, the most important of which is going with Laney to her chemo treatment tomorrow.

"Why the fuck not?" he growls.

"Laney has chemo tomorrow. I have to be there, Mase. Can we go on Saturday?" I ask hopefully, cringing when a string of profanity flies from Mason's mouth. Several weeks ago, Laney and I sat down over dinner and told my brother about her cancer. It was a hard conversation to have, and not just because of the subject matter. Mason and Laney have always been close. She's like a sister to him, and it tore him apart to hear what she's been going through. Since that night, he's been incredibly supportive of the both of us, covering for me when I've needed to be with her and understanding when she needs extra time off of work.

"Levi, listen." A deep sigh passes through the phone and I plop down in a chair, my head landing in my hand. "I know how important it is for you to be there with Laney, but this is important too. This is *our dream*, Levi. Two days . . . we'll be gone *two* days. Can't Luke or Mia go just this once?"

Sitting up, I run a hand along the back of my neck as my eyes fall on a pile of envelopes stacked on the table. I know it's none of my damn business, but I slide them toward me and pull out the papers inside, one by one. Doctor bill . . . doctor bill . . . overdue utility bill . . . doctor bill . . . credit card bill.

"Fuck," I growl, slamming my hand down on the table.

"Jesus Christ, bro. If it's that big of a deal, I'll call them back and—"

"No," I bark into the phone. "It's not that. Listen, can I call you right back?"

"Yeah, sure," Mason sighs then hangs up. I immediately pull up the calculator on my phone and start adding up what Laney owes. As the number gets higher, so does my blood pressure, and by the time I'm done, I'm absolutely fuming.

"*Twelve thousand dollars*," I murmur, and these are only the bills sitting in front of me. I can't imagine what others she might have floating around that I haven't seen yet. My heart clenches in my chest at the thought of Laney struggling financially. She's already been through so much, and on top of it she has to worry about these damn bills.

I toss the envelopes back on the table and tilt my head up to the ceiling, thinking about how I can help without pissing her off. It irritates me to no end that she didn't tell me about this, but I can't say I'm surprised—Laney is one of the most stubborn people I know.

I prop my elbows on the table and rub my thumbs over my eyes, frustration boiling up inside of me. My mind starts racing with all of the small things that I've noticed but stupidly ignored over the past couple of months. Like how she'd sometimes walk to and from work if the weather was nice. I never thought twice about it then, but now it makes me wonder if it was because she didn't have enough money for gas. And all the times she would only eat half of her lunch at work and take the other half home for dinner. She'd said she wasn't hungry, but now I'm not so sure.

"Shit," I hiss.

"Levi?" Her soft voice startles me, and I look up to see Laney's eyes flitting nervously across my face before drifting to the stack of bills scattered in front of me. "Were you going through my stuff?" she asks, furrowing her brow.

"What the fuck is this, Laney?" I snap, instantly regretting my harsh words. But this is important, damn it. She is *mine,* and she shouldn't have to worry about whether or not she can afford to pay her bills.

"Those, Levi, are *my* bills. What the hell are you doing going through them?" She strides across the kitchen and snatches the envelopes off the table.

"Well shit, Lane. If you didn't want me to look at them, you shouldn't have just left them lying around. And frankly, I'm glad I looked at them." She rolls her eyes and turns away from me, ticking me off even more. "How much debt are you in, Laney? Is this it, or is there more?" I ask, knowing I'm probably going to piss her off more than she already is.

She spins around, her mouth gaping wide, and she shoves a finger into my chest. "That is none of your damn business," she growls.

"It is my business. *You're* my business." My phone buzzes on the table, but I ignore it. "You have almost twelve thousand dollars of bills, just in that stack," I say, flicking the envelopes in her hand.

"I'm aware," she grounds out, her teeth gritted together. Her bottom lip trembles and she steps away from me. The anger and annoyance on her face are quickly replaced by resignation and she looks down. Her shoulders rise and fall several times before she looks back up, and when those gorgeous hazel eyes find mine, they're clouded in defeat and brimming with tears. "You don't think I don't know how much money I owe?" Her voice wavers, cracking several times, but my brave girl manages to hold herself together. Any ounce of anger I felt completely dissipates.

I step toward her but she shakes her head and shuffles backward, putting up her hand. I glance down at her hand then back at her face, and it slices me open to see her like this and know that I'm causing her pain. "You're right," she chokes out, tears dripping down her face. "This isn't it. This is only about half." She bats angrily at the tears. "But what the hell am I supposed to do, Levi?" she yells. "I don't really have a choice in the matter. I have to see my doctors, and I have to have chemotherapy—"

"You should have told me," I interrupt as softly as possible, wanting to calm her down. "You should have come to me." I take another step toward her and pull the stack of envelopes from her hand, tossing them on the table. "I love you, Lane, and I don't want you to have to worry about anything except beating this cancer." A harsh cry rips from her throat and she buries her face in her hands. My arms wrap around her seconds before her body goes slack. "I don't want you to have to worry about money or food or gas or doctor bills or the electricity. Christ, Laney . . . I want you to come to me." I squeeze her tighter, which causes her body to shake harder than it already is. "I want to help you. You aren't in this alone anymore—not any of it."

"I just don't want to burden you," she sobs, hiccupping back tears as she pulls away from my chest. Her face is red, her eyes are puffy and her nose is clogged, but she still looks so damn cute. "I don't want you to feel like this is your responsibility—"

I stop her words by placing a finger against her mouth. "First, I don't feel burdened. Second, you are my responsibility; I just need to get you to see that. I want to take care of you, Lane." She offers me a wobbly smile, making me chuckle. "I'm in this, for better or worse. I want forever with you, Laney, and that forever started the second you drove back into town."

I run a hand up the side of her face and cup her cheek while planting a gentle kiss to her swollen pink lips. She sighs, her body relaxing into me, and I'm about to sigh with relief when she takes a deep breath, causing her to break out into yet another coughing fit. She braces one hand on my shoulder, the other covering her mouth. Her lungs wheeze, and after several seconds I become alarmed because she isn't stopping. Pulling out a chair, I nudge her into it and grab a bottle of water from the refrigerator. She takes several small sips but continues to choke and sputter. "Laney," I ask, trying to keep from panicking. "What can I do? Are you okay?" She nods her head with her hand still to her mouth and finally the coughing subsides.

"I'm fine," she squeaks, her voice raw.

"You're not fine." Squatting down in front of her so we're eye to eye, I grip her hand in mine. "You need to call Dr. Hopkins. Didn't you tell me that she wanted to know if you started getting sick?"

"That was when my blood counts had dropped, but they're a little better now. It's just a cold, Levi. I'll be fine," she says, dismissing me.

"A cold doesn't last this long. Jesus, Laney, you've been coughing for weeks and you don't have any other symptoms. This isn't normal. We're calling Dr. Hopkins." Standing up, I reach for my phone, but she snatches it off the table before I can get to it.

"No. I promise, I'm fine." My phone buzzes again while she's holding it, and she looks down and then holds it out to me. "It's Mason."

"Promise me you'll mention it to the doctor tomorrow," I say, disregarding my phone because this is much more important. Laney drops her hand back in her lap when she realizes I'm not answering the call.

"I promise," she sighs emphatically, rolling her eyes. "I promise I'll tell her about the cough."

"Thank you." My phone buzzes again and she shoves it at my chest then stalks out of the room, coughing the entire way. I answer the phone.

"I can't do it, Mason. I can't go."

"You have to go. This isn't an option, Levi." I know my brother, and I can practically hear him pacing around his living room. "Look, I get it. You want to be here with her. But this is important, Levi, and I don't want us to lose out on this opportunity."

"I know. I don't want us to lose out on it either, but she's sick, Mase, and I'm not just talking about the cancer. She's got this cough and it's getting worse, and I need to be here with her to make sure she talks to the doctor."

"She's a grown woman, Levi; I'm sure she can talk to the doctor on her own. And I know that Luke would never let her go by herself. Fucking hell, Levi," Mason grunts, his irritation obvious. "This is important. It's important to me, and it sure as hell is important to our business. You have to go so just make it work," he says with finality.

I open my mouth to tell him to fuck off, but the asshole hangs up on me. I toss my phone on the table. *What the hell am I supposed to do?* Spinning around, I come face to face with Laney.

"What did Mason want?" She yawns and tucks herself into my chest, wrapping me in her arms.

"He wants me to go to Nashville tomorrow to sign paperwork for the investors."

"What? That's amazing, Levi. I'm so happy for you guys!" Her eyes glitter with joy and it's like a punch to the gut because I haven't seen her smile like this in days. I'm realizing now how much I've missed it.

"I'm not going." Untangling her arms from around my back, I walk down the hall and into the bathroom. Seconds later, she comes barging in on me with my sweats around my thighs and my dick hanging out. She doesn't seem at all fazed that I'm standing here taking a piss, and the sassy little vibes she's putting off with her hands on her hips and her chin jutted out is turning me the fuck on.

"What do you mean you're not going? You have to go." Her mouth comes together in the perfect pout, and I fight the urge to bite one of her lips and see just how sassy she can be. I pull my pants back up, wash my hands and push past her on my way out of the bathroom.

She follows me into the bedroom, which is exactly where I want her. I'm declaring our little argument the first fight since we've reunited, and I'm in need of some serious make-up sex. I shove my pants back down my thighs and Laney watches them fall to the floor. Then she looks back at me, trying to appear un-affected.

"I don't have to go. We can reschedule." I stalk toward her.

"What? No!" she says, shaking her head furiously. I grab onto the bottom of her shirt and tug it over her head. She looks down at her naked chest in confusion and then back up at me. "You have to go, Levi. You guys worked really hard for this. You *de-serve* this." She yawns, and as she takes in the deep breath, I hear a faint wheeze come from her mouth. Laney coughs once and clears her throat several times before speaking again. "Why wouldn't you go?"

"Because I need to be with *you.* I *want* to be with you." Bend-ing down, I scoop her up into my arms and carry her over to the bed. As soon as I set her down, she scoots back and buries herself under the covers and I curl up next to her.

"You need to go," she mumbles, resting her head on my chest. "I'll get Luke or Mia to go with me to my treatment." I smile to myself because she didn't mention Benny. Don't get me wrong, I like the guy. But if Laney wasn't with me, I could see her with someone like him.

"I don't know, Laney—" She rises from my chest and shuts me up with a kiss.

"It isn't up for discussion. I will be fine, and I'll be here when you get back." She falls back on my chest and I grunt. "Speaking of that, how long will you be gone?"

"I would leave tomorrow and come back on Sunday. We're supposed to approve a building site they selected." She nods, her smooth head rubbing against my chest. I'm so used to her bald head that sometimes I completely forget she doesn't have hair . . . or eyebrows or eyelashes, for that matter. With the cold weather, she's had to start wearing hats. I tried to take her to get a wig, but she didn't like the way they felt on her head and I didn't care either way, so she decided to go without.

My fingers trace a loop around the top of her head, over and over, and within seconds, a faint snore drifts through the air. *So much for the make-up sex.* She's been so tired lately—more so than usual—and I can't help but wonder if it's because of the chemotherapy or the cold. She slept a full ten hours last night, and it's not even nine o'clock in the morning and she's already back asleep. The small wheeze that I heard earlier starts up again each time she inhales and I prop myself up higher on the bed, bringing her with me.

Laney's breast is squished against my side and her silky smooth legs are tangled with mine. It feels so fucking perfect, except that my mind starts to wonder what the hell I'd ever do if she wasn't here. I've gotten fairly good at shutting off those thoughts because I know they won't get us anywhere. She'll get past this. Laney will survive, and when she does, I'm going to put a huge fucking rock on her finger and change her last name.

There is absolutely no way I'm going to fall back asleep, so I do the next best thing—I watch Laney sleep. Her shoulders rise and fall with each shallow breath, and a few times I lay my hand across her back just to make sure she's still breathing. She's so tiny and fragile, and I have no clue how her body has made it through everything that it's been through. I'm in complete awe of her resilience and strength. I'll never know how she puts a smile on every morning and pushes through each day the way she does, and I think it's one of those things that I'll just never understand. Often times I've thought about how easy it would be for her to be bitter and angry rather than hopeful. I know that she's had her moments, but that's to be expected. I also know that there are days when she just puts on a show, but the majority of the time she seems legitimately happy and upbeat.

"Damn it," I hiss, tilting my head back on the pillow. I don't want to go to Nashville, but I know I have to for Mason. I couldn't forgive myself if he missed out on an opportunity like this because of me. Shifting Laney ever so gently to the side, I roll her onto her back, making sure she has a pillow under her head. I slip out of bed, tuck the covers around her body and throw on my sweats, wondering where in the hell I left my phone. I backtrack through the house and find it sitting on the kitchen table with three missed calls from Mason. Tapping his name, I hit 'talk' and he picks up almost instantly.

"Well?" he snaps, not saying another word.

"What time does our flight leave?" Grabbing a glass out of the cabinet, I fill it up with water and take a drink.

"It's like a four or five-hour drive, douchebag. We're not going to fly." Damn it. I fucking hate driving long distances. I take one more drink and empty the cup into the sink.

"Whatever," I growl. "What time do we need to leave?"

"Cheer up, Buttercup," he quips. "This is a good thing. We leave at eight in the morning. Where should I pick you up at?"

"Pick me up at Laney's."

"You got it."

"And Mason . . ."

"Yeah?"

"Don't fucking call me back today." I hang up the phone before he has a chance to respond, but right before I hit 'end,' I hear his booming laugh come through the line.

My eyes rest on the stack of bills on Laney's table, and suddenly the only thing I can think of is making things right for her. When I grab the pile, a folded piece of paper falls to the floor. Bending down, I pick it up and unfold it. Laney's bucket list is staring back at me, and I smile at all of the things I've been able to check off of it. I laugh out loud when I see the line drawn through number six and recall the way she blushed when I changed the wording. My cock stirs when I remember the day we checked off number eight. I'll never forget the look on her face or her tinkling laughter when she took off running from me at the quarry, and the way she squealed when I finally caught her and tossed her into the cold water. My eyes slowly make their way down the page and my breath catches in my throat when I find number fourteen. It wasn't there before so she must have added it. I grab a pen off the counter and scratch through that one, making a small note next to it.

Laney's Bucket List
1. Go Skydiving
2. ~~Get a tattoo~~
3. Make love on a beach in Bora Bora
4. Kiss my husband under the Eiffel Tower
5. ~~Make a significant positive impact on a stranger's life~~
6. ~~Dance in Levi's cage~~ — Have sex in Levi's cage
7. ~~Have a picnic under the stars~~
8. ~~Go skinny dipping~~
9. Go cliff diving
10. Visit the Grand Canyon
11. Go to New York
12. Get married
13. Have children
14. ~~Make Levi fall in love with me again~~ I never stopped loving you

Folding the list up, I put it back on the table then grab the stack of bills and start fixing things the only way I know how.

Chapter 27

Levi

"I'M NOT GOING. END OF discussion, Laney. I'm *not* going."

It's three o'clock in the morning. I spent the entire day yesterday checking on Laney because she literally slept all afternoon, only waking up once around five o'clock in the evening to eat, drink and go to the bathroom before she crawled back into bed, seemingly exhausted. Okay, I can understand that. But when she wakes up in the middle of the night with yet another coughing fit and a fever to boot . . . yeah, not happening.

"I'm fine," she stresses, curling up into a ball after taking the fever reducer I gave her. "You're going. I told you, it's just a cold."

"Cold, my ass. It's not just a cold."

"Trust me, babe," she yawns, pulling the covers up to her chin. "Your ass is far from cold. In fact, it's pretty darn hot." A wistful smile touches her lips as her eyelids bob heavily. I crawl into bed, wrap my arm around her scalding hot body and pull her toward me.

"Now's not the time for jokes, Lane," I mumble into the top of her head before kissing it twice.

"Mmmmm . . ." she moans before drifting off to sleep.

I, on the other hand, stay up through the wee morning hours, constantly monitoring her temperature, which finally breaks around six o'clock. It's now seven and I'm standing next to her bed, completely fucking exhausted, trying to figure out what in the hell I'm supposed to do. There's no way I can leave her like this . . . I just can't. My meeting will be a complete waste of time because I'll spend the entire time thinking about Laney and wondering how she's doing.

Right when I'm about to text Mason and tell him I'm not going, a soft knock sounds at the bedroom door. I crack it open and Mia looks at me, concern marring her face. "How is she?" she whispers, crossing her arms over her chest.

I slip out the door and Mia follows me into the kitchen. God bless her, she already has a pot of coffee ready to go and I fix myself a cup. "Her fever finally broke, but she coughed all night long."

"I know. I heard her." Mia walks across the kitchen and refills her coffee mug. She brings it to her mouth and takes a sip.

There for a while, Mia had been sleeping on Benny's couch when I would stay the night, but the past several weeks she's insisted on staying here. I'm not sure if it's because something happened between her and Benny, or if she's just as concerned about Laney as I am and wants to be here in case she's needed. I suppose it doesn't really matter. She's a great friend, and I'm just glad that Laney has her.

"She's going to be okay, Mia." I wrap an arm around her shoulder and she nods her head.

"I know. I just want her to be okay *now*." A couple of tears slide down her face. "I can't stand to see her go through this. It makes me sick to watch her lose weight and to see the bright light in her eyes dim. I'm not sure how much more of this I can take," she cries, setting her mug down so she can wipe the wetness from her face.

"I know. I feel the same way." I fold her into my arms, and her shoulders tremble and shake. "We have to stay strong for her, okay?" She nods weakly against my chest and then pulls back, her face red and splotchy from crying.

"I'm trying," she says, her voice cracking as another batch of tears roll down her face. "It's just hard. I want this to be over for her."

I pat her back awkwardly. I'm not sure it's doing any good, but I really don't know what else to do. It's one thing to comfort Laney, but trying to comfort her best friend is something entirely different.

"She's almost done. Only a few treatments left," I remind her.

"I know. But then she has radiation every single day for six weeks. What in the hell is *that* going to do to her?"

"We'll cross that bridge when we get there. She's a fighter, Mia."

"Trust me, I know that better than most." She sniffs, grabbing a Kleenex to wipe her nose. My phone buzzes with a text and I look down.

Mason: I'll be there in 30 minutes.

"Shit," I hiss, running a hand along the back of my neck. "There's no way I can go to Nashville."

"You have to." Mia smiles at me, her eyes still watery. "I have strict instructions from your woman that you are not allowed to bail on Mason."

I shake my head and chuckle. "Of course you do. When did she tell you that?"

"She got out of bed last night to get a drink and I heard her stumbling around in the kitchen. We stayed up and talked for a couple of minutes."

"I don't know, Mia. What if something happens? What if she needs me and I'm not here?"

"I'll be with her, and so will Luke. I promise that I'll call you right after she sees the doctor, and then as soon as she gets done with her chemo, I'll call you again." She pauses, her eyes softening. "She wants this for you, Levi. So even if you don't want to go for you . . . you should go for her. You know," she continues, a nostalgic look on her face, "she used to talk about you all the time. I felt like I knew you long before we actually met. She was always so proud of you. Luke would call, and the first thing out of her mouth was always, 'How's Levi?' followed by her begging him for information. She told me once what happened between the two of you, but I always had the feeling she wasn't giving me the whole story. But I never pushed her or questioned it because I knew it wasn't important. She loved you, and that was all that mattered."

My heart is jammed in the middle of my throat and I swallow hard, trying to push past it. There is no way I'm going to lose my shit in front of a chick, but just hearing Mia say that does something to me. It touches me in a way that I can't even explain.

"Okay, I'll go," I concede, although a sick feeling in my gut is telling me to stay. "But you promise to call constantly?"

"I promise." She gives me a friendly push toward the bedroom. "Now go get ready."

Laney is still asleep when Mason pulls up thirty minutes later. "I don't want to wake her up," I whisper, looking over at Mia, who's hovering over Laney right along beside me.

Mia places her hand gently on the top of Laney's head. "She doesn't feel warm. Maybe just let her sleep and I'll have her call you as soon as she wakes up?"

"Sure," I say with a massive amount of hesitation. Bending forward, I place a soft kiss on Laney's cheek, but it's not enough so I do it a couple more times and then whisper, "I love you, pretty girl." She doesn't move or make a sound as Mia and I head out of the room.

"Will you sleep in here with her while I'm gone?" I don't want Laney to be by herself.

"I was already planning on it." She gives me a quick hug, and after I double and triple check that she has my phone number programmed correctly into my phone, I finally make my way out to Mason.

The second I close the car door, I officially begin the count-down of when I'll get to come back. Mason is bright-eyed and bushy-tailed, and it takes everything I have not to slap that damn smile off of his face. I know he's excited but I'm cranky and tired, and this is the last thing I want to be doing right now.

The drive is long and boring, and despite Mason's multiple attempts to start up a conversation, I just don't have it in me. He finally gives up, and about two hours into our drive—after our first and only bathroom break—I manage to actually fall asleep.

Mason shakes me awake when we hit the city limits of Nashville, and the first thing I do is check my phone. There's a text from Mia waiting for me. I'm a little concerned that Laney didn't call, but given the circumstances, I really didn't expect her to.

Mia: We're heading to treatment center.

That text came in about an hour ago. Since there's nothing after it, I assume that Laney is still going through the usual pre-chemo blood work and doctor visit.

As Mason pulls up to Mark and Brady's office, I turn my phone on vibrate and shove it in my coat pocket. Then I give my brother a congratulatory fist bump and step out of the car. "Let's do this."

Chapter 28

Laney

MY LUNGS ARE BEING RIPPED from my chest—that's the only explanation for the way I feel. I heard Levi tell me goodbye a little while ago, but I pretended to be asleep because if I'd opened my eyes and told him that I felt like I'd been hit by a Mack truck, then I'm certain he would've stayed. I've screwed with his life enough in the past and there is no way I'm going to screw with it now.

Speaking of being screwed, my head is pounding, I'm freezing cold and I'm short of breath. My entire body aches, and it hurts to even *think* about getting out of bed.

"Mia," I croak, attempting to suck in a deep breath, which causes me to cough. She comes running into the room.

"You look horrible, Laney," she says, appearing as if she's seconds away from panicking. "You didn't look this bad last night."

"I feel horrible." My hands find my head and I rub gently at my temples, trying to alleviate the pain behind my eyes.

"I'm going to call Levi—"

"No. Please don't," I whisper. If I talk any louder, my head will explode. "Let him have this." She nods, but her lips are pursed and I can tell she isn't happy about it.

"Can you get up?" she asks, helping me swing my legs to the edge of the bed. She offers me her arm and pulls me to a sitting position, and I manage to push myself up the rest of the way. Slowly, I shuffle toward the bathroom and collapse on top of the toilet seat. "Laney, there is no way you can get in that shower by yourself."

"I know," I grunt, sucking in the deepest breath I can. "Will you call Luke or Benny?" She scurries from the bathroom and within seconds she's back, the phone to her ear. It doesn't matter that she's three feet in front of me; I don't hear a word she's saying. My lungs feel like they're on fire, and despite my concentration on taking slow, deep breaths, I still feel like I can't breathe.

"Luke is on his way." She squats down in front of me. "Do I need to call Dr. Hopkins?"

"No." My eyes drift shut and I lean forward, resting my elbows on my knees because the strength it's taking to sit up is just too much. My body is aching, my muscles loose like noodles, and right now my head is spinning so fast that I may very well throw up if I try to move. "We'll just go in a little early. Can you help me get dressed?"

Mia jumps up from the floor and runs into my room. When she comes back, I don't even bother to look at what she picked out for me. I brace my hands on the sink as she slips my sweat pants from my body, lifting each foot when she needs me to so she can put my clean pants on. Letting go of the sink, I raise my shirt over my head and drop it on the floor next to me. When Mia doesn't make a move to help me put my shirt on, I look up and find her staring at me. Her eyes are quickly filling with tears and her hand is covering her mouth. My brows knit together and she lowers her hand.

"I'm sorry," she says, shaking her head. "I've never seen your scar before." I look down at myself and back to her.

"I'm sorry." I move to cover myself up and she grabs my arm.

"No, don't be sorry. It's just . . . ." Her eyes search my face and a small smile touches her lips. "You've never offered to share this part of your cancer with me, and I just wasn't expecting it." She kneels down in front of me and grips my hand in hers. "I shouldn't have reacted like that. I'm so sorry. I just . . . it's just . . ."

"It's a lot to take in when you see it for the first time," I interrupt, fighting back the cough that's tickling my lungs.

"It is," she nods. "Thank you for showing me." Without saying another word, she helps me into my bra and pulls my t-shirt over my head just as the front door slams. Footsteps bound down the hall and then a gentle knock sounds at the bathroom door.

"It's open," Mia hollers as she bends down to help me with my socks and shoes. Luke peeks his head around the corner and when he sees it's all clear, he walks in. I look up at him, the movement causing a sharp pain to radiate across the front of my head. I suck in a quick breath and squeeze my eyes shut.

"What the fuck," Luke growls. "Laney?"

"She's feeling worse," Mia answers for me.

"Well, no shit," he snaps, and I crack open an eye. "You look like hell, Laney. Why didn't you call me sooner?" I hate seeing this look on Luke's face. I hate seeing him hurt because of me. "Have you called Levi?" he asks. Mia leaves the bathroom and returns with my coat. My arms hang limply at my sides as she gently squeezes me into it.

"No, and we're not going to," I tell him firmly. "He needs to do this, Luke. It's important." Luke rolls his eyes, but I continue. "And I didn't call sooner because I was going to see the doctor anyway."

"Luke, will you go get Laney's purse and I'll help her get to the car?" Luke grunts and bends down to pick me up, cradling me in his arms. "Okay, never mind." Mia rolls her eyes and walks out of the bathroom. "I'll get her purse."

My head flops onto Luke's chest and he pulls a hat over it before kissing my cheek. "I need you to get better." His voice is thick, but I don't look up at his face because I'm not sure how much I can handle right now. A whispered *"I know"* is about all

I can get out.

Mia opens the front door and Luke follows her out to the car. He slides me into the back seat and then props my body up next to his with an arm around my shoulders. My teeth are chattering nonstop and Luke snaps at Mia to turn up the heat. My eyes bob heavily as I concentrate on my breathing, which seems to be getting worse. *In. Out. In. Out.*

"You okay, sis?" I try to move my head, but it feels too heavy and I can't seem to get it to move. "Drive faster, Mia," Luke shouts.

"We're almost there." I can hear the fear in their voices, and for the first time since I've gotten sick, I'm *truly* afraid. My body feels like it's shutting down . . . throwing in the towel . . . giving up. It's as if I'm completely helpless—an outsider looking in, watching it all unfold, one labored breath at a time.

Luke

"Damn it, Mia, how much further?" I stretch my neck to look out the window, but it's useless—I can't see a damn thing.

"Almost there, so don't fucking yell at me!" Her voice breaks at the end and normally I'd roll my eyes and tell her to 'man up,' but I'm about a minute away from losing it myself.

I put a hand to Laney's forehead. She's burning up. A fine sheen of sweat is dabbled across her forehead and her body is shivering uncontrollably next to mine. Her eyes are closed and I fight the urge to shake her awake. *I just need to see her eyes so I know she's still with me.*

"We're here." Mia whips the car into a parking spot and throws it into park. "Want me to get a wheelchair?" she asks frantically, grabbing everything we need out of the car.

"No," I bark. "Open the damn door so I can get her out of here."

Mia's movements are jerky as she yanks the back door open. I pull Laney onto my lap, cradling her to my chest, and push out of the car. We walk at a clipped pace to the entrance of the Cancer Treatment Center and the automatic doors slide open. When the woman at the front desk sees Laney in my arms, her eyes go wide and she flies out of her chair and disappears behind the wall. Suddenly, two nurses meet us and we're quickly ushered into an exam room.

I hate these fucking rooms. They're chilly and sterile, and there is no way in hell I'm laying Laney down on that crinkly-ass paper when I know she's much safer in my arms. Folding into one of the chairs, I bring Laney down with me and adjust her body so I can keep a hold of her while one of the nurses begins taking her vital signs. Mia is standing against the far wall with tears running down her face and she scoots out of the way when the door opens. Dr. Hopkins rushes into the room and starts firing off questions to the nurse.

"What's her blood pressure?" She pulls a light out of her pocket and checks both of Laney's eyes.

"BP is 82/50, pulse 132, respirations 34, temperature 102.8 and oxygen level is 94 percent." Frustration and apprehension are building up inside of me with each number that's thrown out, because I have absolutely no fucking clue what they mean. My eyes stay focused on Dr. Hopkins' face, looking for any indication that she likes or doesn't like what she's hearing, but she stays impassively calm, which does nothing for my growing anger.

"Call upstairs, I want her admitted to the ICU," she says, glancing over at me. When I open my mouth to talk, she holds up a finger and starts firing off more orders. The nurse is writing furiously on a pad of paper, and I have no idea how these people are able to look so goddamn composed when my skin is crawling so fucking bad I want rip it from my own body. "Order a chest X-ray, PA and Lateral, ABGs, CBC, CMP, blood cultures, and a sputum culture, if we can get one. Let's get her on two liters of oxygen to start." Dr. Hopkins brings her stethoscope to Laney's chest. "STAT!" she hollers and the nurse hurries out of the room.

My heart is pounding against my ribcage, adrenaline and fear are running rapidly through my veins, and I'm on the verge of completely losing control. I look down at Laney's tiny frame wrapped in my lap and I remember all the times she used to hold me like this when I was sick. Her fingers would make long, slow strokes along the top of my head, and she would hum . . . she would always hum. I squeeze my eyes shut to try and remember the song, but for the life of me I can't.

Dr. Hopkins motions for Mia to sit down, and she slides into the seat next to mine. When I see her hand shaking in her lap, I reach over and lace my fingers with hers. She looks up at me with sad eyes and I give her a slight nod, silently indicating that together we'll get through this.

Dr. Hopkins clears her throat and we both swivel to look at her. "Can you tell me what symptoms Laney has been having?" she asks. Her voice is soft and calm, and once again I want to scream.

"She's had a cough for a couple of weeks," I answer, looking at Mia for confirmation.

"Probably three to four weeks," she agrees, wiping the tears from her face. "Her cough has gotten worse the past couple of days, along with her exhaustion. She's been sleeping almost non-stop." Dr. Hopkins is watching her intently. Mia glances at me and I squeeze her hand, urging her to continue. "She's had a fever and chills, and this morning she was complaining of a headache. She also just started breathing a lot faster and harder than normal, and she's been really weak."

Dr. Hopkins rests a hand on Mia's knee. "Thank you." Mia nods, a fresh batch of tears falling down her face. Laney groans and I adjust her on my lap, wondering where the damn nurses went and why they haven't started her on the oxygen yet.

The door busts open and everything erupts into a flurry of

activity. Laney is taken from my arms and placed on a gurney. Clear plastic tubing is placed around her head and inserted into her nose. She's immediately whisked away and I jump up from my seat to run after them, desperate to stay with my sister. Laney needs me, and there is no way in hell I'm leaving her side.

Several of the nurses are rattling things off to each other as they wheel her down the hall, but what they're saying doesn't make sense to me. My eyes stay focused on the sight of Laney's frail body lying limp on the crisp white sheet. A set of double doors fly open and shut in my face, and I'm left standing in the hall, staring through a small rectangular window.

So this is what it feels like . . .

Tears burn the back of my eyes and I swallow hard. I've walked past people crying in a hospital before; I've even seen people wailing over a loved one. But never in a million years did I think it would be me. I've never known how it feels to watch your loved one carted off and have absolutely no idea what's going to happen to them, not knowing if the next time you see them they'll be alive or . . . gone.

A gentle hand lands on my back and I whirl around, grabbing onto Mia, burying my face in her hair. Mia's arms wrap around my neck, and for the first time since I found out Laney has cancer, I cry. My tears soak through Mia's shirt, but she doesn't move. She just stands there like the rock I need her to be.

Chapter 29

Levi

"GENTLEMAN, YOU MADE THE RIGHT decision." I grip Mark's hand firmly in mine then move to Brady, and Mason follows suit.

"We've already signed, Mark. You can stop the ass-kissing," Mason quips, earning a boisterous laugh from our two new business partners. We've spent the last two hours going over the contract and ironing out every little detail. My eyes hurt, my ass hurts and I'm ready for some grub. "We're starving," Mason says as if he read my mind. "Where can we get something to eat?"

Mark rattles off the address of a steak house down the road as we grab our jackets and walk toward the front door. I drape my coat over my arm and reach into the pocket for my phone, aggravated at myself for not checking it sooner. I know I should have, but I got caught up in the meeting and completely lost track of time. My hand comes up empty and I instantly begin to panic.

"I'll be right back." Spinning around, I take off down the hall to the conference room we just left. I frantically search the room but come up empty-handed. "Shit," I mumble, running toward the door.

Mason is already outside and getting in the car when I come barreling out. "What's up?" he asks, arm propped up on his door.

"I can't find my fucking phone." Yanking the door open, I sigh deeply when I find my cell wedged between the seat and center console. "How the fuck did that get there?" I growl, pressing the side button to turn it on. My screen flashes with five missed calls, but I scroll past them and click on the first text.

Mia: Laney is really sick. They're admitting her to the hospital. Please call.

My stomach drops. *Laney.* Fuck, this is not happening. "Get in the car—now. Let's go!" I yell. Mason must register the panic on my face because he doesn't waste any time jumping in the car and peeling out of the parking lot.

Mia: Where are you, Levi? You need to come home.

"FUCK!" I roar, slamming my fist into the dash. "Step on it, Mason. I need to get home." He glances over at me but doesn't say a word. *Smart boy.*

Luke: They're admitting Laney to ICU and running a bunch of tests. I'll keep you updated.

That was an hour ago. What the fuck is going on? How did things go from bad to worse so fast? Is she okay? I can't believe they needed me—that *she* needed me—and I wasn't there.

Pulling up Luke's name and number, I hit 'talk' and he answers on the first ring. "Took you long enough," he growls.

"Cut the shit, Luke. What's going on?"

"What? You're the one who didn't even have your goddamn phone on!" he yells, causing me to hold the phone away from ear. "Are you fucking kidding me, Levi?" His voice cracks and the phone is muffled.

"Are you on your way home?" Mia asks. I close my eyes at the sound of resignation in her voice.

"Yes, I'm on the way. Will you please tell me what's going on, Mia? Please. I need to know. This is killing me. My phone fell out of my pocket in the car, and I didn't realize it until the meeting was over. There's a shitload of messages telling me that Laney isn't okay, so please—"

"We're still waiting," she interrupts gently. A lump forms in my throat, nausea churning deep in my gut. "They took her a while ago to go run some tests and they haven't brought her back yet."

"What did the doctor say?" *Please tell me she's going to be okay.*

"All the doctor said is that chemotherapy causes the white blood cells to drop and that makes Laney more susceptible to infection. So they're trying to figure out what's wrong with her, and they're going to keep her here until they can get her better." A sob breaks free from my chest and I lean forward, my shoulders heaving. "Shhh . . ." Mia croons. "Just get home. Okay?"

I don't even have it in me to respond. My mind is focused on one thing and one thing only—*Laney.* Handing my phone to Mason, I bury my head in my hands and cry like a fucking baby. If I make it to the hospital and something has happened to her, I'll never forgive myself.

Time passes, as do the mile markers. Slumped down in the seat, I keep my eyes focused on the constantly changing scenery that is flying by. Mason doesn't say a word the entire drive and that's probably for the best, because right now I'm so furious at myself for leaving that I'm liable to say or do something that could irreparably damage our relationship.

At some point along the way, my phone beeps and I look at it strangely, wondering when I got my phone back from Mason.

Mia: She's in the room. They have her on oxygen and a heart monitor, but we're still waiting for the tests to come back.

Oxygen? A heart monitor? *Oh God.*

Me: Is she awake? Has she talked to you?

My phone beeps almost instantly.

Mia: I'm sorry, no. The doctor said that her body is under a lot of stress and she'll probably fade in and out quite a bit.

Me: Let me know if anything changes.

The next few hours are the longest of my life. Although they creep by at a snail's pace, Mason somehow manages to make a five-hour trip in a little less than four hours. When the car screeches to a halt, I bolt out the door before Mason even has time to shift into park. I can hear him running after me, but there is no way I'm slowing down. The doors open automatically and the woman at the front desk smiles when I run in, then her eyes quickly widen. "ICU?"

"Fifth floor. Take the elevator up and then turn left." She's shouting the directions at me because I'm already running toward the stairs. Fuck the elevator. I bound up the steps, two at a time, and when I reach the fifth floor, I shove through the door and fly down the hall, looking for anyone that might be able to help me.

"Levi!" Turning around, I find Mia, Benny and Luke walking out of a room.

"Is she in there?" I jog over to them, but Mia shakes her head.

"This is just the waiting room." I follow the three of them in the room and Luke immediately starts pacing, his hands planted firmly on the top of his head.

"Any news? Where is she at? Can I go see her?" I ask. Mason strides into the room, heaving and out of breath.

"We haven't even seen her," Luke growls. "We've been sitting in this goddamn room for the past five fucking hours, waiting to hear something . . . anything."

"But Mia, you made it sound like . . ." She shakes her head and my words trail off.

"I didn't get to see her, Levi. The nurse just came to give us an update. The ICU has really strange visiting hours and we have to wait another two hours before we can see her. And even then, we can only go in one at a time."

"Fuck that." I dig my phone out of my pocket, thankful that my best friend's fiancé is a doctor here at the hospital. And right now, Tyson might be the only one who can help.

Me: Are you working tonight?

I slouch into a seat and breathe in for what feels like the first time since I found my phone. My knee is bouncing furiously. I need to see her and hold her and tell her I love her. I need to see with my own two eyes that she's okay and that she's still here. My phone vibrates in my hand and everyone stops to stare at me.

Tyson: Yup. What's up?

Me: I need you to get me into the ICU. It's Laney.

His reply is almost instantaneous.

Tyson: I'll see what I can do. Give me ten minutes. Where are you at?

Me: ICU waiting room. HURRY.

"Well—?" Luke's broken face is looking at me like I hold the key to all of life's answers.

"Tyson is working tonight. I'm hoping he can pull some strings and get us in there earlier, or at least find out some more information. Did the doctors come down and tell you anything else? Anything at all?"

Luke falls into the chair next to me. "Just that they know she has pneumonia. To be honest, I didn't understand all the medical garbage the doctor was throwing at us. But I understood that they are still waiting on some of the blood work to come back. She didn't look good, Levi. She was so limp and lifeless in my arms, and I—" His words break on a deep sob before he stands up and walks out of the room.

"Levi!" My head snaps up at the sound of Harley's voice as she runs in the room. I stand up in time for her plow into me, and I hold onto her with everything that I have. Her arms wrap tightly around my neck. "Tyson called me. I got here as fast as I could. What's going on? Have you seen her? Have you gotten to talk to her?"

Her words hit me like a ton of bricks when I realize for the first time that I never said goodbye to her this morning. Sure, I told I loved her, but she was asleep. I didn't get to kiss her one last time or tell her that she means the world to me. What if I don't get to tell her that? What if something happens and the last thing I said to her was, *'Now's not the time for jokes, Lane.'* Gripping Harley's shoulders, I pull her away from me, panic now in full bloom. "I need to see her, Harley. *Now.* I need to see her now."

"Tyson is talking to the doctor and he's going to get you back there, I promise. Just give him a couple of minutes."

"I don't have a couple of minutes," I plead, needing her to understand how important this is to me. "What if she—?"

Just then, Tyson walks into the room with another doctor at his side. Luke comes in right behind them and we all crowd together.

"Levi, this is Dr. Byers. He's been overseeing Laney's care in the ICU. Dr. Byers, this is Laney's fiancé, Levi, and her brother, Luke." Warmth rushes through me. *I want that.* More than anything, I want to be Laney's fiancé. Dr. Byers reaches a hand out to me and then Luke.

"You've already been informed that Laney has pneumonia?" We all nod in unison. "Okay, good. Although we're still waiting for some blood work to come back, I believe that Laney may be septic."

"What does that mean?" I ask.

"Sepsis is a complication of an infection—in this case, pneumonia—and the fact that Laney's immune system is already weak from her chemotherapy puts her at even greater risk. As soon as we find anything out, I'll be sure and let you know right away. But for now, we're just going to watch her closely. Her oxygen level dropped quite low a little while ago, but we were able to stabilize her."

"Is she going to be okay?" Luke asks, his eyes filling with tears.

The look on Dr. Byers' face softens. "It's obvious your sister is a strong woman, and I can assure you that we are doing absolutely everything we can. But sepsis can be a life-threatening condition and Laney is very weak right now."

"Is she awake?" I ask, desperately needing to see her.

"No, she's not. And when she does wake up, she may be extremely drowsy and slightly incoherent, so please don't be alarmed. But I can assure you that she is comfortable."

"Can we see her?" I ask, knowing full well that if he says no, I'll probably do something that could land me in jail. Dr. Byers turns to Tyson and they exchange a look.

"The visiting hours in the ICU are strict for very specific reasons, but I'm aware that you all haven't been able to see Laney since she came in so we're going to make an exception. Just one person at a time, make sure you wash your hands and if you feel even the slightest bit sick, please do not go in there. Laney is our number one priority right now, and we don't want to expose her to anything that may further complicate her situation." We all nod in agreement. "Perfect. Who would like to go in first?"

Luke and I both look at each other. *Please,* I mouth, not being able to recall a time when I've been as desperate as I am right now. We're both dying to see the one woman we both love more than anything in this world, but I don't waver. There is no way in the world I'm not going in there first, and Luke must see the determination in my eyes because he drops his head in resignation.

"Go. You go first," he says, his chin quivering. When he looks up at me with a steady stream of tears running down his cheeks, I take him by the shoulders and pull him in for a tight hug.

"Thank you," I whisper, knowing how much it's hurting him to not be with his sister. His arm comes around my back, and he pats it twice and nods. I pull back and look at him, trying so hard to convey just how much this means to me. "Thank you," I whisper one last time before Tyson leads me toward the ICU . . . toward Laney.

Tyson waves his badge and the doors open. The space is quiet, the lights are dim, and several nurses are sitting in front of a row of monitors. I'm led across the room and Tyson stops in front of one of the doors. "Levi," he says, clearing his throat. "You need to be prepared. They've got her hooked up to a lot of machines, but they're all helping her."

"Please, just let me see her," I beg. Tyson purses his lips and sighs before pushing the door open.

"I'll be out here if you need me," he says, then shuts the door behind him. My eyes instantly fill with tears when I see Laney's tiny fragile body lying in the middle of the bed with a white sheet tucked around her. My chest aches and I swallow hard as I move toward her. Both of her arms are resting at her sides and her head is propped up on a pillow. She looks so peaceful.

My Laney.

Clear tubing is wrapped around her head and positioned inside her nose. Several wires lead from one of the machines and disappear under the neck of her gown. She has an IV in her left hand, which is connected to bags of clear fluid hanging from an IV pole. I don't bother to look at what they're giving her because I won't know what it is anyway, but I make a mental note to ask the nurse later. A small square apparatus is attached to her middle finger and the wire from it disappears under her covers. The room is eerily quiet minus the steady beep emanating from one of the monitors and the faint sound of oxygen as it enter Laney's nose.

I spot a chair off to the side and I pick it up, moving it as close to her bed as I can without disturbing anything that she's hooked up to. I sit down and take her tiny hand in mine. It's so cold and feels so . . . lifeless. And that's all it takes. I bury my face into the side of her hip, her hand clenched between mine, and I bawl. "Wake up, baby. Please wake up," I sob, desperately wanting to feel her fingers curl around my hand.

Why didn't I wake her up before I left this morning? What if I never get to feel her fingers run through my hair or hear her tinkling laughter when I touch her in just the right spot? What if I never get to propose and watch her walk down the aisle? I want to hear her say 'I do.' I want a life with her, a family with her . . . *I just want her.*

Everything hits me all at once. The reality of the situation is like a punch to the gut when I think about all of the things that I never got to say or do—all of the things that the two of us will miss out on if she's taken away from me. The tears continue to flow as my chest heaves and I attempt to suck in air between sobs.

She is my life. I can't exist if she doesn't exist.

Please God. Please don't take her away from me.

Pushing up from the chair, I pepper kisses across her beautiful face. "I love you, Laney. Please wake up. *Please.* I need you, baby." My lips land on hers and I kiss her softly, hating the stillness of her mouth beneath mine. "Please, baby," I mumble, my lips brushing against hers.

I fall back into the chair, her hand still firmly in mine, and I continue to cry as I watch her chest rise and fall with each shallow breath. As I look up at her beautiful face, I see her eyelids flutter and I jump from my chair, placing a gentle hand on her cheek. "Laney, sweetheart, can you hear me?" Her lids bob heavily before finally staying cracked open. "I love you. I love you so much," I tell her, tears flowing uncontrollably down my flushed cheeks. The side of her mouth ticks up just a fraction as though she's trying to smile, and her fingers twitch against mine. "Don't move, okay. Just relax." I nuzzle my face into the side of her neck. "I'm so scared, baby. *So* scared. Please don't leave me." Bringing my face back to hers, I kiss her softly several times, and it doesn't matter that she can't kiss me back because her eyes are open and she's looking at me. Right now, that's all I need. "You're the love of my life, Laney. I'm sorry I left this morning, and I'm sorry I didn't wake you up." A tear falls from the corner of her eye and disappears in the pillowcase, and then another and another. I wipe them away the best I can. "Please don't cry. You're going to be okay." My voice breaks as emotions build up in my throat.

"Love you," she croaks, her voice raw and gritty.

"I love you too, baby. *So much.*" She nods, and her lids drift shut before bobbing open once again. "This is forever, Laney. Promise me this is forever," I beg, wanting to hear her say the words, needing to know she isn't going to leave me. Her eyes squeeze shut and several more tears fall. When she opens her eyes up again, and those hazel orbs find mine, they're full of more love than some people see in a lifetime.

"I will love you forever, Levi." Her voice breaks and her body shakes as she begins to cough. A feeling of dread settles deep in my stomach and I press the call button. Within seconds, a nurse rushes into the room and starts checking Laney. Her coughing stops and I sigh in relief, thankful that I was able to talk to her before she drifts back to sleep.

One of the machines starts beeping loudly and I look up at the monitor, trying to figure out what's going on. Three other nurses push into the room, shoving me to the side, all of them hovering around Laney, their hands moving too fast for me to see what they're doing. The beeping gets louder and my heart starts slamming inside of my chest, adrenaline and fear pumping through my veins.

"What's wrong? What's going on? Is she okay?" I push into their huddled circle and see one of them pull Laney's oxygen tubing out of her nose and replace it with a mask.

"Sir, I'm going to have to ask you to leave." The beeping sound seems to be getting even louder, and one of the lines on the monitor is flashing red. Panic sets in.

"No," I argue, trying to get closer to Laney. "What's going on? Please tell me what's happening," I beg, only to be shoved back further by one of the nurses. *Why won't they tell me what's wrong?* The beeping stops, replaced by a long steady tone, and everything around me ceases to exist . . . everything except Laney. My breath catches in my throat at the same time a sharp pain rips through the center of my chest. Lunging forward, I reach for her—any part of her—only to come up empty when I'm shoved to the side.

Please, God. No!

My stomach tenses, my heartbeat thrashes in my ears and my body shakes as adrenaline pumps through my veins.

NO! No no no. This isn't happening.

I can't lose her.

The only thing I can think about is getting closer to Laney. I weave frantically through the room, trying to see past the wall of nurses. *I have to see her. I have to help her.* Everything around me is moving at warp speed, and my mind is struggling to keep up with the shrill sound of the alarm and the nurses yelling out orders. I'll do anything—sacrifice anything—for her to be okay.

"No!" I yell, pushing my way forward again, desperate to see her and hold her and tell her I love her. A set of strong arms lock around my chest, and I fight but I can't seem to break free. My whole life is lying in that bed. *She can't leave me.* "Laney!" I yell, continuing to struggle. "Let me go. I need to see her. Let me go!" I'm begging, yelling and cursing at Tyson. "Let me go. Laney, I'm here. Laney!" My body is yanked into the hallway and when the heavy door slams in my face, my body sags to the floor as my entire world shatters around me.

Epilogue

One Year Later

Levi

*M*Y FEET ARE DANGLING PRECARIOUSLY outside the edge of the plane. The wind is rushing by so fast that I can't hear a damn thing—but that's okay, I don't need to hear anything. Right now, there is only one thing I need and that's to jump out of this airplane so I can check another thing off of Laney's list. I've made it my mission to complete her bucket list, and I won't stop until each and every last thing is accomplished.

One year ago, my life and everything I thought I knew about it changed in a matter of seconds. In that very moment, I vowed to live my life to the absolute fullest. I swore to live every single day like it's my last, because we never truly know how much time we have left on this earth. I want to enjoy my time. I want to take chances. And someday when my time here is up, I want to die knowing that I wouldn't change a single thing about how I lived my life.

"Are you ready?" Phillip is jumping tandem with me today, and he understands the motivation behind why I'm doing this.

"Hell yes, I'm ready," I yell back so he can hear me over the noise.

"Do you want to have a little extra fun when you jump?" I turn my head to look back at him and he nods, giving me a thumbs-up.

"I have no idea what that means, but sure. Why the hell not?" My nerves are fried. As much as I want to do this, I can't believe I'm doing this. I'm jumping out of a fucking plane at nearly 13,000 feet above the ground. *This is crazy.*

Phillip slides us into position and I look back, giving the other passenger in the plane a thumbs-up. She smiles and waves, and before I can even smile back, I'm rolling head over ass into the sky. Everything around me is whirling by and I have absolutely no sense of direction—it's the greatest feeling in the entire world and now I know what the 'extra fun' is.

Somehow by the grace of God, Phillip manages to straighten us out and all I see is blue. The wind is rushing past us, but surprisingly I don't feel like I'm falling. My eyes bounce around, trying to take in everything that I can. There's no good way to describe this because the sights I see and the sensations I feel are all-consuming. My mouth is agape at the fantastic view before me.

Suddenly, we're upright and everything around me is quiet. The rushing wind has slowed to a dull hum, and I notice that the instructor has pulled our chute. My eyes focus on the varied shades of green and brown patches below that seem to be getting bigger as we continue to float toward the large white banner that's starting to come into focus. The bold red letters stand out perfectly, and my excitement turns into pure giddiness as I think of what's about to happen.

"You ready for this?" Phillip hollers.

"Absolutely." A large smile is plastered to my face and he starts in on the familiar directions to prepare me for our landing. My feet are extended in front of me and the receivers are jogging toward us as we swoop in and sail into a steady walk. "Yes!" I yell, wanting nothing more than to go back up and do it all over again. But that will have to wait because right now I have something a little bit bigger than skydiving to get ready for.

Everyone works to strip me of my harness and gear, and I run to a waiting car to change into my suit, knowing that she's probably on her way down. My hands are shaking, and my mouth is dry, but there's a lightness in my chest that I'm certain I've never felt before.

Emerging from the car, I adjust my pink tie and run to the edge of the banner. I don't even know how big this thing is—I just called a guy and told him that I needed something she could see from up in the air. He didn't disappoint, that's for sure. But I hope like hell she doesn't want to take it home.

"What is that?" I yell, pointing toward the large white thing stretched across the ground.

"I don't know," my tandem instructor responds. The closer we get, the larger the white thing gets, and slowly, little red dots show up against the white background. My eyes squint, trying to see what it says, but I just can't—we're too far away. Clouds are flying past us but I feel like I'm floating, and despite all of the wonderful things that I know I'm missing, I can't seem to take my eyes off that darn white thing.

A feeling deep in my gut tells me that something is going on, and that whatever this is, it's important. So I keep my eyes on the big white thing. As we get closer, the red dots begin to form shapes and the shapes soon become words.

Oh. My. God.

"Get me down there, Dave!" I yell, my heart fluttering in my chest. He chuckles in my ear and it doesn't take me long to realize that he knows exactly what this is. He was probably in on it.

"We're falling as fast as we can," he hollers in my ear. I can feel chest bounce, presumably with laughter.

"Faster, Dave! I need down there now!" My body is trembling

with excitement. My heart is slamming against my ribcage, and it isn't because I'm free falling toward the ground.

WILL YOU MARRY ME? is plastered in large letters on an enormous white banner, and my mind works furiously to try and figure out how I can get that thing home.

"Congratulations," Dave says, patting my arm.

"Don't congratulate me yet. He still has to say the words!" A giddy laugh bubbles from my throat. He directs me on how to land as we glide toward the ground. My feet slip when we the hit the grass, but Dave grabs ahold and manages to keep me upright. The chute floats down around us, but my eyes are locked on the gorgeous man kneeling next to the banner. His beautiful blue eyes are focused on mine and I stand there, completely still, numb with happiness as everyone works to free me from my harness.

"You're good to go," Dave whispers, nudging me in the arm. My feet are moving and before I know it, I'm standing in front of the only person who owns me, heart and soul.

"Hi." Levi's magnificent smile lights up his entire face, and I have no choice but to smile back.

"Hi." My giggle turns into a broken cry and my hand flies to my mouth. Tears burn the back of my eyes as I wait for him to say something else.

"How was your jump?" he asks, sounding calm and unaffected, the exact opposite of how I feel.

"It was amazing," I whisper, removing my hand from my face. "I had the best view in the entire world."

"I was hoping you'd say that." Tears trickle down my face and I let them, because they are happy tears. Levi swallows hard, dips his hand into his pocket and pulls out a black velvet box. "Laney Jacobs, you are the most amazing person I've ever met. I've loved you for as long as I can remember, and I'm going to love you long after I leave this earth. I can't imagine going through this life without you by my side. Will you marry me?"

"Yes," I gasp, catapulting into his arms. "Yes." My mouth

fuses to his, my hands tangling in his silky hair. His arms wrap around me, his warm hands cradling my neck. He pulls back and my mouth follows his, so he kisses me again, swallowing my laugh.

"You're going to be my wife," he says, his eyes bright and brimming with tears.

"I can't wait," I whisper, grabbing his tie and pulling him back to me. Everyone around us is clapping and cheering, and a warm sensation crawls up my chest, infusing my neck.

"Wait," Levi says, digging into his pocket. He pulls out a tattered piece of paper and then looks around. "I need a pen! Who's got a pen?" Someone tosses a pen at us and Levi catches it midair. Holding the paper against his thigh, he makes a mark and then hands the paper to me. My eyes dart to the words and then back to him, my breath catching in my throat.

"My bucket list," I breathe, my eyes darting back down. "You've had this the whole time?" He nods his head and I take the paper from him, my eyes skimming over the words.

Laney's Bucket List
1. ~~Go Skydiving~~
2. ~~Get a tattoo~~
3. Make love on a beach in Bora Bora
4. Kiss my husband under the Eiffel Tower
5. ~~Make a significant positive impact on a stranger's life~~
6. ~~Dance in Levi's cage~~ Have sex in Levi's cage
7. ~~Have a picnic under the stars~~
8. ~~Go skinny dipping~~
9. ~~Go cliff diving~~
10. ~~Visit the Grand Canyon~~
11. ~~Go to New York~~
12. Get married
13. Have children
14. ~~Make Levi fall in love with me again~~ I never stopped loving you

"There are only four things left," he says. My eyes snap to his and he gives me a devilish grin.

"I can't wait to check them off," I say, earning another kiss from—"My fiancé." I smile when the word rolls off my tongue. "I liked the sound of that, although I'll be happier when I have your last name."

"Me too, baby. Me too." Levi steps away, and for the first time I notice all of our friends standing off to the side. Luke, Benny, Mia, Harley, Tyson, Max, Mason and Quinn are all smiling widely, and I wave at them before looking back down at my list.

One year ago I was on the brink of death, and I feel so incredibly lucky that I'm here now. Honestly, I don't remember my time in the ICU, but Levi and everyone else has told me stories about how scary it was. By the time I woke up, the pneumonia was gone, but I was still being treated for the sepsis. I was told it was touch and go there for a while, and that there was even a moment where they thought they had lost me. I don't like to hear that story.

It especially hurts to hear about how Levi was ripped from my room, and Mia and Benny told me that he'd been an absolute mess afterward. Apparently, he became a complete introvert, refusing to leave my side. Mason had to bring him clothes and practically forced him to take showers. He didn't eat and barely slept, and the thought of him going through that breaks my heart.

I'm glad everyone was there for Levi when I couldn't be. We're incredibly blessed to have such an amazing support system. Luke, Mia, Benny, Tyson, Harley and Mason have been there with us every step of the way, and Levi and I couldn't ask for a better group of friends.

My eyes drift over to Levi, who is talking animatedly with his hands. Everyone is standing in a circle, hanging on his every word. My gaze slowly makes its way around the circle. Harley's hand is rubbing circles around her swollen belly, and Tyson's arm is wrapped firmly around her waist.

Benny and Mia . . . well, they're Benny and Mia. They still fight all the time, but when they think no one is looking, they're really quite sweet to each other. Mia finally got a place of her own, and Benny jumps at any chance he gets to go over there and help her out. I just know something is going on there, but I haven't quite figured it out.

My baby brother is still a workaholic. I've tried to set him up with a few of the nurses from the treatment center, but he won't have any part of it. It seems he's forever the self-proclaimed bachelor.

Mason is standing next to Quinn. He thinks that no one notices, but we all see the way he looks at her. I met Quinn shortly after being released from the hospital. Harley introduced the two of us, and we became fast friends.

Speaking of the hospital, I never finished my last few chemo treatments. Once my body was stronger, I went straight into radiation, which was every day for six weeks straight. It was exhausting, but for me it didn't hold a candle to the chemotherapy. I'm lucky, I guess, because I've heard some horror stories about the side effects people can have. It took a while for my body to feel normal again, but I eventually did get there.

I've started the process to get my breast reconstruction which is so much more than simply getting a breast implant. I've had to wear an expander for nearly a year to help stretch out my skin, and I'd be lying if I said it hasn't been painful. But the pain will be worth it. Levi has told me time and time again that he loves me no matter what, but I want it for me, not for him. I hate wearing mastectomy bras and I want to feel normal again. Well, as normal as I can feel. I've done my research, met with my doctors, and I know that it'll never look perfect, but anything is better than this horrible scar over my sunken chest. At first I was worried about the cost of the surgery. I have better insurance now, but I didn't want to get into money trouble like I was.

It wasn't until several weeks after my release from the hospital that I realized Levi had paid off all my debts. I didn't even have it in me to be mad, because I knew where he was coming from. I would have done the same thing if the roles were reversed.

So, I did the only thing I could do . . . I thanked him and promised him sex anytime he wanted it. Let's just say he's been cashing in on that nearly every day, but I'm not complaining. In fact, you'll never hear me complain again. Life is precious and I'll never take it for granted, because I've learned just how fast it can all be taken away.

Closing my eyes, I tilt my face up to the sky, my bucket list clenched in my hand. I thank God for this second chance at life he's given me, for my brother and the incredible friends I have, and for Levi.

Always for Levi.

THE END

Thank you all for taking the time to read Pretty Pink Ribbons. If you have time please consider leaving a review, it is greatly appreciated, even if it's just a few words.

Follow KL Grayson here

Facebook
https://www.facebook.com/pages/KL-Grayson/1403900879892076?ref=hl

Twitter
https://twitter.com/authorklgrayson

Goodreads
https://www.goodreads.com/author/show/8299638.K_L_Grayson

And you can also find me at
www.KLGrayson.com

KL Grayson Newsletter Sign up
http://eepurl.com/6f12n

<u>Books</u>

Where We Belong
Pretty Pink Ribbons

I am currently co-writing a book with BT Urruela and we are extremely excited about our collaboration. We expect to release *A Lover's Lament* in fall 2015. You can check out both of our webpages and social media links for further information.

A LOVER'S LAMENT

IN A MATTER OF SECONDS my entire world changed, and it was in that moment that I stopped living and simply began to exist.

In my grief, I sent a letter to a stranger. I hoped in writing it, I'd find some peace from the nightmare I was living, some solace in my anger.

I didn't expect him to write back. I wasn't prepared for his words, and I certainly wasn't ready for the impact this soldier would have on my life. A deep-rooted hate transformed into friendship and then molded into a love like I'd never known before.

Sergeant Devin Ulysses Clay did what I couldn't: he put the shattered pieces of my heart back together, restoring my faith in humanity and teaching me how to live again.

But now that I'm whole, I have a decision to make. Do I return to my life as I knew it and the fiancé I've left waiting, or do I walk away from it all for the man I've never actually met—the man who doesn't even know that he holds my heart in the palm of his hand.

* * *

I've been living in hell, but you won't hear me complain.

These men depend on me, as I do them, and this brotherhood

276

is the only family I've ever known.

The Army saved me from a callous mother and a life on the wrong side of the tracks that was quickly spiraling out of control. So unlike most of the men in my platoon, going home wasn't something I longed for.

I was content overseas, spending my days defending this country that gave me my life back. Fighting became my new normal . . . *until her.*

A letter from Katie Devora—a letter that I almost didn't open. Her words put a fire back inside of me that I didn't know I'd lost. She gave me hope during a time when I was fighting every day to stay alive, and now it's time I fight for her.

Acknowledgments

Pretty Pink Ribbons holds a very special place in my heart because at the age of twenty-nine, my sister Casey was diagnosed with Stage III Invasive Ductal Carcinoma. Although six years has passed and she is now considered cancer-free, that moment in time is forever ingrained in my mind. There are several people who recognized the importance of this story and encouraged me, plotted with me and helped me get the story to where it is now.

Tom, aka the most wonderful husband in the universe—I absolutely could not have written this book without you. Thank you for making dinner, stepping in to do the dishes and vacuum the floor, and thank you for the countless times you got up at the break of dawn with the kids because I stayed up way too late writing. Thank you for understanding and encouraging my passion for writing and for this story. Thank you for being the best husband and father in the entire world. I've told you before and I'll tell you again, every single good quality I write in a man is written about you. You are, hands down, my number one book boyfriend.

Whitney and Lex—There are not enough words in the English language to express how much your friendship means to me. You both spent countless hours talking to me, encouraging me and plotting with me, and I will never forget the way you both stepped in to help me out and offer your endless support. #TRIFECTA

Michelle and Jackie—It's hard to believe that we've only been friends for a year because it seems like we've known each other for a lifetime. We've spent nearly every single night together plotting, sprinting, laughing and encouraging each other, and I am incredibly grateful that I get to call the two of you my friends. Thank you so much for absolutely every single talk, tear, laugh and smile.

Kristen and Jena—I could not have asked for two better beta readers. It was an absolute pleasure having the two of you read this book as I was writing it, and I treasure your opinions more than you'll ever know. I'll never forget the little notes you sent me or the late-night messages begging me to #SaveLaney.

Grayson's Girls—Each and every one of you have touched my heart and my life in a way I cannot explain. I love that you loved Harley and Ty, and I love that you fell in love with Levi and begged for his story. I can't thank you enough for all of the encouragement and support you've shown me; I'll never be able to repay your kindness and generosity.

Nevaeh—You're the calm to my storm, the person who can talk me down from every single ledge and I can't wait for the day that I get to hug you and tell you this in person. Expect lots of tears, my friend!

Karrie—I'll never forget the way you stepped up with a clear determination to make people fall in love with my stories. You pimped, supported and encouraged me countless times, and I'm eternally grateful for your friendship. *hugs*

A big huge thank you to Love Between the Sheets for putting together and rocking my cover reveal and blog tour.

THANK YOU to every single blog that participated in my cover reveal, release blitz and blog tour. And thank you to every blog for liking, sharing and pimping my teasers and excerpts. I absolutely could not have done this without you.

THANK YOU to the readers. I was flabbergasted by the endless amount of support and messages you showered me with after I published Where We Belong and I truly hope that you enjoyed Levi and Laney's story.

About the Author

K.L. Grayson resides in a small town outside of St. Louis, MO. She is entertained daily by her extraordinary husband, who will forever inspire every good quality she writes in a man. Her entire life rests in the palms of six dirty little hands, and when the day is over and those pint-sized cherubs have been washed and tucked into bed, you can find her typing away furiously on her computer. She has a love for alpha-males, brownies, reading, tattoos, sunglasses, and happy endings . . . and not particularly in that order.

65149969R00170

Made in the USA
Middletown, DE
01 September 2019